The Western Shore

The Western Shore

Clarkson Crane

MINT EDITIONS

The Western Shore was first published in 1925.

This edition published by Mint Editions 2021.

ISBN 9781513283562 | E-ISBN 9781513288581

Published by Mint Editions®

 MINT
EDITIONS

minteditionbooks.com

Publishing Director: Jennifer Newens
Design & Production: Rachel Lopez Metzger
Project Manager: Micaela Clark
Typesetting: Westchester Publishing Services

To F.B. This Volume Is Most Gratefully Dedicated

Contents

EPISODE ONE

I

A Pair of Shoes

There were few people on the ferry-boat, only those who were coming late in the morning from homes in Marin County, no early business men or commuters, and George Towne, feeling sleepy, stood almost alone on the forward deck, his blanket roll at his feet, smoking a cigarette made from Durham and brown paper, and watched the white cube of Alcatraz Prison with the blue sky gleaming over and behind, and a gray mist farther away on the horizon. He loathed the bland, cruel walls. A friend of his who resisted the draft two years before was still confined there; George had been to see him in May, before going to the lumber camp in Mendocino County, and had found him resigned and tranquil The old discontent had left Joe Farely's eyes and voice; folding his arms, he had smiled and quoted the last paragraph of Max Stirner's *The Ego and His Own*, the book that used to lie amid scraps of cloth, pins, and thread on the floor of his tailor shop in Lander, Wyoming, before the Vigilance Committee had driven him from town. George muttered the words now, and let the remnant of his cigarette fall to the deck. The somber quiet of the redwood forest, spattered with sunlight here and there, was still in his mind; but a memory rose against it of Joe Farley in his shirt-sleeves near the broad table, a green eye-shade on his forehead, looking up from his work and saying; "Come in, George. Come in, boy." In those days Joe was the only man to whom he could talk of the books he was reading. He often went to the shop after school: especially in winter he liked to sit on the rickety wooden chair with the round stove drumming and flushing at his elbow, and hear Joe Farley's voice. "He's a queer duck," one of his brothers said. "What the hell do you go there for?" And when Joe Farley disappeared from Lander in July 1917, George's brother and father tried to make him tell what the tailor had said during those afternoons.

"I'll have to go and see him next week," George thought.

"Shine?" exclaimed a Greek boy emerging from the interior of the ferry-boat.

"Shine?"

"No," answered George, "not me."

There would be no use having his shoes shined after having worked in them all summer. The soles were worn through: he would have to buy a new pair. He moved toward the rail and pulled his cap down lower onto his brow and stared at the glitter and dance and bobbing of the small waves.

When the boat crept into the slip and the gangplank descended, he walked over it into the gray ferry building, along the arcade, with the sunlight flashing and cars grinding outside, and checked his blanket roll, and came forth onto the pavement among shouting newsboys. The long green cars swung around the circle, halted for a moment, and then streamed away up Market Street one after another. He noticed that the stonework of a new building, which had only been a red skeleton earlier in the year, mounted now to the tenth or eleventh floor. "They sure work fast," he thought, drawing out his Durham and brown papers; and, standing on the sidewalk before the Ferry Building among hurrying people, a husky blonde youth in a flannel shirt, he rolled another cigarette, and struck a match on a stone column.

"I might as well get a pair of army shoes," he thought, "They're cheap and affordable." Then he strolled west, hands in pockets and shoulders drawn a trifle forward, across the car-tracks to Market Street, and along the north side of Market Street. The stores and people and automobiles were all blatantly new to him, for the monotony of forested hills occupied his mind; and each young woman started a creeping sensation in his entrails. There had been few women in the lumber-camp, just Emily, a frowsy wench from Ukiah, who helped with the laundry, and Mrs. Jackson, the superintendent's wife. Of course there were two or three prostitutes in town, about eight miles away. Every Saturday night some of the men would visit them; but George had not gone to town all summer. He feared disease, and knew that he would be unable to restrain himself were he to accompany the others and take a drink or two. Accordingly, he had more than a hundred dollars in his pocket with which to enter the university.

He planned to get a job as waiter or dishwasher in a Greek restaurant in Berkeley. It was a long narrow room with a counter on one side rimmed with stools and a dozen tables beneath a mirror along the opposite wall. Steam and clatter issued from the kitchen at the farther end, with now and then a long pounding hiss when water gushed from the faucet into a hot pan. The year before, during the autumn semester of 1918, when the university resembled an armed camp, he had washed

CLARKSON CRANE

dishes from six o' clock in the evening until one in the morning; some of his friends ate there, and, when he finished, they would all go to his room and play poker until the day arrived, and then sleep into the afternoon. Little time remained for study; George drifted with the crowd, though it occurred to him now and then that he had not come all the way from Wyoming to play poker and wash dishes. At the end of the semester he received his marks and learned that he had "flunked out." Now in August, 1919, after a spring working in Oakland and a summer in a lumber-camp, he was ready to try again. "I'll go to the chop-house this evening," he thought, stretching his body and legs in the fresh sunlight and feeling limber once more after the cramped, long night in the box-car. "I guess Pete will gives me back my old job."

When he reached Kearny Street, he paused under the clock protruding from the Chronicle Building to watch a girl in a dark suit buy violets from a flower stand on the corner. She pinned them onto her bosom, standing for an instant with chin lowered, and then walked away up Kearny Street, her slender figure very straight and trim and her head lifted. For a while George pondered whether or not to follow her. "They all dress like tarts these days," he thought, taking a few steps along the pavement where newsboys were waving green afternoon papers. "You can't tell one from another." But she was too far away now, nearly out of sight behind people mingling on the sidewalk, and George turned and crossed Kearny and strolled up Market Street, thinking that he would telephone over to Berkeley to see if Dan Wilkens or Herb Storey or Tuppy Smith had returned. It was only the fifth of August and there was more than a week yet before registration. "But they may be there," he decided; "one of them might come over and we could eat in some Dago joint."

While he was in a drug-store turning the leaves of a telephone directory, he pulled out his handkerchief. The cloth bore odors of redwood (he had stuffed a sprig of it into his pocket,) which made him see all at once a path leading to the bunk-house, and his own room in the bunk-house, a small, square, unvarnished room with obscene penciling on the walls. "I have not written home for two months," he thought, "I'll have to write Emma pretty soon." There had been a hush over the forest when he last scribbled a letter; the men, newly shaven and fresh after soaping, reading old magazines and talked. He closed the door of the booth and took down the receiver. The high school in Cheyenne where Emma taught English would not open until the first week in September, and Emma was doubtless still in Lander where she had gone for the summer. "I'll write to the whole family at once," he thought, putting a dime into the slot. While he stood there waiting for the number to be given him, with the crackling and buzzing of the telephone in his ear, and a faint mint smell of some disinfectant coming from the transmitter, he remembered a letter from his father which he had received in Mendocino County. "Your sister, Emma, is with us," the old hotel proprietor had written in his wavering scrawl, "and your mother is happy to have her." There had been three sheets of paper, all of them with a dark picture of the Tower Hotel as a heading, and on the last page his father had said: "Jerry and Art are still in Coblenz. They don't know when they'll be sent home."

No one he knew was in; he wasted thirty cents telephoning; the landlady of the house in which Tuppy Smith had lived last year said that Mr. Smith had moved into a room with another young man, but that she did not know where. "They're in Berkeley anyway," said George, leaving the drug-store. "I'll find them this evening." The noon sun spread a calm, hot flare over Market Street; he was no longer stiff; throwing back his head, he walked more rapidly, beginning to feel hungry: after all, he had more than one hundred dollars in his pocket. The heavy languor of Mendocino County was dropping away from his mind, and he listened to the sound of his feels on the sidewalk, and felt sorry that his friends were not still with him. He wanted to do something, no matter what, something to make up for those flaming days in a forest clearing, with a multitude of stumps round, and pieces of bark tickling his sweaty forehead under damp hair. "What the hell!" he exclaimed, swinging his arms. "I don't want to go over to Berkeley tonight."

Around him warm sunlight flashed on broad windows, on polished brass rails that followed white steps downward into the basement cafeterias, on the smooth bodies of automobiles. He paused for a while to contemplate rows of shoes with lowered prices arranged behind glass in a store, tan shoes and black, low and high, many of them with curving humps near the toes and glanced down toward his own, scuffed and bulging, and decided that must be the pavement he felt beneath his sole when he moved his foot to and fro. It was hard and cooler: the hole, he knew, was large and by this time his sock must have gone. "It's the pavement all right," he thought. "I guess I'll go and buy the army shoes." But he did not move, for he saw his face in the window, with dark lines under the eyes (he had slept little during the night in the box-car) and yellow bristles on cheeks and chi; and the languor came over him again, a sleepiness in which all the noises, crashing of street cars, voices, and croaking of horns, sounded like one great, black noise, widening before him.

He walked away. "I might as well go to Berkeley," he muttered, "and get a night's sleep. I want to start fresh tomorrow." A year filled with study and work, in which his life, he knew, would be unified and controlled, opened before him. He felt sure that he would find the intellectual realm he had always imagined, a magic environment from which he would absorb energy and desire to study. The high school Latin teacher who had urged him to enter California, a slender, stooping man named Baird, often told him of students' clubs and meetings, where all questions were talked over. "Why, yes," he would say, piling together exercises in Latin composition and smiling at George, who had wandered into the classroom, "why, yes. We discussed all those things. Why, we'd talk all night. Say, I'll never forget it." And so the University of California became in the boy's mind a sort of enchanted forest from whose branches knowledge fell gently and surely upon all who entered. "I was a fool last year," he thought, hesitating on the corner of Powell and Market.

A girl in a dark blue suit passed by him, walking rapidly northward. George found her legs attractive and followed her along Powell Street, remaining about twenty paces in the rear. She wore a small round hat; her figure was slim and graceful; he wondered if he might not speak to her; but she turned suddenly into a music store, and left him mournfully regarding Victor records in the window. He felt sleepy again. At this time last week, even three days ago, he had been swinging an ax in the hot redwood forest, during those last long minutes before they knocked off for lunch; and yesterday morning he was crouching in the freight car he had jumped before sunrise when the train slowed down on the long grade up a canyon. His eyelids drooped, and standing there on Powell Street he heard the faint noise of the pale, tumbling river in the darkness, barely emerging above the clicking and rumble of the freight train. He looked up and rubbed his eyes.

"I guess there's no use waiting for her," he thought, "Maybe she works there." Yawning, he crossed Geary Street, loitered for a moment on the corner, starting across Union Square at the gray lopsided bulk of the St. Francis Hotel. Then he went into the Square and sat down on a green bench and drew out his Durham and brown paper. He would eat lunch and catch the one-forty boat. "I ought to be able to catch the one-forty," he thought, "if I eat right away." He almost rose from the bench; but he was so comfortable in the heat that he leaned back again, and wondered if Dan Wilkens were still sleeping with the girl he picked up last April on the Key Route.

"I might as well take that German course over again," he went on, ideas following one another like lazy clouds in his mind. "I can surely get by this time, because I'll remember some of the stuff from last year. I wonder if I can find the book."

After a long time, during which he dozed for a quarter of an hour, he left the bench, not without effort, and emerged from Union Square onto Post Street, and strolled eastward on the shady side. Halfway down the block he remembered that he had lent Tuppy Smith his German book to use during Summer Session. Tuppy might have sold it, as he sold all his other books. George frowned. "Damn him," he said, "if he's sold that book I'll be sore as hell. Why did I lend it to him anyway?" Until he reached Kearny Street only dark thoughts of anger and revenge were in his mind. Tuppy would shake his red hair and say: "Well, I had to eat, didn't I?" "Well, whose book was it in the first place?" "Oh, for the love of Mike, it wasn't worth anything." "Well, what'll I do now without a German grammar?"

He entered Holmes' bookstore on Kearny Street, and stood near the counter in the middle of the long narrow room, and pawed over many volumes of the *Modern Library*, peering into some and reading a few lines, and glancing occasionally at the price-mark on the last page. The proprietor was in the rear of the shop opening a wooden box with a hammer and chisel; a young Japanese nearby took down books of American poetry; George noticed that he read for a long time *The Vision of Sir Launfal*. The shop was a quiet recess, opening shell-like to the thunder of Kearny Street, and darkened by placards in the window announcing book sales. "Well," he thought, "Where's Max Stirner." He read the paragraph his friend Joe Farley so often quoted. Then, having ascertained that the proprietor's head was lowered over the box, that the young Japanese was remote in Lowell, and that no passerby was opposite the doorway, he slid the book into his pocket, and after waiting a few minutes longer before the counter marched out onto the sidewalk, head back and thighs swinging, filled with new energy, triumphant, Nietschean, and free.

CLARKSON CRANE

Having eaten ham and eggs in a White Lunch, he lit a cigarette and walked down Market Street toward the ferry, planning to buy his army shoes at the Spiro Harness Company, two or three blocks above the Embarcadero. He no longer felt sleepy, for coffee had revived him, and great, clamoring trolley-cars that pounded along four parallel tracks stirred his mind. It was good to be in the city once more; from the red framework of a new building a rapid clatter of riveting hammers drove into the roar of charging street cars, and one overwhelming, beautiful turmoil crashed into his ears. People with taut faces hurried by shouting to one another. "Gee," he thought, "this is some town after all." And he tossed his head and strode onward, exalted and gay.

When he reached the corner where Bush Street slants into Market, he heard someone cry, "Hey, George!" and he turned and saw Tuppy Smith running toward him and waving his arms. They stood for a while beneath the bronze statue calling to each other. "When d'ja get here?" asked Tuppy. "This morning," shouted George. "This morning?" "Yeah." "Going to Berkeley now?" "I guess so." "Say, listen here," exclaimed Tuppy, seizing his arm, "come along with me. I'm just going to the Flood Building on Powell." George hesitated before his friend's lively blue eyes. "I gotta get some shoes," he said. Tuppy drew him along Market Street. "We'll get 'em on the way down." "Aw hell, I—" "Just up the line," concluded Tuppy, and George said no more.

While they followed Market Street westward, Tuppy explained.

"It's this way," he said, gesticulating with a freckled hand. "There's a guy I gotta see up in the Flood Building. There may be something pretty good in it. Crawford his name is, and he owns a lot of land up near Yuba City. If I can get in with him, to hell with school. I won't waste any more of my time around that joint."

"But you haven't taken any 'Ag' work yet."

"Oh, that's all right. Wasn't I raised on a farm? I guess that's better than all this theoretical crap."

"Where'd you meet him?"

"Crawford? Why, down in Pescadero."

"Whenj'a go to Pescadero?"

"Why, I just came back from there," Tuppy exclaimed in surprise. "Didn't you know? I went down after Summer School to see the old man. Hadn't seen him for three years."

"Oh," said George. "I thought you knew I was down there."

"Naw, I didn't know," George answered. "The store's on the fritz and I guess the old boy often wishes he hadn't sold the ranch," Tuppy continued. "Anyway, I'm glad I cleaned out when I did Pescadero is sure the rottnest hole in creation."

When they reached the Flood Building, George said, "I'll wait down here," and, planting himself on the corner of Powell and Market, he began to smoke a cigarette. For almost half an hour he stood there and contemplated, rather sleepily, the women who passed by. He noticed them in the distance, and muttered to himself as they approached: "Seventy-five per cent," and then changed his estimate, perhaps, after seeing their backs. Gradually erotic images trooped into his mind, increasing his bodily heat, and causing him, now and then, to shift from one foot to the other. When Tuppy struck his shoulder, he was mentally undressing a young blonde who strutted eastward with a leather bag in her right hand.

"Nothing doing," exclaimed Tuppy. "Let's go."

"What's the matter?"

"Oh, I don't know. He doesn't want anybody. Say, listen, George, let's go out to Tony's and get a drink."

"Aw, hell, I have to buy my shoes."

"That's all right. We'll get 'em on the way back."

During the ride in the Powell Street car toward North Beach, George explained that he must return to Berkeley immediately in order to see Pete before dinner and "strike him" for his old job. "But I have to get my shoes first," he added. "Absolutely," Tuppy agreed, "we'll go right back."

"Say," asked George, "did you sell my German book?"

"Sell it? No. Why?"

"Oh, I don't know. I thought you might have."

Tuppy arose. "Here's where we get off. Hey, stop."

They jumped to the pavement as the car swung around a curve, and went north on Powell. The street was bordered with gray wooden houses of one and two stories; a few of them were shops with Italian names in white letters on the windows; some were restaurants, others just dwellings. After a time, they paused before a low ancient saloon, coated with dust, and Tuppy rang a hidden bell.

"He's got some damn fine cognac," he said.

Nearby footsteps thudded inside. The door opened. A tall thin man with dark hair and a long nose smiled, after a moment, and exclaimed in a slightly Italian way:

CLARKSON CRANE

"Come in, friends, come in." His eyes glittered. "Haven't seen you for a long time," he said to George, taking a mop from against the bar and thrusting it into a closet. George told him where he had been Tony said in his rather high voice:

"You can sit out in the kitchen. You know my wife, don't you?"

"Sure," answered Tuppy. "How are you, Madame Tony?"

When they were seated before an oilcloth-covered table with bread sticks before them in a tall glass, and a gray cat passing to and fro between their feet, Tony brought two small glasses and set the bottle nearby so that they might take more if they desired; and Madame Tony, laughing silently, remained near the stove and spoke now and then to the cook, a bald-headed man with a brown mustache. George liked to drink cognac and lean back in his chair: the room was so familiar to him: he had been there often the year before, and knew all the tawdry decorations on the wall, During one month when he was not working in Pete's restaurant, he had come over here three or four evenings a week, usually bringing a book and sitting until midnight over a bottle of wine. He had read *The Way of All Flesh*, while a traveling salesman and an ex-navy officer told dirty jokes at his elbow, their women giggling beside them. The story, for weeks afterward, remained in his memory. Some day he would read it again. He asked Tuppy what Herb Storey was doing.

"Damned if I know. He's in love."

George started.

"The hell he is."

"Yeah. The girl's an assistant in Econ. Herb read for her all last semester. He's a damn fool."

"Oh, I don't know," said George. When he was seventeen, he had loved a high school girl in Wyoming. She had not returned his affection, and the feeling had died, but he remembered the affair with a heavy tenderness, and often wondered if he would ever fall in love again. "Oh, I don't know," he repeated, and refilled his glass.

Madame Tony sat shelling peas, the cat prowling to and fro across her feet. George felt languid in the warm air. Had it not been for Tuppy's monologue he might have dozed, for the cognac had befuddled him; but his friend's voice kept sleep away, and George entered upon a calm reverie.

He thought for a long time of all the books he was going to read during the year. There were novels by Hardy, Meredith, Conrad, Henry

James. Bowing his head onto his chest and touching the wine-glass with his right hand, he listened to Tuppy and the rustling fire in the stove, and the tapping of shelled peas against tin, and smelt the odor of boiling meat. He would try also to write, which he had always intended to do, and would go on seriously with German in order that he might speak and read it easily before finishing college. With his hundred dollars he would be able to buy all the clothes he needed, and then—

Tuppy was shaking his arm.

"Let's go, George."

"Mmmmmmm?"

"Come on Let's get the hell out of here."

The air outside was gray. George did not know they had remained so long in the kitchen.

"Gee!" he exclaimed. "I gotta get my shoes."

They turned south on Grant Avenue, an undulating street that crosses Chinatown, and walked slowly between shops that gave forth odors of fish and incense. Men and women with yellow, tight skins surrounded them.

"You know what," began Tuppy, turning his face toward George, "I'm all for this guy Burton."

"Yeah?"

"He's got something on the ball. Had a long talk with him about that English paper I didn't write last year. I don't have to do it now. He asked about you."

George did not listen; a dim sense of well-being pervaded him: all those faces in the narrow streets were grinning at him, and fragmentary glimpses of Mendocino County and the night in the box-car were crossing his mind. Voices around him tangled. Once more be heard Tuppy, as if he were far away.

"I know where we can get some fine gin. The real stuff. Absolutely—"

A glistening automobile passed them, and George paused for a moment against a wall that felt cool and rough on his hands. "Get my shoes," he thought He was not certain whether or not he had spoken the words, and so he uttered them aloud, smiling at Tuppy and grasping his arm.

"Sure," answered his friend, "this way."

They entered a corner saloon and leaned forward against a mahogany bar behind which George could see his face in a large mirror.

"Shoes," he said, and then, lifting his voice, repeated: "Shoes. Goddam it. Shoes."

The door was waving and flopping behind him, now and then clicking softly, and he was walking along a sidewalk that seemed strange beneath his feet. "Crisp," he kept thinking, "the sidewalk is crisp," and he explained to Tuppy just what he meant, holding one arm out before him. But automobiles were crawling by with high golden noises coming from them, and he had to see where he was going. For a long time they sat somewhere drinking.

Now they ate. A little thin man in a derby hat was with them. George was telling about his shoes.

"You know," he said, "down by the ferry building. An army store."

He leaned back against a house wall so that an automobile might go by without touching him, and then he went on, hearing Tuppy's voice behind. He remembered all at once that he was going to see Joe Farley very soon, and that Joe was still in Alcatraz. He went downstairs.

She was beside him at the table. Her face was warm, her hand rough. She said: "I think you're a sweet kid."

For an instant a room took form around him, many tables, clangorous music, layers of smoke rising toward lights, eyes of men and women, hands, voices, smell: then all of it melted into the woman's head near him, and he was dancing with her, wrapping and unwrapping himself in the strands of music.

"Sure," she was saying, "sure, you'll get 'em, kiddo. A nice pair of shoes."

The air was cool outside and the cobbles on the street were rough and made his ankles turn first outward and then inward. He tried to remember where Tuppy was, and he halted and muttered in a voice that he could not hear: "Oh, Nellie," and she answered: "I'm with you, kiddo," and kept adding, as they went on: "Now be nice, dear, be nice."

He climbed stairs. The room smelt of old perfume. He felt sick.

"Come on, now, sweetie. You're all right."

His shoes fell one by one to the floor and soon he was naked. The room was warm. Nellie, naked too, was waddling to and fro. He laughed. Her hips were fat.

A long thick darkness was slowly disintegrating from around him, bits of it going here, bits there, and he kept dabbing at the pillow and thinking that Joe Farley had called him, and that the ferry-boat would bump when it moved into the slip. A few commuters were passing, and he tried to open his eyes so that he might see more clearly what he was doing. But his would not come open: his lashes were brown and the together.

A clear window was before him, with a curtain that stirred a trifle, and beyond, a dense blue sky glistened with light. He raised his head and saw his clothes lying on the floor, and felt that a great time had gone by, days, perhaps even weeks, and here he was alone in this small room with stained walls. A dented brass knob at the foot of the bed caught a line of sunlight and glittered. He lay back, for a slow ache was rising through his neck into his head, and he laid a bare fore arm across his eyes, and listened to the noises that rose from the street. Then memory returned, little by little.

He got out of bed, stretched himself, filled the basin, plunged his head into cold water, and dressed. As he went downstairs he found that his pockets were empty, but he thought nothing in particular. The book was still there, Max Stirner's *The Ego and His Own*, and, oh yes, there were two dimes in his trousers. She had left him enough to get to Berkeley. But the hundred dollars!

He felt the pavement under his worn sole and thought:

"Guess I'll have to borrow money for the shoes."

Then, with his cap pulled forward over his blonde hair and his shoulders hunched a trifle, he walked down to the ferry building.

II

MILTON GRANGER

Milton threw his hat into the straw rocking-chair, dropped the new books he had purchased onto the green blotter that covered his table, and sprawled for a few minutes face downward on the bed. The brown quilt smelt dusty. His watch ticked sonorously: *cluck, clung, cluck, clung*. The curtain on the south window brushed over the sill and the grind of a Euclid Avenue trolley-car came with the afternoon sunlight into the room, "a sort of jagged, bronze noise," Milton thought, quivering for a moment. Then a door opened and closed farther down the hall, and another student in the boarding-house went into the bathroom nearby, and soon Milton heard the swish of the water closet.

If he got up and went out, he knew that he would smell cooking, which was a damn rotten smell, especially when it was of cabbages. The odor had been in the hallway downstairs when he entered, an odor that reminded him of a house in Santa Barbara where he had gone years before to take lessons from a pale, caressing young man with yellow hair and red lips and restless, peering eyes; and Milton had hurried up to his room, after pausing briefly near the desk until the girl looked up from her book and said: "No mail for you, Mr. Granger. This was Tuesday. Saturday, Sunday, Monday: his mother couldn't have written Sunday, or he would have received the letter yesterday Perhaps mail from Southern California would reach Berkeley early in the morning, and he would find a letter waiting for him after he returned from his first eight o'clock, a letter written on the *loggia* of the villa at Montecito (his mother insisted on saying *loggia*) with the murmur of the blue and white Pacific filtering in among roses under the luminous sky. His mother was living on raw food now, having traversed Theosophy and Christian Science. He could see her before the tall open window, rather florid under glossy hair, sitting with a book in her lap and her legs crossed, moving rapidly and minutely the toe of one white shoe. Unless his Aunt Caroline returned from Los Angeles, she would eat dinner alone, chewing her food well and lovingly, while Noa moved near the sideboard in ber black dress and white apron and cap. Slowly, Milton rose and sat on the edge of the bed.

It was almost six o'clock, the hour when we would be returning home from tennis or an afternoon on the beach to dress for dinner. He always liked the weaker sunlight of late afternoon, with less glare on the white houses and yellow sand, when the mountains behind Santa Barbara were darkening, and their outlines growing more clear-cut. At this season the sun did not vanish until they had left the table and were smoking on the *loggia* from which they could see the sky walled with gold and the gray ocean. During that summer Miltan had begun to smoke, and his mother had given him for his eighteenth birthday a dark briar and a large red can of Prince Albert. Having set forth the Prince Albert on the living-room table, he bought real tobacco at a shop in town, and he would draw out his pipe, while his mother and aunt were lighting their cigarettes, and fill it, standing near the rose-bush and looking off into the deepening night over the sea.

Almost six o'clock. Beneath his window, he heard water sizzling from a hose onto a lawn. At six o'clock a man named Grooshen, Groshen, Goshen, something like that, a man he had met a few days before on the train from Santa Barbara, was coming to take him to a fraternity house for dinner. "They're a fine bunch of boys," he had said; "they'll be glad to know you." Groshen was an alumnus of the house; he had left the university four years before, in nineteen-fifteen, and after two years in the artillery was now in a San Francisco bond-house. Milton wondered if his name could be Grover, and felt once more in the inside pocket of his coat for the card he had surely put there. "Anyway," he thought, "I'll hear his name. Some one will call him something." He remembered a speech a master at school had made on the importance of fixing in one's mind the names of people. "It is probably Groshen," he decided, rising from bed and standing before the bureau; and he ran a comb through his brown hair and put on a fresh collar. Then he yawned and sat down in a chair to wait.

The hose stopped on the lawn beneath his window. He noticed that a few layers of afternoon mist were passing over Berkeley. His mother's picture on the bureau no longer reflected the low sun: he could see the face plainly now, the eyes regarding him pensively, as if they were saying: "You're not so very much after all, are you?" He had never seen his mother's eyes so calm as they were in the photograph. Usually they were vague, and he always felt that she was thinking far more of God than of him.

She would be disappointed if he failed to join a fraternity. He knew

CLARKSON CRANE

that her notions concerning them were indefinite. His father, Albert Granger, who died when Milton was eight years old, had been a Yale man, a member of Skull and Bones, and Mrs. Granger conceptions of fraternities were based more or less on memories of what he had told her. In a recent letter she had said: "Wire me as soon as you have been tapped. I do hope you will join a nice crowd."

The clock on the campanile struck six, and then the chimes began slowly and heavily to play a waltz, the notes drifting out into the still air. "Groshen is late," Milton said, rising from his chair. He rested his arms on the upper end of the window-sash and gazed out over the campus toward the west. The fog was vanishing, only a few wisps having blown over, and a flush was mounting gradually into the sky. He wondered if Groshen had forgotten. "I'll wait until a quarter to seven," he decided. He felt homesick again, and all at once loathed the bare walls of the room, stained yellow here and there, and pitted with white crumbling holes where tacks had been, and the stuffy brown bed-cover that had been darned in one corner. He heard his alarm-clock ticking (hitherto he had not been aware of it), a pudgy gilt alarm-clock like a short man with a bloated paunch, tilted a bit to one side. The damn thing would wake him up tomorrow. Some times a feeling of disgust flowed through him in the morning when he first opened his eyes, and he would lie in bed watching a swift lattice of sunlight wheel along the wall as the branches outside moved, and wonder why he had come to this place instead of going to Yale as he had always planned. He might be still in Santa Barbara. Yale did not begin for another month. But when he got out of bed he felt all right again.

"It'll be better when I join a fraternity," he thought. "There's no use being in this place if you're not in a fraternity. All the best men are in fraternities."

There was one fellow in his German class whom he liked, a husky fellow of about his own age with dull yellow hair and a tanned face, who sat usually beneath the window a few seats away. Milton had been regarding him so thoughtfully that the instructor pronounced "Mr. Granger" twice before he turned his head, and two or three girls bent forward and tittered. George Towne was his name. He would like to know him. He had lost sight of him after the German class, and had gone to a section of Freshman English in Wheeler Hall where a blonde, jovial and round-faced young man just back from France informed the stu dents with a wide smile that what they would learn was of no value, but probably would not hurt them very much. The class had giggled, and Aaron Berg, a young Jew whom he had seen before in the infirmary during a physical examination, said to him on the way out:

"Hopkins seems to be a good scout."

Goshen probably had forgotten. Milton hoped that he would not come, for he felt uncomfortable going to a fraternity house among a lot of strangers, where he would be as shy and silent as ever. The western sky was deep crimson now. Milton pulled down the shade over the window, He liked to shut out the moment that was neither day nor night.

The yellow light, which he turned on, blurred his mother's picture, drove shadows into the corners, hid the stains on the brown bed-cover, touched the books on the shelf above the table, the books he had brought with him from home. There were only a few of them. Milton felt more cheerful with the shade drawn. He had brought with him a volume of poems by Robert W. Service, *The Beloved Vagabond* by W. J. Locke, and *The Broad Highway* by Jeffery Farnol. He liked to read and think of wandering along highways and stopping for the night at old-fashioned inns, where he would eat beefsteak before a fresh snapping fire. These were his two favorite novels. Near them, lying flat on the shelf, was *Sapho*, which his Aunt Caroline had given him a week before his departure. "You must keep up your French," she exclaimed, "holding out the yellow book. Daudet is splendid."

At seven-thirty his mother and Aunt Caroline (if she had returned from Los Angeles) would sit down in the dining-room at the small round table that was lighted by two candles with frail pink shades, and Noa would bring in plates one after the other, giving Mrs. Granger only raw vegetables moulded into the sem blance of cooked food. Aunt Caroline always drank before dinner a golden cocktail brought to her solitary upon a polished tray. "I like people who eat," she once said with a snort, "and drink," tossing back ber long head with the mass of hair that was becoming gray. "We like our meat, don't we, Milton?"

He wished he were now in that soft dining-room which had always seemed so commonplace, where candle-light made a sort of pale yellow pyramid over the table, and the swinging door murmured and thudded as Noa entered from the pantry; and he began to count the weeks that must elapse before he would return home for the Christmas holidays. Eight, nine, ten—Aunt Caroline was planning to go to France next summer. "I should like to go with her," thought Milton Then he started. The muffled bell over his door buzzed savagely. "Good lord, there he is."

The bell sounded again. When he opened the door and smelt the dry hall with odor of cabbage still in the air, the girl's voice from beneath called:

"Some one to see you, Mr. Granger."

"Be right down," he answered, taking his hat. Aunt Caroline would remain all summer in Savoy and then go to Italy in the fall to visit an old friend living in Siena. Milton closed the door behind him and walked down the stairs, and imagined her striding, jovial, erect, and defiant over Europe, with her graying hair, her long face, and her snort. "Hello there, Granger. Guess you thought I wasn't coming. Sorry to be late." Groshen, Goshen, Grover was shaking his hand. "Oh, that's all right," Milton said. People talked in the front room. Somewhere else billiard-balls were clicking. "Oh, that's all right," repeated Milton, stammering a trifle, "I didn't wait long."

I've just come from the house," Groshen explained, as they descended the steps and followed Euclid Avenue toward the campus. "Oh," said Milton. "The boys are late too," Groshen continued. "A water pipe burst in the kitchen and the plumber took several hours to fix it." "Oh, I see," answered Milton. He wanted to go on talking, but could think of nothing further to say. "Dinner ought to be ready when we get there," Groshen said. They were passing among dark trees. Suddenly, Groshen seized his arm and exclaimed:

"Well, what d'you know?"

"Oh, I-why—"

"How are you making out, I mean?"

Milton was shorter than his companion and had to glance up at his smooth-shaven face with the rather wide mouth and big lips. Groshen smiled and waved a long arm toward the library and other buildings. "Registration and getting going in your classes," be said. "It's hell to begin with. You never know where you're at."

"Oh, I guess I'm getting started all right."

"You're in Letters and Science, aren't you?"

"Yeah."

The high grove of eucalyptus around the Greek Theater darkened the road along which they were walking. Milton thought again of the loggia in Montecito with vines black and twisted on the sunset.

"I was in Letters and Science," Grosben said. "It's a good college for a fellow who don't know what he's going to do. I majored in 'Econ' and took Philosophy for a minor. What are you going to major in?"

"English, I guess," Milton answered.

"Yeah? Who're you taking it from now?"

"Mr. Hopkins."

"He's all right. I thought you might be in Burton's class. He's a helluva good scout. I know him well. We were in France together."

"I don't know him," said Milton.

They passed the tennis courts, where a few men in the twilight were encasing their rackets, proceeded along College Avenue to the south, and turned westward on Durant, a street bordered with meager trees. Half-way down the block they came to a wooden house, bulbous and many-windowed, with a small porch on one side upon which a door opened. "Here we are," said Groshen, taking Milton's arm, "this way," and he led him up the steps to the doorway, and into a narrow hall filled with the clangor of jazz music and the rattling of drum-sticks. "The boys have a fine orchestra this year," he shouted, leaning forward and placing a hand on Milton's shoulder. "They got a frosh who sure can play the saxophone. Say, isn't that great?"

"Hello, Gresh," some one called from the next room.

Other voices repeated: "Hello, Gresh. Come on in, Tommy. Well, old Tom Gresham." Young men surrounded Milton and his companion in the hallway; the music stopped; the saxophone youth came forward slowly, with his instrument held under his left arm. "Gresham," thought Milton, while he shook hands with a multitude to whom he was being introduced, "Gresham. I'll remember that," and he went aloud: "Glad to know you, Mr. mumble-mumble, glad to know you, Mr. mumble-mumble."

In a few minutes the music began again, and Milton stood beside a large table near an empty fireplace, talk ing with a serious, broad-faced young man about the climate of Santa Barbara. Gresham, seated not far away in a brown leather morris-chair, was taking Durham from a skull on the table and letting it dribble into a yellow paper. "When it rains down there, it sure does rain, the broad-faced young man said, regarding Milton with melancholy brown eyes. "Yeah," replied Milton, thrusting his hands behind him against the edge of the table and giving a little laugh, "it sure does."

The saxophone in the other room brayed amid rattling drum-sticks and clanging cymbals; a round boy with glasses smote the piano; two fellows were dancing together, having rolled back the carpet, and now and then they whirled through the wide doorway toward Milton and his companion, and forced them back against the table. "Mr. Granger— meet Mr. Pollock." "Glad to know you, Mr. Pollock." "Did Shoomey let you by that 'Zoo' course, Poll?" "Hell, no, the old bastard rolled me."

Milton saw a tall, red-haired youth in a white coat and apron appear in the doorway and begin vigorously to shake a cow-bell; for a time the sound blended with the music and no one else observed him; he stepped forward and leaned against the wall and grinned at Milton; then the broad-faced young man turned around and started. "Oh, say!" he exclaimed. "Let's eat. Yay. Let's eat."

The red-haired youth opened sliding doors and exposed a long oval table set with many places. For a moment Milton was carried onward amid straining bodies. Then a hand grasped his arm and he heard Gresham's voice shouting into his ear: "Mr. Granger, meet Mr. Wendell." "Gresh tells me you're from Santa Barbara," said

Wendell, leading Milton to a chair near the head of the table. "Here's a clean napkin, I was in Santa Barbara last summer for a while. Played in a tennis tournament." "Oh, yes," answered Milton, and peered for an instant at the senior's thin face, "I remember you. You played in doubles with Nesbit. There—" He stopped. George Towne, the blonde fellow whom he had noticed in the German class, emerged from the kitchen with plates of soup along his arm. He wore, like the red-haired youth, a white coat and apron; Milton watched him, thinking that he liked his looks, and, when he had vanished again to fetch more soup, fell to dreaming that they might become friends, brought together by German grammar. An opaque reverie settled over his mind.

He lifted his head suddenly and felt himself grow ing hot, for Wendell and two other silent fellows were regarding him. "What?" he exclaimed. "I—I—did you—?" "It spurted all over the kitchen," said Wen dell, and we couldn't get a plumber for more than an hour. Some leak." "Oh, yes," Milton replied, "it must have been a bad one." Some one yelled: "Get that phone frosh!" and the saxophone youth, at the other end of the table, slid back his chair and hurried from the room, trailing a napkin from one hand.

After all the food had been eaten, Wendell leaned toward Gresham and said: "You start 'em, Tom." Gresham nodded, drank a last bit of coffee, wiped his mouth, cleared his throat, drew up his head, and bellowed forth the commencement of a song about the tummy of the golden bear. Ignorant of the words, Milton uttered vague sounds, A great seriousness dropped over the singing youths, and for a quarter of an hour songs followed one another, some of them about the university in general, others praising the fraternity, and having to do with stars, friendship, eternity, and good old college days. At last silence came; Wendell pushed back his chair and arose; the others did likewise; and, standing there around the table, they chanted very slowly the university hymn, beginning: *All hail, Blue and Gold.*

"Gee!" exclaimed Gresham, when they had finished and were going forth into the other room. "It's good to come back and sing the old songs again. Often I wish I was beginning all over. You don't know what a good place it is until you're out of it."

Milton noticed tears in the alumnus' eyes, and he felt a tender and proud surge in himself. The words of the song returned to him: "Loyal Californians whose hearts are strong and bold." He was glad, after all, that he had not gone east to college, for he felt certain that a spirit existed here (he had heard it proclaimed as California Spirit) which surpassed anything else of its kind, something mysteriously virile and superior, peculiar to this university. He remembered another song: *Fight, fight, fight for California*, and he felt tearful, bold and chivalrous. What a fine bunch of fellows this was! He would like to go through college days with them, shoulder to shoulder, carrying banners, chanting sonorous anthems, intrepid and warlike, battling for vast causes, and then through life's journey—"That was great!" he exclaimed to Wendell, who sat on the edge of the table stuffing his pipe with Prince Albert. "What?" asked Wendell, peering up. "Oh, the singing? Yes, we've got some good voices in the house this year." "Wonderful," said Milton, bringing out his own pipe. "Have some?" said Wendell, offering the red tin. "Oh, thanks," Milton replied, and he leaned against the table with the senior beside him, filled his pipe, took the match that Wendell held out to him, and puffed out smoke toward one of the cracked globes on the chandelier. It seemed to him that something good was commencing.

Two or three hours later he walked home alone through the campus, following the dim road that led beneath the hill on which eucalyptus trees surrounded the Greek Theater. They rose tall and somber upon the stars. Milton paused in the open beyond the chemistry building, and looking over the campus towards San Francisco in the distance, a shimmer of golden lights under still mist, let his thoughts drift back to the house he had just left. Many of the fellows had gone out after dinner, and he had passed the evening with Gresham, Wendell, and the saxophone youth, listening and talking. Soon the room grew cold, and the saxophone youth made a fire in the grate. He was tall and slender, with a thin freckled face and curly hair. His name was Burt Hudson, and he came from Honolulu. Milton smoked eight or nine pipefuls, and now, as he stood in the cool air, his mouth felt charred and stiff.

While they sat before the grate fire, Tom Gresham told of his experiences in France as a lieutenant in the artillery. He had seen no action, for the armistice had arrived when his outfit was in reserve behind the Argonne; but he had spent a furlough in Paris during the late summer. "Believe me," he said, "that's some town." Milton had lived two years in Paris as a child, and found at once a subject of conversation with the alumnus.

Emerging from beneath the trees, he turned west on Hearst Avenue, which borders the campus. There were lights in a few windows, "Fraternity houses," he thought, and walked more slowly. Music came through an open door, the rattling of a drum and piano, but as he went by, the noise ceased, after a few discords, and the yellow lights vanished from the room. Milton paused. In a moment he muttered: "Crickets," and stood a short while to hear their rhythmic chirping, the frail, insistent, white sound, for which he had so often tried in warm Santa Barbara nights to uncover the fitting word. Once he had written a sonnet, but Aunt Caroline found a copy of it on his table and exclaimed with her snort: "It makes me sick at my stomach."

Milton walked on, hands in pockets. A feeling of intimacy had grown in him regarding the house he had just left. Instead of dragging him to Oakland or Idora Park, they had been content to remain all evening near the fire, with tobacco-smoke in layers above their heads, and the warm red coals before them. "They're a fine bunch," he thought, and knew that he would no longer feel ill at ease among them. "Till join if they ask me, he said, as he turned north on Euclid Avenue. Had not Gresham left about midnight, Milton might be still by the fire, for he had been warm and comfortable, and exuded a vague good will toward his companions. "A fine bunch," he repeated, and remembered as he arrived before his boarding-house that Gresham had said, quite by chance: "We're very strong in the east. Especially at Brown. I guess we run the place." "Abso lutely," Wendell put in, nodding his head, "absolutely. We're strong as hell there." The saxophone youth, chin sunk in both palms, regarded the flames.

Only one light glowed in the hall of the boarding house, where there was no longer a smell of cabbage. Miton glanced toward the wire rack near the door to see if a letter from Santa Barbara had come while be was away; but the rack was empty, save for a postcard which had been there three days, and Milton went up the stairs as quietly as he could, and opened the door of his room. "There's no mail in the evening," he thought, "I knew that all along. When he had found the switch and turned on the light, he sank into the straw chair, and listened for a while to the pudgy alarm-clock ticking nearby. The curtain rustled before the window and he felt cool air on his cheek, and rising quickly he knelt before the low sill and thrust forth his head. Oh, what a night! Multitudinous stars trembled in the sky. The trees were dark. He sniffed the dampness of near fog. "I wonder if Mother would like the crowd," he thought. They had invited him again for the following night: if they should bid him, he would not know what to say. He would like to see more of other houses before joining any of them. His mother might exclaim: "Why *did* you join them? Really, Milton, you know nothing of any other fraternity, and now—" He continued the scene in imagination, but finally began to feel sleepy, and yawned in the darkness. "Oh, well," he thought, "I'll see what happens." Many stars bad vanished behind the fog, and the street lamp was blurred. Milton yawned again. "Oh, well, I guess it will be all right." He remembered the saxophone youth. Then he arose, turned from the window, pulled the brown cover from the bed, rubbed his eyes, stretched, and, with one of the songs heard after dinner running in his mind, began slowly to undress.

III

RENEWAL

C arl felt angry with her for coming this way: why couldn't she leave him alone? Tall, somber, expectant he stood with hands in pockets looking from his apartment window at the foliage outside, so clean-cut and motionless in the dense air of this September hot spell. She had written that she would come about two-thirty.

A car from San Francisco had passed along College Avenue and stopped beneath him on the corner of Haste Street about two-twenty-five: Mabel Richards had not been on it. He awaited the clear, hard ring of the bell, thinking he might not have seen her when she got off. But five or ten minutes went by, and he remembered how she had often kept him waiting in the room in Paris, nearly an hour before she would appear. "The fool," he muttered, "the fool." If he should go now, and pretend when he saw her (if he ever saw her again) that her letter had not arrived in Berkeley until two days later, he would at least avoid this meeting, and she might perceive (though he knew she would not) that he didn't want to see her any more. With head down and hands behind his back, he walked slowly into the other room, around the dining-table, then back into the front room, thinking that he might be studying (he knew simultaneously in a corner of his mind that he would not), and what nerve Mabel Richards had to write to the university for his address as soon as she returned to San Francisco. Then he heard a light rapping on the apartment door.

"Come in," he called, as gruffly as he knew how.

She came in slowly, closed the door behind her, and walked toward him, smiling in her melancholy way, her head, which was covered by a low, round hat, held slightly to one side.

"She has grown fatter," Carl thought, as he said: "Hello, Mabel."

"I didn't see your name on one of the mail boxes outside, and I came right in. I asked a man with a beard downstairs where Mr. Werner lived. He told me on the third floor."

She held her bag in joined hands before her and lowered her eyes.

"That's the landlord," Carl answered. He thought: "She wants me to kiss her. She acts as if she were sixteen. She must be at least thirty-five." He was saying aloud: "Sit down, Mabel. Yeah, over there."

She sat down on the sofa, having placed her gloves and purse in a small crumpled heap on his desk, took the cigarette he offered, accepted a light, leaned back among the cushions, and said, after contemplating him for a moment:

"You're looking well, Carl. Still brushing your hair in the same way. So stiff and black sticking up above your forehead. I've often thought of it."

He replied: "Um," then went on: "Have a good trip out? Awfully hot, I'll bet."

"No, not until we reached Sacramento. It was quite warm in New York the day I left, but Chicago was beautiful and cool."

Reclining there, smiling now and then in that rapid manner of hers, and dabbing her cigarette frequently against the ash-tray, she told him of a day in Chicago with Amy Carter, whom she had known for years, of the delay near Omaha behind a wrecked freight-train, of the first autumn colors in Michigan (which she adored), of the poor food in the dining-car. "I'll go Santa Fe next time," she said, "I love the Harvey System. And then the Indians you see are so picturesque. How did you come out?"

"Troop-train," answered Carl. He had been wondering, as she talked, where she got the money to dress so well. Of course, she received alimony from that fellow Richards, but not very much after all, considering the way she always lived. He had an unpleasant feeling at the thought that some one had been keeping her, some rich man in New York whom she had met after leaving the Red Cross. She had written him only once since they separated in Paris.

She asked: "Are you all right now, Carl?"

He shook his head. "Only fair. Same trouble I had in the army. Mostly my stomach, I guess. I'm trying to get compensation from the government. If I do, I'll go on studying here."

"Oh," she said, a shadow in her eyes, "I'm sorry. I thought you'd be all right." For a moment she was silent. Then, all at once, she popped forward, spilling cigarette ashes onto the couch-cover, took his hand, squeezed it, exclaimed: "Poor old Carl, he's a nice boy, but he's so gloomy," and then relapsed into her former position with that short little laugh, and drew her skirt away from the ashes strewn beside her. "On your nice couch-cover," she added, glancing up at him from under her low hat.

They sat in the warm room with the cars droning by occasionally along College Avenue below, and the sunlight, as the afternoon advanced, streaming more and more through the windows which faced the west; and Mabel talked on about the good times they had had together in Paris during the winter following the armistice, of the little restaurants they had found in narrow streets after Carl had finished his work in the headquarters office, of Sunday excursions to St. Cloud and Versailles, of the Grand Trianon silent, tinted, and melancholy in damp gray air. He listened without enthusiasm, and noticed that her skin was no longer so faultless as it had been, or as he had believed it to be: her complexion seemed almost pasty now, with one or two pimples on her right cheek; and her voice had a disagreeable, hoarse quality. He tried to imagine what she had been like more than six months before in the plain Red Cross uniform. "Give me a cigarette, Carl dear," she exclaimed suddenly. Offering his open case, he remembered the charm her voice always had for him in these same words, and how he had wished to preserve on paper some indication of the way she went down the scale and then half-way up, ending on a note plaintive and long drawn out; and he examined her now more closely, almost expecting to see her as he believed that she had been. But it was as if the quality of voice and mannerism of accent had come from somewhere else to emerge only for a moment from this per son who resembled the one he had once loved. "I guess I never loved her very much," he thought, and then said aloud, almost to his own surprise: "Take off your hat, Mabel." When she removed it quickly, as a boy would snatch off a cap, and laid it beside her on the sofa, he could not understand how he had ever been attracted to this woman who sat now before him. She was not even dark as were most of the girls who had drawn him hitherto; there was no real color in her hair: one could merely say that she was blonde; and then her nose and cheeks had a certain fleshiness, which even repelled him.

"What are you thinking about, Carl?" she asked.

A line of Verlaine came into his mind: "*Deux formes ont tout à l'heure passé*," and he tried to recall the rest of the poem, but it was gone somewhere. He answered: "A poem of Verlaine's. I can't remember it."

"Oh, say it, please. I adore Verlaine."

"I can't remember it," he repeated.

Mabel went on: "Carl, do they still want you to go into the store? Your father and brothers?"

He nodded.

"But you're not going to, are you?"

"I should say not."

She was looking at him earnestly, her eyes blinking now and then. Finally, as if after profound reflection, she said: "No, I think it's best didn't."

"Why should I go into the store?" he exclaimed, preoccupied now with his own affairs. "There's something more in the world than business. A fellow has a right to lead his own life. I—" He paused, half conscious of the stupidity of his words. Mabel was looking at him calmly, holding the cigarette in her left hand, her legs straight out before her with ankles crossed. What the devil was she thinking? Clearing his throat, he continued: "I want to study for a while, psychology mostly, and then have leisure to read." He considered it not worth while to go into details before her vague little mind. As a concession, he added: "I'm reading Dostoievsky."

"Mmmmm," she replied, her eyes lighting up.

"As if it were something to eat," he thought. "Little fool."

"What does your mother think?" Mabel asked.

"Oh, she's for me. That is she agrees with Father. But—ah," he spoke slowly, "she feels sure that I'll come around to their way of thinking, and is perfectly willing for me to go on at the university. Of course," he paused thoughtfully for a moment, "of course, they don't understand me at all."

"Poor boy," said Mabel.

Carl looked toward her. She went on:

"But don't you think that most of the men who were in the war have a hard time readjusting themselves to ordinary life? I know a young man in New York who doesn't know what to do. He wants to go back to Europe as soon as he can. I mean-oh, well, every one seems so restless."

Serious, she awaited his opinion. He answered finally: "Yes, maybe that's so," rather pleased at being victim of an epoch. "Child of the century," he thought, and repeated: "Yes, maybe that's so."

"In the meantime," she said, glancing around the room, "you're comfortable here, aren't you? It looks like a nice place." She slid from the sofa, went to a closet and drew aside the curtain covering the door way. "What's in here? Oh, the telephone. What a lot of shoes you have. And all so well arranged. I never knew you were so neat, Carl."

He replied: "Um."

"You sleep in the other room?" She peered through the door. "Do you sleep in there, Carl?"

"No. Out on the little porch. It opens off that room."

"Oh, yes, and you eat there." She walked in. Carl heard her moving about. Finally, she reappeared, laughing. "I never saw such a vile kitchen. Come on, we'll wash the dishes." She was removing her coat.

"Oh, no," Carl said, "not now."

Why did she have to trouble about such things? They had been sitting there, talking of important matters, and suddenly she had to leap up and wash dishes. "Not now," he repeated, but he followed her into the small kitchen where soiled dishes lay in piles in the sink and caught the towel she tossed at him.

She rolled up her sleeves; hot water from the faucet rushed drumming into the pan; one by one she held toward him moist plates that steamed slightly.

"It seems to me," she began, "that enough of your family are in the store. Three brothers. What is Henry doing?"

"Writing ads at McCann's."

"I went into the store the other day, Carl."

"Did you?"

"Yes. I was on Market Street and all at once I saw Werner's written across a huge building. I wondered if it could be your father's place, and I went in and asked for some ribbon. I looked all around for men like your brothers. I think I should have recognized them from what you told me. I thought I might get your address from one of them."

Carl let the towel drop away for a moment from the dish, and raised his head, wondering if she had been hanging around the store asking for him. She caught his eye and laughed.

"No, I didn't ask any one there. I got it from recorder's office, just as I said." She laughed again. "Poor old Carl." Then: "Are they all married?"

"Hugo and Henry. Hugo has a kid."

"Oh, really?"

"He's about five years old. Billy his name is."

"And you're an uncle. I don't know why that sounds so funny. Uncle Carl."

He smiled. "It does, doesn't it?"

"Here, be careful of these glasses. Look out, they're hot." She remained for a moment idle, dish-mop in hand, watching him. Then she took a greasy platter from the table and slid it under the bluish water.

"Does Henry like writing advertisements?"

Carl nodded. "He always wanted to be a writer," he answered, "and this is the next best thing to it. He kids himself along that he's doing creative work. Wait a minute, Mabel, I want to light a cigarette."

"Oh, you'll get ashes all over everything."

"No, I won't. You see," he went on, shaking out the match, "Father thinks Henry's gone to the dogs too. He doesn't like his wife."

"What's she like?"

"All right. Paints fairly well and she's a good cook. You see, Henry has known her for a long time. Met her several years before he went into the army."

"You and he get on well together, don't you?"

"Oh, yes. I'm over there a lot."

She asked slowly: "Does he understand you?"

"Oh," he said, "I guess so." They glanced at each other and laughed.

Most of the dishes were washed now. As he dried them, Carl had been putting them one by one on the shelf in the cupboard; and when they were all there, and only a few round puddles of water remained on the table, Mabel wrung out the mop and, removing the dish-towel from Carl's hands, spread it out along the wire near the window. Then she wiped off the table with a rag found beneath the sink.

"Aren't you glad now we did that?" She stood rolling down her sleeves.

"Yeah, thanks, Mabel."

When they were going into the other room, after a few more dishes and pans had been set in order, Carl began to tell Mabel of a good little restaurant he had found in San Francisco, where one could get wine without paying too much, and where the food was well cooked. The discovering of "good little restaurants" had been a constant occupation during their friendship in Paris. Carl would meet her and announce, more or less with joy, that he had learned of a place where one could eat well for only half as much as it had cost the night before. As Mabel sat down again on the sofa in the front room, Carl said: 'It reminds me of that place in the Rue Jacob. You remember it, don't you?"

"Of course I do. The little American with the nostrils was in there."

"And that tall woman, La Tour Eiffel. I wonder what's become of her."

"Oh, yes, and the room behind the partition. We never could find out who the people were that went in there."

"Oh, by the way," said Carl, "Steffins is in Berkeley."

"Oh, really? He *was* a funny person. With that awful laugh. Do you remember how he was always talking about the *péniches*?" Carl nodded.

"You were too," Mabel continued. "One day you told me that you'd like nothing better than spending a summer on one of them. Do you still want to go to sea?" she asked, after an instant.

"Sometimes. The other day I went aboard the F. W. Wilkens. That's the windjammer I made the trip to Honolulu on several years ago. Have a cigarette, Mabel."

He noticed, as he held a lighted match toward her, that her cheeks had more color, and that she still had the habit of beginning a series of rapid and futile puffs before the flame touched the end of her cigarette. The room was cooler now, though the late afternoon sunlight blurred the framed pictures on the walls. As he sat down in an armchair near the desk, she picked up a book that lay beside her on the couch and said, opening it:

"You're not studying too hard, are you, Carl?"

He laughed and answered: "No." Then it occurred to him all at once that he had asked her nothing about what she had been doing since her return to America. For a moment he hesitated, fearing to seem over anxious, but finally he began, gradually:

"Uh—how have you been, Mabel? Like New York?"

"Oh—yes. It's been all right. I've been terribly busy. With my course."

"Your course?"

"Yes. In short-story writing at Columbia."

"Oh, I see."

"I thought I might go on with my work here. Do they have courses in short story writing at California? That was one of the things I wanted to ask you."

Carl was silent. "I guess so," he replied at length.

Oh well, suppose she did live near him in Berkeley. After all, she wasn't so bad.

"I'll find out for you," he added. That curious feeling of displeasure at her coming to see him was fading now, and he wondered why it had been so strong.

Mabel observed a clock on the wall. "Carl," she asked, "what time can I get a car for San Francisco?"

"In about ten minutes," he answered. Suddenly, instinctively, he said: "Why don't you stay over for dinner?"

She shook her head.

"I must go back. I have an engagement in the city."

For a minute he felt relieved. Then, as he sat watching her there on the sofa, slowly, imperiously, brutally, a desire grew in him to possess her. Why not? She had been his often enough. What else had she come for? His face was becoming hot. He looked at her.

"Well," she exclaimed, taking her hat and rising quickly, "I must go."

While gathering up her gloves and purse, she kept her eyes averted.

"Don't," Carl said.

"Yes, I must."

Her voice was higher than usual. The moment passed.

"Well," Carl said, "all right. I'll ring you up one of these days. I think I can find out all about the short-story course. A friend of mine over in the fraternity house is majoring in English and he knows all about things like that. I suppose you want one of the advanced courses. I've noticed some of that kind in the catalogue. I'm sure you will be able to find just what you want." They had passed through the door into the hallway, which was darker, and began, one after the other, to walk down the stairs. Carl went on talking in a loud voice. "I've tried a little writing myself, but not very much. I met a fellow last week down where I was bowling who writes for some of the college papers—" They were on the ground floor, and the door was open.

"Good-bye, Carl," Mabel said, turning and thrusting forth her hand. "Call me up some time."

"I certainly will."

He stood on the threshold while she went down the front steps and crossed College Avenue to the corner where the car that ran to the ferry would stop, and he thought he was glad he had not started anything; for he did not want to get entangled with a woman just at this time, when he had so little money and was beginning to work. Yet Mabel was not so bad after all. He was glad she had not asked at the store for his address; it would never do for Hugo to know of such things as this. Standing in the doorway, he looked at her over there on the corner, slender, darkly clad, against the yellowish wooden house with white steps; and he waved his hand in answer to her smile and nod. Then the long car, passing before her, ground to a halt and when it started again, he saw her for just an instant on the rear platform, opening her bag.

He had seen her for an instant only, as there were other people on the platform. Having received her change, she walked through the car into the forward compartment, holding the ferry ticket in her gloved hand, and sat down between two men who were smoking cigars. She could no longer see Carl. Poor Carl. He was a nice boy, but a little—she looked down at the spittle and cigar-ashes along the corrugated floor—just a little stupid. Yet there was something awfully nice about him, in spite of his ill temper and awkward ways, a certain—she did not know what, perhaps youthfulness, which made her want to do things for him: she wondered now, as she thought of him in the untidy apartment, whether she might not darn socks for him or do mending of some kind. The car was drumming along at high speed. She was rather glad, nonetheless, that she had visited this boy whom she had decided, on reaching San Francisco, never to see again (she drove down once more the thought that she had come all the way from New York merely to see him,) and sat watching the wooden and stucco houses of Berkeley go by, thinking quite suddenly that she might in no time have washed out the dish-towel. She remembered Carl's expression of fear when he believed that she had asked for his address in the store. It was always that way, seeing herself in his eyes, or seeing there what he considered her. Even in Paris it had been the same, but not so much. Paris and the war and the armistice: all that was different. When the car stopped for the last time where she had to change onto an electric train, she arose and followed the men with cigars to the front platform. Stepping down, she saw her face for an instant in the mirror which the motorman uses to see behind him, and she thought that she must seem old to Carl who was only twenty-four. She found a seat in the train.

Carl would probably end in his father's store with the rest of his brothers; he would never be happy if he were not making money, and the best way to do that was in the store. He had often been so cheerful in Paris. She had had a feeling of surprise, almost of repulsion, on first seeing him in the apartment. Did he really look like that? As the train glided out along the mole, she noticed the dark, oily mud-flats, tinted here and there with gray and blue, glossy black often. For a few minutes other memories dimmed Carl in her mind.

She was on the ferry-boat at last, crossing the bay. Yes, she was glad that she had gone to see Carl: he was a nice boy, and she might not see him again. Of course he was not a person to think about as she had thought about him in New York: that had been silly (she walked over to the rail when they passed Goat Island;) but he had some nice qualities, and then what else was there in her life? There must be some one. She felt sad. Her life. She smiled. A nice mess it was. Jim Richards, then the French officer, and now Carl. Slowly she paced to and fro on the deck.

When the ferry-boat thudded its way into the slip, and the crowds moved about her, she thought: "Good heavens. How foolish I am."

It was only six-thirty: the fog had not come in and the air was warm, and Mabel decided to walk up to her hotel which was on Geary Street, not far from Union Square. Why was she troubling herself about that idiot Carl? She would never see him again. Crowds were on Market Street; the great cars pounded by; a few early lights were appearing. In a few days she would go down to Los Angeles to visit her sister, and she would remain there all winter in the little white bungalow with the row of fat-bodied palms along the street outside. She felt like laughing at Carl now, sitting there gloomy in that ridiculous apartment. How *could* she have cared for him? Those heavy eyes rimmed with dark shadows. Really, he was unhealthy, and she had pictured him as being so fresh and young. She walked faster along the sidewalk. People went by. There were more lights. She was free, free. All at once hatred rushed through her for this stolid dark faced young man with the awful bristly hair over his forehead. "The fool," she muttered, "the fool." Love that. She nearly laughed aloud.

She walked more slowly after she had turned off onto Geary Street. There would be time to lie down in her room before dinner, and then she would eat in the hotel and go to bed early. The gray mass of the St. Francis rose above Union Square. Thinking of her sister and her brother-in-law (he was in the oil business in Los Angeles,) she walked on to her hotel, and through the revolving door into the narrow lobby with the red carpet, brass cuspidors, and imitation marble pillars. And when the clerk handed her the key to her room, as she was moving away, he added:

"A gentleman just called you up, Mrs. Richards."

"Yes?" she said, turning back.

He left his name. Mr. Werner. He said he would call again.

Mabel said: "Oh, yes, thank you." She walked over to the elevator and stepped into the car. Then all at once she felt happy and wanted to cry out:

"He's coming. He's coming."

But she only stood there smiling, while the elevator climbed swiftly to her floor.

IV

INTERIOR

The window was open, and the shade moving slightly admitted noon sunlight that swelled across the floor nearly to the wide bed and then withdrew, leaving the garments sprawled over the carpet again in shadow The edge of the shade scraped now and then upon the wood-work. But the two young men in bed, both lying on their backs, did not stir, and George Towne, asleep on a couch nearby, went on snoring, mouth open, blonde hair disheveled against the pillow, one bare arm drooping downward to the floor.

The golden patch of sunlight advanced and retired and advanced again. It hesitated halfway to the large bed, trembled for an instant and then, as the shade bulged and rustled, glided forward, covering two or three empty beer bottles that lay among shirts and shoes. One of the young men in bed moaned, lifted his red hair from the pillow, turned over, lay down once more, and pulled the clothes higher around his neck. The shade clicked on the wood-work; George Towne snored. Rapidly, the red-haired youth lifted his head again and peered to and fro. Then, flat on his back, he extended his left arm, and without seeing where the hand went, pawed over the carpet, touching a coat, a book, a shoe, two bottles that clicked together, a neck-tie, and finally a pair of corduroy trousers. Slowly, he drew them toward him. When they were on the bed clothes, he leaned on one elbow and with his other hand touched a watch gradually from a pocket, looked at the face, and then let himself fall heavily back onto the pillow, where he remained for a while, limp and with his eyes closed.

At last huskily he called: "Dan! Hey, Dan!"

There was no reply. George Towne snored. Tuppy stretched his arms upward and dropped one of them onto Dan's shoulder. "Wake up," he cried. "Hey, Dan, wake up."

When Dan uttered no sound, but only rolled onto his right side, half burying his head with oily black hair beneath the pillow's rim, Tuppy flung away the bed clothes and stepped to the floor and stood for a moment stretching his arms. He wore B. V. D. underwear rather soiled and torn: he bent forward to find his socks among the empty bottles on the floor, he smelt an odor of stale perspiration emanating from himself and thought: "Gee, I gotta take a bath pretty soon. The first sock he pulled on was torn, so that all his toes emerged, and the garter, faded and limp, was so extended that he had to tie it around his leg. Thinking of the problem in book-keeping he had not done (the course was at one o'clock,) he finally uncovered the left sock, fought his way through a flannel shirt, which he smoothed down over his body, breathing rapidly, his hair mussed. "Hey, Dan, come on, you've got a one o'clock." Before putting on his shoe he passed the heel of it slowly along Dan's forehead.

"Come on," the black-haired youth snarled, shaking his head. "For Christ's sake, cut it out, Tuppy."

"Well, you've got a one o'clock, haven't you?"

"Mmmm rum rum," answered Dan.

Tuppy could not find his necktie. With his foot he swept aside the empty beer bottles. They tinkled for a moment and one of them struck the table leg. Across the room, without moving on the couch, George Towne asked: "What time is it, Tuppy?" "Twelve- thirty. Got a one o'clock?" For a long time George was silent: Tuppy thought he had gone to sleep again, and nearly spoke to him. But finally he answered, laying one arm across his face: "No, haven't got a one o'clock." He breathed thickly few seconds before continuing: "But gotta write a paper." "What about?" asked Tuppy, pouring refuse from the waste basket to see if his necktie were beneath it. There was another long silence. Tuppy lifted two or three chairs, stooped down and peered under the bed, dropped a towel onto the floor, finally exclaimed: "Ah!" and lifted his tie from under a pair of scuffed shoes that bulged near the door. "Say, George, what did you put your shoes on my neck-tie for?" "Mmmm?" "Oh, hell, get up." Standing before a tall mirror that rose from a low, marble-topped bureau, Tuppy adjusted his tie, and then, before combing his red hair, walked over to the window and raised the shade, letting the full sunlight into the room.

"Let 'em get up," he thought. "Why shouldn't they? They've slept long enough."

Dan lay with his back to the window, only a portion of his head emerging from the bed-clothes, but George was sitting up, regarding without expression the yellow wall opposite.

As he tied his shoes, Tuppy asked again: "What do you have to write a paper about?"

"*Duchess of Malfi.*"

"What the hell's that?"

"A play."

Tuppy thought: "George is wasting his time with all these English courses. Why doesn't he take something practical?" He turned toward him, as he sat in bed, still blinking in the fresh light, hair falling to his eyes, and said: "Got any money?"

George shook his head. "Not a damn cent."

"Well, how are we going to eat?"

George pondered, knees raised and arms about them.

"I guess I can borrow some. I don't owe Burton anything."

Having tied his shoes, Tuppy went out and started down the hall toward the bathroom, an old towel over his shoulder. Half-way there he paused: before one of the doors stood a quart bottle of milk and a long thin loaf of bread.

"Fine," thought Tuppy. He took the bottle and the loaf and returned to his room.

George had risen and was standing near the window, with his underwear in tatters around him, and the sunlight falling onto his skin. A dark tan descended along his neck, and his arms were burned nearly to the shoulders. But over his back were clusters of small pimples.

"Look," said Tuppy, showing him the food.

George started. "Where'd you get it?"

Tuppy nodded his head sideways. "Down the hall. It was against the door of that two-room place where the girls live."

Momentarily, an expression of uncertainty passed through George's eyes, and Tuppy thought: "What's the matter with him anyway? He's got no nerve at all." Then George's face collapsed into a baba laugh; the uncertainty returned for an instant to his eyes; he laughed again and said:

"Holy Christ! Do you think you ought to do that?"

"Aw, why not? Gimme your knife so I can open the bottle."

There was a round table littered with books near the window, and while George was putting on his shirt and trousers and shoes, Tuppy cleared away the books, which he piled one upon another near the door, and set forth the loaf and the bottle beneath the lamp that was screwed down and could not be removed. A spatter of milk fell on the table when he dug out the cap: rapidly, he wiped it off with the sleeve of his flannel shirt; then, with the short blade of George's knife, he cut five or six chunks of bread and arranged them in two piles on either side of the bottle.

"All right," he announced, "let's eat."

George finally came to the table, shirt open and trousers unbelted, and the two students emptied the milk bottle, drinking from it one after the other. While they were crunching bread, a clock somewhere sounded one. Tuppy swallowed and said: "I gotta go," and went quickly to a corner of the room and began to paw among some clothes and old newspapers. "Seen my notebook?" he asked, stooping over. When George answered that he had not, Tuppy straightened up and saw it on the bureau. "Well," he said, putting it under one arm, "I'm off. See you later." Erect, hurried, a trifle out of breath, thinking: "I gotta make time." he strode through the door and slammed it behind him.

S eated before the table, George heard his footsteps grow fainter along the hallway. Tuppy would not return until late afternoon, for he had classes until five. "I'll see Burton," George thought, breaking a piece of bread, "and borrow ten dollars from him. He ought to be in his office about two o'clock." In the stillness of the room abandoned by Tuppy, George could hear Dan snoring with a faint click now and then, and the noise made him wonder if Dan owed Burton any money. If he did not, he too might borrow some, not very much, just seven or nine dollars, an uneven number that would not sound so full and much as ten or twenty. The young instructor in the English Department had lent money previously to all of them, but last spring, before departing for the lumber-camp, George had won heavily at poker, and had repaid, which he rarely did, the money he owed. "Damn glad I did," he thought, "because I can borrow more now."

He sat with elbows on the table and jaws moving. Soon he began to think that he should get to work, and, having lit a cigarette, pushed the empty milk-bottle and the bread crumbs away from before him, opened a drawer, and took out a few sheets of paper and a pencil.

It was not difficult for him to write the paper once he began. He had enjoyed the play, especially the somber last act in which the Cardinal, Ferdinand, and Antonio all follow separate ways of death to the great cold hall where Bosola, a "wretched thing of blood," stabs in frenzy. He wrote five or six pages summarizing the plot and describing the chief figures. When he had half covered a seventh page with his big, irregular scrawl, a misgiving entered his mind: would it not too obvious if he went to Burton's office and asked for the money? How much better it would be were he to meet him, as if by chance, on the campus, and, after accompanying him a short distance, to say: "I wonder if you could lend me ten dollars? I just happened to think you might—you see—" George pondered, drawing tiny figures with his pencil. Frequently, Burton went to the swimming pool about four o'clock and lay around on the warm stone. He might find him up there and ask him, or else learn when he would emerge from one of his classes and wait for him outside, in order to meet him by chance. "That might be the best," George thought, looking down once more at the written page. He felt sure Burton would give him the money, for the young instructor had been very friendly all the preceding year to the entire group who lived more or less together, but especially he had favored George.

During another half hour, leaning on the table and breathing thickly, George continued his paper, while Dan Wilkens, black hair on the pillow, snored minutely. But foreign ideas mingled with what he was composing about the *Duchess of Malfi*. It occurred to him that Burton might have no classes this afternoon, and that he might be at home, away out on Euclid Avenue, up the hill. "I can't go out there," George thought, commencing to recall someone else from whom he might borrow, "Let's see. This is Tuesday, and Burton has section in California Hall on Tuesday afternoon, I'm dum sure." He stared for a while at the yellow wall beyond the bed. Or was this Tuesday? He had left that fraternity house where he had a job as waiter last Thursday,— no, before that. He had left it after dinner on Monday. He was sure of that, because the men in the house were just going downstairs to the meeting (one of the under classmen had struck a gong in the hallway,) and Monday was the evening all over the campus for meetings of fraternities and house-clubs. Then on Friday and Saturday he had the job arranging papers in the recorder's office. "Let's see," he muttered, "that leaves Sunday, Monday—yes, that's right. Today is Tuesday. Of course, last Tuesday he had met Burton on the campus in the afternoon and had told him that he had lost his job at the fraternity house the day before. And Burton had asked: "Do you need any money? I'll lend you some if you're broke." George had refused impulsively without knowing why, having five dollars in his pocket. Later in the day he regretted that he had not borrowed the money (he always used the word "borrow,") but now it seemed fortunate that his credit was still intact. "Burton's a good scout," he thought, bending forward once more over the paper.

He wrote on for another thirty minutes, but the parade of irrelevant ideas kept prowling through a back hallway of his mind. He was fairly sure now he had caught nothing from the woman he slept with that night in San Francisco. Pete had told him that he could have his job as dishwasher the first of next week: he wondered if the old cook were still there; then he remembered the Greek waiter with the popping name and the high bush of hair with whom he would shoot craps at one o'clock in the morning, just after the restaurant had closed for the night. He could see the kitchen again, the floor near the wide sink wet from the water he had slopped over while washing the dishes. He would be still wearing the gray apron that he took off before going home, and tossed toward the black hook near the door opening onto the basement stairs. A smell of grease always hung in the air.

He jerked up his head and began to write. A picture came to him of the dying Bosola, holding a bloody dagger aloft in one hand, and shouting: "Revenge Revenge for the Duchess of Malfi—" What was the remainder of that speech? He turned pages until he found it, and then repeated, with a certain relish, "Arragonian brethren," and decided to end his paper with a brief description of the scene. He wrote: "The dying Bosola lifts his dagger and shouts—"

"Say, George! George!"

Dan Wilkens was sitting up in bed calling to him.

"Yeah?" He peered up.

"Say, what time is it, anyway?"

"I don't know. About two, I guess."

"Two! Well, my God, why didn't you wake me up? Didn't you know I had a one o'clock? Sweet Jesus! What's the matter with you fellows anyway? You're a fine gang. Letting me sleep on when you knew damn well I had a one o'clock."

He swung his legs to the floor and sat on the edge of the bed in his underwear, which was yellowish and had long sleeves and legs. George answered:

"Tuppy woke you up. You went back to sleep again."

"Oh the hell he did."

"Yes, he did."

"Aw, he didn't."

Dan rose and went to a pile of garments in a corner and extracted a rumpled pair of trousers into which slowly he inserted his legs, grumbling meanwhile: "This is the third time I've missed this course. Tuppy knew that. You did too," Dan exclaimed, raising his voice, and reaching for a soiled pink and white shirt that lay among the rubbish on the floor.

Head close to his paper, George answered: "Mmmmm," accustomed to Dan's early morning ill humor. He knew that he needed three large cups of coffee, and, if possible, a drink of bootleg whiskey before he could enter the day with serenity. When Dan roared: "Where'd you get the milk, huh?" George did not reply until the question had been repeated. Then he said, without looking up: "Down the hall."

"Hum," Dan grunted, stamping his foot into a tight shoe. "Why didn't you save me some?"

"You wouldn't get up. We called you."

"Like hell you did."

George glanced at the line he had written, "The dying Bosola lifts his dagger and shouts—" and then read over the entire paper, thinking it might be long enough without the final paragraph. It was nearly time for him to seek Burton, who might be in his office between two and three. "I guess it will do," he thought, "six and a half pages." He knew the reader in the course, a graduate student in English with whom he had played poker the year before, and he felt sure he would be lenient. "He ought to give me a two anyway," he decided, "even if it isn't very good."

Across the room, Dan was plunging his face into a basin of water, splashing the floor, a chair that stood near, and the foot of the bed. Then he drew a comb from his pocket, and, spreading his legs apart before the mirror, lowered his head as much as possible, and combed out his wet hair. The water from it slopped onto the marble top of the bureau.

"You know," he said, turning from the mirror and wiping off the comb on his trousers, "I think I'll go to my two o'clock today. Swanson doesn't call the roll, but I might as well go anyway. He's all right, that fellow."

Long, lean and dark-haired, he peered earnestly at George. "It's a damn good course," he went on. "He's talking about Whitman now. You ought to take it."

"Mmm," answered George, who was thinking again of Burton. Dan gathered a few books from the wash. stand. "Well," he said, "I gotta go. It's damn near two o'clock."

As he pulled a cap over his eyes, there came a low knock at the door, which was repeated after a few seconds, a trifle more loudly. A voice said very slowly: "May I come in?"

"It's Burton," exclaimed Dan. "Sure, come in."

The door opened. "How the hell are you?" he demanded, and strode forward and held out his long hand to a stocky man of about thirty who hovered uneasily on the threshold, touching one end of a short brown mustache. "Have a good summer?" Dan continued, shaking hands with energy. "When I last saw you, you were going into Yosemite."

"Oh, yes, thank you. Had a great time." Burton spoke nearly with a drawl. "We were in the mountains six weeks." He walked over to the table and laid his gray hat beside the milk bottle. "I'm awfully glad to see you again. You're looking well. I saw this fellow (he touched George on the shoulder) "last week. You haven't found another fraternity house job, have you?" He grew more serious. "I've been wondering what you were doing."

"No. Haven't got any job now." George laughed. Then he added: "Oh, hell, I'll find something."

A clock struck two, and Dan Wilkens, who had been stirring restlessly near the doorway, said: "Awfully sorry. I've gotta go. Have a two o'clock. Listen, you'll come around again, won't you? Absolutely. We still eat in the same place. There, almost every night."

Burton had been regarding George. Now he turned to Dan and answered: "Oh, yes, I'll be around. When Dan had slammed the door, he asked George: "You don't have to run off, do you?"

"Oh, no, I've got no class this afternoon, at all."

"Good," said Burton. "Good."

Silently he lifted one or two books from the table, glanced at the open and disheveled bed, thrust his hands in his pockets, and strolled for a minute or two about the room, peering with a slight forward movement of his head (George knew that he was nearsighted) at several photographs on the bureau.

"Isn't that the damnedest thing," George was thinking, "just when I wanted to see him. How shall I work it now?"

Burton halted. "By the way," he said. "You don't need any money, do you? If you're broke, you know—"

George pondered.

"Oh, hell," he answered, with a brief laugh, "I don't know. I hate to borrow money from you. I guess I'm broke all right, but I can get along.

It's damn decent of you, but perhaps it would be better if I didn't." He knew he could go as far as this in refusing. He waited. Had he gone too far?

"Here," said Burton, drawing some bills from his pocket. "Let me lend you fifteen." He put the money in George's hand, which he squeezed for a moment. "No hurry about paying it back."

"Oh, no," George stammered. "Oh, no. Really, I don't need it." He became red.

"Go on, go on, go on, take it."

Burton turned away: George looked quickly down at the bills; then he put them into his trousers.

"Well, thanks very much," he said. "I'll pay it back as soon as I can. Thanks very much."

Burton swung around suddenly and approached the table.

"What are you writing?"

"Oh, nothing in particular. A paper for an English."

"What about?"

"*The Duchess of Malfi.*"

"Oh, yes. It's good, isn't it? The Elizabethans are lots of fun." He picked up the sheets. "May I read it?"

"Sure, if you want to." George was very cordial. He admired Burton's calm opinions and his urbanity. The instructor, though born in Kansas, had lived in London and Paris, and, aside from his work in the English department, wrote book reviews for the weekly literary section of a New York paper. In his rooms, which were far out on the hillsides of North Berkeley, be had many volumes in French, German, Italian, and English, a piano, and always a bottle of port or sherry, which he brought forth about eleven o'clock, when they were sitting on the lounge before the fire. George had been to his rooms three or four times during the past year. Wait ing now for Burton to finish the paper, he wished that the instructor would invite him to come up after dinner.

"Mmmm," said Burton, nodding over the pages. "Mmmm. Been reading anything else lately?" He laid down the paper, went over to the window and exclaimed: "What perfect weather!"

"No." answered George, "only the *Duchess of Malfi.* I'm going to read one of Massinger's next."

"Yes, and Cyril Tourneur," Burton muttered slowly, and John Ford. I must go though some of those chaps again. It's been years since I read them." He was silent. Then he asked: "What's Dan taking this year?"

"Oh, the same sort of thing, mostly English. He's gone to Swanson's course now."

"Good heavens," Burton said, "does he like that man?"

"He said he did. Likes him very much. But I don't know (George felt his soul ooze toward Burton,) "Dan likes anybody other people don't like. Then Swanson is all for the stuff Dan writes. Says he's the only genius on the campus."

"Oh, then Dan is writing again? That's good."

"Yes, he's going to have a story in the *Occident* next month." George grinned and added: "It's about a pimp. But it's written in such a way that you'd never know what it's about. Dan is clever all right."

"Where is Herb Storey?" Burton asked, sitting do in a rocking-chair that swayed to one side and taking a square-bowled pipe from his pocket. "Have you match?"

"Sure." George pawed among some fallen garments for a box; then, having found them, sat near the table. "Herb Storey? Oh, he's around. Lives down west of Shattuck in a basement. He's in love with a girl who's a graduate student in Econ."

"The devil he is! And how about Billy Schwartz Is he any better?"

George shook his head. "Worse, I guess. Both lungs are affected now, and he's gone down onto the desert. Still writing though. He had a long poem in the *New Republic* last week. Didn't see it, eh?"

"No, I didn't. By Jove, that's bad—bad, bad. He has talent, that boy."

"He wasn't getting enough to eat up here last year," George said. "I know damn well. That's what put him under again."

After a few minutes of silence, Burton knocked out his pipe and asked: "So you're going to live with Dan and Tuppy Smith, eh?"

"Well, for a week or so, until I get a job. This room is really just meant for two."

"So you'll be looking for a room before long?"

George nodded.

He knew that in Burton's apartment, which was really a cottage partially attached to a larger house there was a small room, well furnished, under the roof; and he had often hoped that Burton would offer it to him, instead of storing books there, and keeping it for a friend who arrived occasionally from Santa Barbara. "It would be just right," he thought now, staring down at the cigarette stubs on the carpet. "I don't know where I'll find one," he went on. "Berkeley is crowded this year."

"Yes, I know." Burton nodded. "A friend of mine has been looking around for a place to live. He wants to be here six or seven weeks. He could find nothing, so I've stowed him away in that little box up under my roof."

"Oh, yes. That's damn nice. Is that the fellow from Santa Barbara?"

"Yes. He teaches in a school down there. It doesn't open until the first of October, and he'll stay with me until then."

"Oh, I see," George replied.

The sunlight was entering the window at a greater angle now, covering the bureau and making the mirror shine. Burton arose and walked about.

"How would you like to go up swimming?" he asked finally. "I was starting up there, but thought you might like to go with me. It's perfectly lovely up there these late afternoons."

George thought of the paper he had not finished, but remembered the fifteen dollars, and decided it would be better to do as Burton wished, even if he did not feel especially like swimming. Perhaps if he came to know the instructor very well, he might offer the small room, after his friend had left for Santa Barbara. Moreover, he never knew when he might want to take another snap English course; and Burton, if they came late from swimming together, would doubtless invite him to dinner, and might even urge him to come up the hill afterward to have a glass of port. The water would be nice in this hot weather: his head felt stuffy after working so long on the paper. Why not go swimming? It wouldn't cost him anything.

"Sure," he said, "that's a fine idea. Just the thing in this hot weather." Then: "I wanted to ask you about one or two things."

"All right." Burton took his gray hat from beside the milk-bottle. "We'd better go right away so that we'll have time to lie around in the sun. It's bully."

"Let's go," said George. "Where the devil is my cap?"

While he was reaching under the bed, choking a little the dust, Burton asked: "Going anywhere for dinner?" And when George, after coughing, answered that he was not, Burton said: "Better come and eat with me up at my place. Joe likes to cook up messes. He's the fellow from Santa Barbara, you know. He's got something good for tonight. He's working up there now. And we have a lot of dago red we bought in the city. You'll come, won't you?"

"Yes." George replied, "I'd love to." He had found his cap far back against the wall and stood, red-faced, brushing off his trousers. "That sounds good."

Burton opened the door. "All right. That's fine. I think you'll like Joe. I've told him about you."

George felt a momentary surprise that Burton should tell any one about him. He drew on his cap.

"Come on." Burton said, "let's get started."

They stepped into the dark hallway together and George slammed the door behind them. Then, walking lightly, he followed the instructor downstairs.

V

Tom Gresham

From where he sat near the head of the long table, Tom Gresham could see all the members of the fraternity, the seniors on either side of him, then the juniors and sophomores, and finally the freshmen in a semi circle at the lower end. The swinging doors into the pantry flapped behind them: a Japanese boy in a white jacket carried in dishes. Tom wondered where that blonde fellow, Towne, was, whom he had seen waiting on the table a month before, and he asked the man next him. "Oh, we fired him long ago. No good. He came late for every meal." Tom Gresham ate slowly. He felt contented to be once more in this dining-room with the gray chipped plaster walls and the college flags and fraternity shields. "Good to be back now and then," he thought, laying down his book and listening to the conversation among the freshmen. "That guy? Hell, no—"; "I was coming out of the gym—"; "I think I'll drop that damn Zoo course." He remembered his own freshman year, and thought, not with out melancholy: "They have the best four years of their life ahead of them." The fellow next him said: "You're coming over for initiation two weeks from Saturday, aren't you?" "Yes," be answered, "I'll be here."

He had a room in San Francisco, out on Taylor Street near Russian Hill, which he had occupied for a year, ever since bhe began selling bonds for Morton, Dunlop & Company. On one of the pale walls hung a calendar advertising an insurance company to which a friend of his belonged, and on another a California banner drooped from two thumb-tacks. Lying in bed he could see through the window, provided he had drawn the limp curtain aside, the back of a white stucco house with a kitchen door half open and a few feet of clothes-line. Frequently, when the sash was raised, he could hear voices in the kitchen and water drumming against tin. But he could not make out what the voices were saying.

"Yes," he repeated, "I'll be here. About seven-thirty?"

Wendell, the blonde tennis player with the narrow head and closely cut hair, answered in his hurried way: "Yes, I think so," and then, bending forward with one hand against a tumbler, called out to

Dick Folger, the robust president of the house, who sat on the other side of Tom Gresham: "Initiation about seven-thirty, eh, Dick?" "Yeah," answered Dick, and went on talking with the man next him about a course in book-keeping that he had just begun.

"Been to any of the games yet, Tom?" Wendell said.

"No? Say, you ought to go. Got a wonderful backfield. Even better than last season. Chippy Griggs is gone, but that fellow Spook Taylor is a wonder. Old Scrubby's doing fine too. Say," he turned away from Tom, "I wonder if they've saved anything for him." There was loud conversation at the other end of the table. Wendell hesitated for a moment, mouth a bit open, and then called: "Hey, freshmen. Did you save any food for Scrubby?" No one heard him; they were shouting at one another. A sophomore broke in: "Freshmen! Wake up!" Still they did not respond. "What woman?" one of them cried. "The red one? Oh, for Christ's sake, Bert, not the red one." Resting both forearms on the table and joining his hands, Wendell thrust his head slightly forward (Tom noticed that his neck was growing red) and bawled: "Fresh-mun." There was silence, then a meager tinkling of knives and forks, finally silence again. "What the hell's the matter with you down there?" Wendell demanded, looking keen and terrible. "Damn bunch of logs." His voice fell, and he added in a rather grunting tone: "Good cold bath wouldn't do you any harm." Then, having cleared his throat, he repeated: "Did you save any food for Scrubby?" There was an open-mouthed quiet, but at length the Japanese boy said: "We keep food for Meesta Martin." "Oh, you've got it, have you, Frank? That's fine." Wendell glanced toward Folger. "The freshmen ought to look out for that, eh, Dick?" he asked in an earnest voice. "Yes," answered Dick with majesty toward the freshmen. "Wanna look out for that. A fellow's hungry when he comes in late from practice." The freshmen returned with bowed heads to their food.

While the others were talking, Tom looked down at them, wondering if he would ever know them well, these newcomers who were not yet members of Alpha Chi Delta. It was difficult to keep in touch with the boys when one was working in the city, and when the girl to whom one was engaged lived in Oakland, where one had to go three or four times a week. In town there was only the weekly graduate luncheon to which the undergraduates rarely came; every semester more unknown faces were appearing in the house; and now there was this new group of freshmen down there a the other end of the table, the class of nineteen twenty-three. He murmured the numbers again. Nineteen twenty-three. His own class was fifteen; it was nearly the end of September nineteen hundred and nineteen, and he had been out more than four years. Two of those years he had spent in the army, six months in France. As he sat there, regarding the freshmen, he wanted to be back in the house, living here in the old way, studying now and then, going to courses, playing bridge in the afternoons and evenings, swimming during the warm weather in the cool green pool up Strawberry Canyon. He watched one of the freshmen, that stout, dark, little fellow from Chile, leave the table to answer the telephone. He had it all before him. After all, what was the good of this bond-selling? Suppose he did make money and marry Ethel Davis and finally enter the firm? Well, what then? Beside him, Wen dell in his brisk voice was saying: "Business pretty good, Tom?"

"Fair," be announced, "fair. Ought to be a first rate year, I guess."

Wendell, he knew, would make good. He was coming into Morton, Dunlop & Company next spring, after he had left college. The Alpha Chi's sent a lot of men into Morton, Dunlop & Company. For a moment Tom had a feeling of comfort and pride that he was making good in the bond business, but that same kind of intimate desolation followed. Why was he doing it? Why was he doing anything? "People are beginning to buy," he said aloud. "Don't know why. Everybody's buying bonds. All over the country."

The Japanese boy was bringing in coffee now, and the fellows were lighting their cigarettes and pipes. Tom looked once more at the freshmen. Tony Barragan, the little Chilean, was back from answering the telephone Soft-voiced, sleck, muscular in a pudgy sort of way, he was leaning toward Bert Hudson, speaking with his slight accent, Bert Hudson rolled a Durham and nodded his head, and on the other side was that fellow from Santa Barbara, Milton Granger, whom they had pledged three weeks before. He was filling his pipe from a brown leather pouch, and when he caught Tom's eye, he smiled.

"Cigarette, Tom?" asked Wendell, offering his case. "Thanks, I will." "Light?" "Mmmmm."

Puffing out smoke with his under-lip slightly advanced (a trick he had acquired during his freshman year from the senior who was president of the house,) he contemplated the two remaining freshmen. One of them, Jarvis Smith, was slender and dark and had been to school in England; the other was a rangy youth with pale hair whose father owned an orange ranch near Los Angeles. Paul, his first name was, but Paul what? Tom did not know. Shaking out a match, Paul said something to Milton Granger, who nodded and replied: "All right, let's go about eight o'clock. There's a good picture down at the T. & D."

Just then Dick Folger shoved back his chair and all the brothers arose, and there was a great thumping and rasping. Tom Gresham went into the living room and sat down near the empty fireplace in a brown leather morris-chair, the same one he had occupied so much when he was in college; Wendell was on the davenport that stood against the table on which five or six men were sitting; and one of the sophomores, Pollock, leaned on the chimney, both raised elbow spread like wings along the mantelpiece and his hips writhing with the music that clutter from the adjoining room

"How's business, Tom?" he shouted, not ceasing to squirm.

"First-rate," answered Tom, slowly.

Pollock nodded his long head. "Good. I'm glad to hear that." Then, lifting his face toward the cream colored globes on the chandelier, he opened his mouth and bellowed: "Ta de dee, ta ta dee dee."

Tom liked all this friendly noise: it made him feel at home. "They're a fine bunch of boys," he muttered, "a fine bunch of boys." He lay back against the leather cushion and inhaled a puff of his cigarette, and looked up through rising tobacco smoke toward mirror behind the black clock on the mantelpiece. A jumble of moving heads was reflected there: he could see the back of Dick Folger's neck, rather thick, red and bristly, and Tony Barragan's stubby hair. Nearby, was that freshman named Paul who had said something at dinner to the Santa Barbara fellow about a moving picture show. He was dancing with one of the juniors whom Tom did not know, a new man who had transferred this year from Wisconsin; and, not far away, also dancing, were two sophomores, both from Sacramento, who were inseparable. Milton Granger stond in the doorway watching them. The saxophone wailed over the rattling drum and piano, Tom thought: "A fraternity will do that man Granger a lot of good. He hasn't been around much with fellows, He's a nice kid." On the davenport Wendell was saying earnestly, in his rapid manner, to another senior: "We'll have to watch Bert Hudson. He's out chasing every night and for three days now he hasn't gone to an eight o'clock."

Tom continued to examine Milton Granger, whom he found interesting and exotic; for he knew that Granger, though born in Chicago, had lived a number of years abroad, and he surrounded him with impressions he had gathered during his months in France. When he was in Paris on furlough, he had admired the children playing in the Parc Monceau or in the Gardens of the Tuileries, or crossing one of the bridges with their nurse-maids. He had thought: "They certainly dress their kids up well"; and he had often turned around, planning to tell Ethel of the costumes, so that they might remember them when they had children of their own. Now, as he sat in the brown leather morris chair, surrounded by tobacco smoke and clangor, it occurred to him that Granger had probably been like one of those children. "I guess his folks have money," he decided, tossing away his burnt cigarette. And, while he was rolling a fresh one, dribbling grains of Durham onto his clothes (his long legs were extended toward the empty fire-place,) a series of images drifted across his mind of France and above all of Paris.

He had been there in the summer, and it had been a dream for him of stone and leaves and crowds and gray buildings. Nothing remained distinct, save perhaps an enormous and varied dinner in a restaurant with brown cushions, many glasses of what one of his companions called a "swell vin blank," and then an interminable, rattling drive in a taxi, through mysterious, curving streets lit dimly with blue. The following day be had returned to the front, and he had never seen Paris again: it was still the vague region of crowd bridges, taxis with horns that tooted single monotonous notes, blue lights and military police. Somehow it did not seem like a place where one lived, and the thought that Granger had lived there for two or three years stirred him. He'd like to talk to the kid some day: damned interesting kid to talk to. But he always felt a slight uneasiness in his presence.

The music was swelling, and resembled a wagon loaded with iron rails bumping over a cobbled street. Tom breathed deeply. The boys certainly had a fine orchestra this year. He looked up at Pollock, who was still against the mantelpiece, and grinned rather widely and said: "Damn fine music, eh?" Pollock nodded.

When Tom came to the house for dinner, he usually went on down to Oakland afterward to see Ethel Davis, who lived in a small apartment with her cousin, an elderly woman also from Monterey. He always arrived there about seven-thirty, after the dishes were all done: she would open the door, wearing her gray checked apron, her black hair parted in the middle and drawn down on both sides of her face, and would say in her low voice: "Just a minute, Tom." In the living-room, which contained a wall bed behind a tall mirror and was also a sleeping room, Jessie would be seated firmly, both shoes flat on the floor and a heap of sewing in her lap. She would mutter: "Hello, Tom." And he would roam to and fro smoking a cigarette, while the click of dishes in the kitchen went on.

"I ought to be going," Tom thought, wondering what Ethel would say if he came much later than usual. Above him, leaning against the mantelpiece, Pollock said:

"I was talking with a friend of yours today."

"Yes? Who was that?"

"Burton. I'm in one of his English classes."

Tom nodded largely. "Well, rather. Phil Burton. He's a good scout."

"You were in the same outfit in France," he told me.

"Yes," answered Tom, head against the cushions. "Yes." Then, after a chuckle: "He can put a lot of liquor under his belt, that fellow." He assumed the tone and vocabulary of a man who had been an upperclassman during his freshman year the man in turn had acquired it from one still farther back) and went on, in a measured way: "We've been on lots of good parties together. I remember one in Bar-le-Duc. All afternoon we had been drinking cognac and we all had a good lead on For dinner we had champagne, seven bottles for five of us, and after that—"

He repeated immemorial phrases describing the deeds of heroes. The music had stopped; some of the brothers were going upstairs, others to the library; a few came into the living-room and wandered over to the empty fire-place and stood charmed before Tom Gresham narrating. He finished the first tale, and began another, and then, as the sacred frenzy possessed him more fully, inserted details that he had heard from other men. Most of his stories dealt with liquor. Long drawn "Wee-e ells" occurred frequently, he used "Goddam" everywhere as an adjective: "Well, we went back to the goddam hotel—" Certain that he held his audience, he spoke with gusto, spreading his arms apart now and then, and glancing from time to time into the faces of Milton and Bert Hudson, who leaned side by side on the mantelpiece. "Well, we cranked up the Lizzie and went back to Cha(accent over a)lons. One of the goddam tires blew out half-way there—" After one story, he paused to roll a fresh cigarette (he enjoyed talking with a scrap of charred paper hanging to one corner of his mouth) and a red-haired senior near him on the davenport said: "That reminds me of something that happened when I was in the aviation camp in Georgia." Another story began, which led on to still another, and nearly an hour went by before

Tom could once more talk. He had barely listened to the tales of his companions, though he moved his head and chuckled occasionally. He wanted to tell, as if it had befallen him, the adventure of a lieutenant he had met on the transport returning to America. When silence came, he commenced his story.

It was pleasant to sit here talking amid friendly tobacco smoke. Only five or six of the brothers remained now, just those who really enjoyed being here. (Tom had heard Milton Granger say to the freshman named Paul: "Let's not go to the movies. This is too good.") The others had gone away, and one by one each of them told a story. The black clock on the mantelpiece ticked on, and the hours passed, and soon the skull of Durham on the table was empty, and a freshman had to go upstairs for a large sack that was stored away in a closet. When he was in college, Tom Gresham often spent evenings in this fashion. It was known as a "bull-fest," and when the character of the stories changed, as always happened, it became a "smut-fest."

About eleven o'clock Joe Pollock, the long-headed sophomore, looked up and said:

"Did you ever hear the story about the negro wench and the big buck from Tennessee?"

"No!" they all exclaimed, though they knew it well.

The sophomore began: "Once there was a negro wench who—"

There was a straightening up of chairs and a lifting of heads, and soon five or six stories of the new kind had been told. Gresham remembered three or four heard in the army, which he recited gravely in a rather heavy voice, changing his expression only after the final word had been uttered, as if it were the merriment around him that made him laugh; and when he could think of no more, he listened with nodding head and smiling face, exploding now and then into a preparatory guffaw several moments before the definitive storm of laughter. He liked to know that every one said: "Tom Gresham is a good scout."

About midnight, after a few stories paler than the others, they all became still, and lay back in their chairs, steeping in the created world peopled by traveling men, negro wenches, Irishmen, Jews, high-school girls, and sailors. Tom Gresham wanted to sit there always. He was thinking: "It's great to have a place like this to come back to." It made no difference that he had not been to see Ethel this evening, for he had been down three times already during the week, and she might not even have expected him today. He wondered slowly if it were not almost time to get his car for San Francisco, and after a while, moving heavily in his chair, he led out his watch and whistled, after noticing the time.

"Say," he exclaimed, and rose to his feet, "I gotta go. What time does the next Key Route leave for the city?"

No one knew. Some said there were no more trains: others, that the last one would leave about one o'clock Pollock suggested:

"Come on down to *The Dirty Spoon* and get some coffee."

"Let's go," a freshman said.

"Say, that sounds good, doesn't it?" Tom muttered through a yawn, turning to Milton. "Eh?"

"Yes," Milton answered, "let's go."

In the night, under the mist, they went along the dark street in a talking group toward Telegraph Avenue, two blocks away, their footsteps sounding loud in the stillness. And Tom Gresham, hands in pockets and shoulders bent a trifle forward, walked among them, filled with happiness and good will, almost believing that he was an undergraduate once more.

VI

INITIATION

When the Saturday arrived on which Milton Granger was to be initiated, one of the upper classmen told him to leave the house and to be on a certain North Berkeley corner at seven-thirty in the evening; and so he went for the day with Bert Hudson to San Francisco, where they idled in Chinatown, sat for two hours in the lobby of the St. Francis, and then climbed Telegraph Hill about four o'clock, planning to come down for an early dinner and to catch the six-forty boat to Berkeley. Silently, they walked among gray board houses and up wooden steps to the yellow hill-top, each one preoccupied. To the westward Milton noticed fog swelling over Twin Peaks, and he paused near the de caying parapet, feeling melancholy, and wondered where he would be at this time tomorrow, after the initiation.

"Some view," he muttered.

"Gee, yes," answered Bert Hudson.

Tall buildings stood below in light haze. With distance around him Milton felt more tranquil. Locomotive bells and whistles rose from the water-front, but they came to him thinned, "almost worn away," he thought, watching smoke belch from a moving yellow ferry-boat, and hearing long afterward, as if from nowhere in particular, the softened croak.

"If they try any monkey business on me," exclaimed Bert Hudson, "I'll be damned if I'll stand for it."

Milton answered: "Oh, hell, I guess they won't.

"Well, they'd better not," Bert said, agitated.

Milton wondered at Bert Hudson's attitude. Way did he join a fraternity if he felt that way? There were certain things, naturally, one had to accept: he thought, almost with a shudder, of his Aunt Caroline's indignant snort should he ever, in her presence, make such a remark. "What ever happens to you, Milton she had often told him, "be a good sport."

"There goes the Vallejo boat," he said, extending his arm. "See, just coming out from behind Goat Island."

"Where's Goat Island?" Bert asked.

"Why, right there. See? With the white-washed rock."

"Oh, is that Goat Island?" Bert said, "I never knew."

It was strange, thought Milton, that a fellow could live around the bay for several months (Bert had come up from Honolulu in May) and not know Goat Island; and he had a sudden feeling of the stupidity of this fellow who stood now beside him, wrinkling his narrow forehead. Yet he liked him immensely all the same, ever since that first evening at the Alpha Chi Delta house, when they had sat near the fireplace until nearly twelve. Bert had a way of coming to him in perplexity and saying: "Look here, Milt," or "I don't know what to do, Milt," and his feeling of displeasure gave way now to a surge of friendship, which made him imagine all at once a situation in which Bert Hudson, because he did not "stand for monkey business," would be abandoned by all save Milton Granger.

"Dick Folger's a good scout," Bert said all at once.

"Oh, yeah, wonderful."

Milton had never questioned the supreme value of Dick Folger, who was president of the house. Dick was a Big C man, having played guard for two years in the Stanford game, and one of the prominent figures on the campus. It went without saying that he was the glory of the Alpha Chi's.

"And so is Wendell a good scout," Milton added mechanically, sure that Bert would agree with him. But his companion answered, with one of his uncertain, rather twisted laughs:

"Aw, he's always shooting that make-good and college activity crap around. Where does he get that stuff? What the hell's he ever done?"

"Aw, that's not much," said Bert.

They walked around to the northern side of the hill from where they could see Tamalpais against a deep blue sky, and Milton was growing melancholy again at the thought of the coming initiation, when Bert remarked, with another small laugh:

"Dick Folger could hit an awful wallop, couldn't he?"

Milton nodded.

Somewhere, out near the Golden Gate, a fog-horn hooted sadly. Milton wanted to go miles away, to catch a train for Los Angeles, for Seattle. But he said: "Oh, there won't be anything like that."

"The-hell-there-won't," Bert replied, stopping for an instant between each word, and nodding his head up and down. "You just wait." Then, facing Milton abruptly, eyes grave, he asked: "Were you everbinitiated into a high school fraternity?"

"No," said Milton.

"Well, then"—Bert turned away—"you've got some thing coming to you."

Milton walked on silently, a faint clamor of locomotive bells in his ear. "Maybe," he said at last.

A black-haired Italian girl in a red sweater walked unevenly along the slope of the hill, and Bert Hudson stared at her until she went behind a house lower down. At length he said, kicking a loose stone:

"He's too damn puritanical."

"Who? Wendell?"

"Yeah. All the time telling me to stay in and study. Why, I was in four nights last week, wasn't I?" He fixed appealing blue eyes upon Milton. "Wasn't I, Milt?"

"I guess so."

"The juniors are all right. Take Hawkins now. He doesn't say anything." After a pause, he added: "I wish I was rooming with him instead of Jeffries. Of course, Jeff's all right, but he studies so damn late. I can't go to sleep with his light burning. Sometimes he don't go to bed until three o'clock. And then he's always telling me to clean up the room. Why should I clean up the room?"

Milton was thinking more of the imminent initiation than of what Bert was saying, and when his friend said: "How do you like Pollock?" he did not answer for a moment But finally he started and said:

"What? Pollock? Oh, he's all right. We get along well enough. He's hardly ever in his room."

"He's a crazy bastard," said Bert.

"Oh, yes. But he's not so bad when you get to know him. Like Tom Gresham. I didn't like Tom much at first. But now I think he's a helluva good scout."

They were standing again near the parapet that nearly circled the hill. Milton glanced at his watch, afraid that they would not have time for dinner if they remained too long.

"It's almost quarter to five," he said. "Maybe we ought to be getting something to eat. We have to get the six-forty, you know, and there won't be time for anything on the other side."

"Oh, hell, there's lots of time."

"Yes, I know. But it will be after five by the time we get to a restaurant, and dinner will take an hour, won't it?"

"Half an hour," said Bert.

"Well, three-quarters. Anyway, I think we ought to be going."

"All right, Milt," Bert answered quietly. "If you think so."

They walked over the hard yellow ground to the stairs and began to descend. The mist was rolling over Twin Peaks.

"Do you know of a restaurant?" Bert asked.

"Let's go to the California Market."

More than two hours later, on his corner in North Berkeley, a trifle chilly in the late air, Milton was strolling to and fro along the sloping sidewalk under dark trees. He remembered Bert Hudson's remark: "They'd better not try any monkey business on me. I'll be damned if I'll stand for it," and wondered if Bert really meant what he said. "Probably not," he thought, looking at his watch.

It was seven-forty-five. The sky all around him was still tinted with frail colors. To overcome his nervousness he looked westward over the darkening roofs of Berkeley below him to the somber bay and the hills beyond. "Lavender," he thought, "green. Light blue." The fog had not come over.

An automobile rounded a corner and swept toward him, two pallid lights staring, and Milton halted weakly; but the car went on down the hill, and he remained trembling, conscious all at once that his bladder, which he had emptied on the boat, was full again.

"It's not dark enough yet," he decided. There was a women nearby in a doorway.

After all, considering the number of men who had gone through initiations like this, the ordeal could not be fatal; perhaps there was no horse-play at all, as one of the other freshmen, who knew no more about it than Milton himself, had stated. Bert Hudson was waiting somewhere down below Shattuck Avenue: what would happen if he should fight back? The sophomores had often talked vaguely of "tubbing." Another automobile glided down the curving hill, motor at rest, brakes squeaking now and then; and when it vanished, Milton thought he might relieve himself, as the woman was no longer in the doorway. He walked over to a stone embankment over which vines were drooping. But some one took him by the shoulders and slipped a blindfold around his head.

It was Wendell's voice that kept saying: "Step up, down, up, up, now down."

As he was getting into an automobile, his right foot slipped and he scraped his shin on the running-board. A fellow said: "Wuuup." Several others crowded against him on the back seat, and he heard some one breathing rapidly, almost panting, and wondered if there were other freshmen in the tonneau. The car moved. He knew by the familiar noise, and because he had touched a hole in the cushion beneath him, that he was riding in Hawkins's Dodge. For five or ten minutes no one uttered a word; the car swung around curves; then it stopped, and hands descended onto his shoulders and pushed him gradually to the sidewalk, where he stood patiently, while voices whispered around him. Finally, they guided him stumbling up wooden steps (he knew he was entering the front door of the fraternity house,) and then up the staircase, along a hall, and into a room, which he felt sure was Bud Folger's, at the end of the hall. They sat him down on the bed and went away, locking the door.

He dared not remove the blindfold. He heard beneath him a distant noise of conversation, a sort of grumble which he visualized as being all on one level, shooting upward from time to time into a peak of laughter, and then often sinking straight down, until he could barely make out the undulations. Alumni were talking. Alumni, alumni, alumni, alumni. He repeated the word over and over, and soon it decomposed into meaningless syllables: Ny-alum, ny-alum, ny-alum, which reminded him of the wheels of a train clicking along a track, as one lies in a berth behind green curtains. He heard some one running upstairs, then along the hall. He waited stiffly, but a door nearby opened and closed, then, in a moment, opened again (there was a rapid, shrill squeak,) and the person, whoever it was, ran down the hall, and the door, from the force of the small push he had given it on leaving, moved for a moment on its hinges with a thin wail. Milton lay down on the bed. He thought of the open door, Bert Hudson, Santa Barbara, his mother, a game he used to play in his childhood, all this suffused with fear, somnolence, even a bit of pride. Then he remembered that he wanted to relieve himself.

He could not go now, for the door was locked, and even if it had not been, he would have feared to take off the blindfold unbidden. He felt better, absolved from the necessity of action. The grumble of conversation beneath him seemed now like a black plain humped with boulders; his own breathing formed gray lines, like upright layers of mist, often leaning toward one another, their points touching; and he began to count them, trying at the same time to separate words from the flow of noise downstairs, and turned his face to the wall, which he could feel with one of his knees. But the odor of dry sweat that came from something hang ing there made him roll once more onto his back. Perhaps it was a jersey Dick Folger had worn during practice.

He wanted to go to the bathroom. All at once he hated the whole crowd. Why had he joined this rotten fraternity? Why hadn't he waited? He pictured himself for an instant rising up, banging the door until some one released bim, then crushing his pledge button under his heel and speaking proud words. Dick Folger was a fool; Wendell was an idiot. The rest of them were no good. The house was an ugly, unpainted old shack with rickety stairs and smelly, vile rooms—

A few minutes later, when two or three persons entered the room and took him by the arms, he murmured his need to them and was permitted to do as he wished. The light dazzled his eyes. When the handkerchief was once more around his head, the two sophomores led him along the hall and then upstairs to the third floor, where a room existed, he knew, whose door was always locked, and which he had heard referred to in mysterious words. "I'm in for it now," he thought. But when he stumbled, one of the sophomores helped him forward and asked, "All right, Milt?" in so solicitous a voice that he felt reassured, certain that no evil would arise from so brotherly a tone. Suddenly, he remembered a passage in Virgil that he had read the preceding year in which Æneas encouraged his men by saying that they would some day be able to look back upon the ordeal they were traversing. The two sophomores pulled him to a halt, and there was a low knocking.

He could not hear what one of them whispered. A door whined. He stumbled again with a great thud; the air was warm and smelt stuffy; he stood without moving, hearing now and then a rustling near him. Then some one slid away the blindfold from his eyes. What he saw first of all was a greenish frame, about six feet before him, in the midst of which, like a sort of melon, hung a round yellowish face with eyes that blinked toward him. Heavy silence surrounded him. As he waited, his vision cleared gradually, and he saw that the face belonged to Dick Folger, who was standing, clothed in a green robe, behind a kind of altar, also dark green, and wearing on his head a tall cylindrical hat of the same color. Green light came from hidden electric bulbs. Dick cleared his throat, and Milton expected him to say something, but nothing came forth, and his eyes went on blinking in the same nervous way Milton had noticed at table. Other members of the fra ternity (Milton hardly dared turn his head) were sitting along the green walls of the room (he could not see how far behind him they extended,) wearing all of them robes of green with pointed hoods drawn over their solemn faces. In a sidewise manner Milton looked into the eyes of Hawkins, who had always been so friendly to him, hoping now for a glimmer of sympathy; but the glance the junior returned him remained metallic, and Milton stared once more toward the green altar and the round face of Dick Folger.

Knock, knock, knock. There was a scuffling outside. Knock, knock, knock. A door opened: some one whispered, then slow steps came over the floor, and Milton felt some one standing beside him. It was Bert Hudson, owlish in the dim light, his eyes newly uncovered. He did not turn his head.

Knock, knock, knock. There was more whispering. This time it was Tony Barragan who stood on the other side of Milton, looking up and slightly grinning. One of the sophomores shook his head and frowned savagely.

Standing there, Milton heard more knocking, and soon other forms were behind, pressing against him. Some one breathed loudly: he dared not look around. Then all at once Dick commenced to speak, and Milton tried to keep his eyes fixed on the round, yellowish face beneath the green hat, and the fat moving lips Dick seemed to be reading something from a book for he peered downward continually, and every now and then hesitated and cleared his throat. What he read made Milton think of the Episcopal service he had been to church three or four times as a child,) and the same oppression came over him as on those occasions He wanted to move about, for his belly was itching: but he pressed his arms to his sides, kept his head rigid, and tried to fix his mind on the droning voice. He caught a number of scattered words, all of them abstract, and many third person singulars in *eth*; and soon the closeness of the atmosphere, the monotony of Dick's reading, the slow, regular, interwoven breathing of the fellows behind him, which was like some mysterious, murmuring chant, induced in him a restful calm that made him love the greenish light, the kindly, august presence of Dick Folger, the brotherly shoes of the sophomores, which he could see by lowering his eyes, protruding from beneath green robes, the copious and measured stream of words that issued from the holy shrine.

Gradually, he became aware that Dick's voice, a trifle hoarse now, was ascending in a long question. Silence came. Some one poked him from behind. Instinctively, he uttered: "I do," and heard Tony Barragan echo, with his foreign intonation: "I do." Another question began. "Do you swear—" Again, when Dick stopped, a hand poked him. "I do," said Milton. He felt safe now, for he knew what to answer. During the next question he wondered why he had by instinct replied "I do," instead of merely saying "Yes," and what would have happened if he had replied "Yes," "I do," he muttered again, and heard Bert Hudson beside him say: "I do."

CLARKSON CRANE

Two or three more questions followed. Then the tone of the reading changed, abandoned its solemnity and old-fashioned tense endings, and became detailed and practical. Looking away from the book, Dick told in a more normal voice by what signals one might recognize a brother in a strange land, what words to speak, what answers to expect, and the fashion in which the fraternity "grip" was given. "I remember once," he said, and recounted a chance meeting in a Seattle hotel which had had regal consequences. Then he explained the significance of various symbols, and described the knocks and whispered words needed for admission into the chapter room, which was called the *ogoura*, this being the Greek word, Dick added, for the senate chamber of ancient Athens. When he had finished this exposition, he told a long story of two members of Alpha Chi Delta who fought during the Civil War, one in the Northern, the other in the Southern army, and how the Northerner had come upon the Southerner lying wounded after a battle, and, hav ing recognized the Alpha Chi pin, had carried him three miles on his back to safety.

The air of the *ogoura* was becoming hotter and hotter. In the mysterious portion of the room behind Milton, which he was unable to see without turning his head, feet were beginning to shift to and fro, and there were many sniffles and coughs. For a minute or two, after the war-story, Dick paused and remained majestically silent. Then, looking directly at Milton, he said:

You have now been received into Alpha Chi Delta, and have learned the grip, and—ah—have learned what some of the—ah—things mean. I shall now tell you the origin of our fraternity and explain the meaning of the three Greek letters, Alpha—Chi—Delta."

A few of the brothers were coughing. After clearing his throat, Dick continued:

"In 1853, in Choate College, a little group of five or six students of theology gathered together one evening and formed a reading club. They named it Vespers. Every Thursday night for a year the club met and they would read the Bible and other classics. At the beginning of the second year, two more members were taken in, and it was decided that a constitution should be drawn up. They drew up a constitution and by-laws, and the new society was named Alpha Chi Delta, which means—" Dick paused for a moment: there were no more coughs. "Which means *Arete charis dynantai*. In English that is: Virtue and kindness prevail."

As soon as he had uttered the words, a multitudinous rapping began all around the green-walled *ogoura*. Turning his head, Milton saw that the brothers were all lightly striking the benches with the knuckles of their right hands. The noise went on for some mo ments; then Dick spoke once more from the greenish glow of the altar.

"Will the P. R. kindly lead out the candidates."

Immediately, hands seized Milton from behind; the blindfold once more descended over his eyes; and he thought: "It's coming now." But he heard again the solicitous voice that had previously reassured him, and felt a fraternal pressure on his arm. Slowly, guided tenderly, he walked forward. Soon the voice said: "Look out—stairs." He descended cautiously. After a long walk along the hallway, he crossed another threshold, and the sophomore pushed him gently onto the bed and whispered: "Wait there."

He could hear again, even more distinctly than before, the murmuring and raucous sound of conversation rising from below, and he thought that it had grown much louder, and wondered how many alumni had gathered there. Was something else coming? Perhaps this was only the beginning of the ordeal which would continue throughout the night, in the presence of the laughing crowd downstairs. Lying flat on his back, he shut his eyes and heard slow footsteps passing by along the hallway outside. "One of the other freshmen," he thought. Where were they taking him? He tried to remember the meaning of Alpha Chi Delta and when the fraternity had begun, but the facts were gone from his mind, and all he knew was that some students of theology had formed a little club called something or other. Stray portions of the initiation service filed through his brain. "Ways of life," "the hidden stars," "an eternity of friendship," "he who giveth will receive and he who turneth his eyes from love—" After all, it was great to belong to something like this, to have a bond that would hold him all his life. He remembered the majesty of Dick's face in the green light, with the robe hanging from his shoulders and the cylindrical cap towering above his brow, and he de cided as soon as possible to wire his mother that he was now a member of Alpha Chi Delta, one of the "Big Six" among college fraternities. She had been glad when he was pledged. Downstairs, there was a crash, the breaking of glass, laughter. Was something happening? Would his turn come next? Bert Hudson's words returned to him: "They'd better not try any monkey business on me. I'll be damned if I'll stand for it." There was no more noise downstairs, nothing exceptional, that is, only the usual clamor of conversation. Perhaps the crash had not been part of the initiation. Oh, well, what difference did it make?

CLARKSON CRANE

Others had come through all right. He felt weary now, and found it delicious merely to lie there with his eyes closed on this soft bed, with the noise below swelling and then decreasing, in large gray curves, broken here and there into golden patches that kept interchanging with one another like the Japanese cook at home when he stood behind the house under the pepper tree scraping off a platter—

He opened his eyes. Some one was shaking him. "Yes," he answered. "Yes."

"Gone to sleep?"

"No, I was just lying here."

The light was on; the blindfold seemed golden. Then it was removed, and Wendell said:

"Congratulations, old man. Congratulations, old man."

Dazzled, blinking, he sat up and tried to return the "grip."

"Like this," said Wendell, his narrow face red with joy. "See?"

"Oh, yes," Milton answered, "I guess I can do it now, all right."

Wendell was leading him out. As he went downstairs into the light, still drowsy, his vision blurred, young men crowded toward him from all sides exclaiming: "Congratulations, old man. Congratulations." One long table extended across the entire house. Older men were pushing back their chairs and coming toward him with crumpled napkins. Nearby, he saw Bert Hudson, very red, shaking hands. Then, among other alumni, Tom Gresham pushed forward and dropped a long arm over his shoulder.

"Damn glad, Milton. Damn glad," he muttered.

There were tears in the alumnus' eyes.

The brothers all rose late the next morning, and many of them came down in bathrobes, as was customary on Sundays, and sprawled over chairs, discussing the initiation and banquet of the evening before. The sheets of the Sunday papers lay trampled along the floor. Wearing corduroy trousers, slippers, and a blue sweater with a great golden C, Dick Folger reclined in the brown leather morris-chair, legs extended toward the empty fireplace, and stared at the pictorial section of the *Chronicle*, in which were photographs of the California team in action. "Say," he began to no one in particular, "Wally Cuzzens sure has a boot. Look at the leg on him. Jee-sus!" Nearby, Bert Hudson looked up from the table over which he was bending and said: "Yeah, damn good picture, isn't it?" He returned to his own paper, but the telephone bell rang in the closet under the stairs, and he hurried off just as some one shouted: "Get that phone, frosh!" A moment later he emerged from the closet, brushing the dinner gong with his shoulder as he went by, and shouted: "Eh! Milton Granger! Yay! Milton Granger!" Soon Milton appeared from the room at the back of the house—it was known as the card room— and went to the closet, shutting the door, and Bert went back for his paper, which some one else had taken.

Coming at last from the closet, Milton walked over to Bert Hudson.

"It's my Aunt Caroline," he said; "she's in San Francisco. I'm going over for dinner this evening."

He stood for a while, hands in pockets, regarding the pictorial section over the back of Dick Folger's chair. "Where'd you get the white sweater?" asked Bert, touching Milton's chest with closed fist.

"Los Angeles. I used it for tennis last year at school. Good to warm up in."

"Yeah," said Bert, "it's class." Then he went on:

"Let's take a walk up the canyon past the swimming pool. There's time before we eat."

It was a clear warm day; sunlight streamed through the windows; from indolence, Milton hesitated a moment. But he knew that he would feel better after exercise and a bath. "All right," he said.

They left the house without caps and walked up to the end of Durant Avenue, and then climbed a few stairs to the beginning of the canyon road. As they started off at a good pace, between dry, odorous bushes, Milton glanced at Bert Hudson, who strode along beside him, head back, curly hair glinting in the sunlight, and thought he was a nice looking fellow. Now, as frequently happened, he felt constrained in Bert's presence, and did not know what to say. Soon Bert said:

"I thought it was going to be worse than that last night, didn't you?"

"Yeah," said Milton, "I certainly did. Especially when they put on the blindfold."

"I was as scared as hell. I don't mind saying so," Bert continued, running his hand through some reddish leaves.

"Look out," Milton exclaimed, "that's poison oak."

"The hell it is. What'll it do?"

"Oh, nothing much. Sorta make you itch."

"Oh, hell, I won't catch it. You know," Bert said, rubbing the back of his hand on his khaki trousers, some of the houses still have horseplay. But we don't," he added, not without a certain pride. "And I think that's damn fine."

"Dick Folger looked wonderful, didn't he?" said Milton.

"I'll say he did."

For a while they walked on under the thick blue sky. All around them the dry hills were tawny. Finally Bert said:

"The whole thing was damned impressive."

"It certainly was," Milton agreed.

Bert picked up a branch and dragged it a few steps.

"It makes a fellow realize what the fraternity means. The ceremony and all that. And then to see all the old fellows sitting around the table. Were you scared when they asked you to make a speech?"

"Well, rather."

"So was I. Scared as hell. Say, that fellow Tavish is sure a card. Remember that story he told?"

"Yeah," said Milton. "Damn good, wasn't it?"

They both laughed at the memory and walked on, and then paused for a few minutes to look over the fence at the fellows in the swimming-pool below. The green water glittered under the hot sun.

"Some of them certainly have wonderful tans," Milton said, as they started on again.

"Well, they ought to have. Do nothing all summer but lie around up here. I'll bet the water's fine today."

After going on a few hundred yards, they came to the end of the road and lay down in a dry, yellow field. Warm, sweaty, comfortable, they stretched their legs in the heat. A buzzard made circles against the blue sky; flies buzzed; close under his ear Milton heard an insect of some kind moving with a tiny crackling through the dry grass.

Bert rolled toward him and said: "Did you hear what Tom Gresham was saying last night?"

Milton, one arm across his eyes, answered slowly:

"No. What?"

"He's coming back to college in January. Yeah, that's a fact. Says he's tired of the bond business and wants to study law. Guess he'll move in with Hawkins."

"But, my God," said Milton, "that's about a three-year course, isn't it?" "Damned if I know. Anyway, he's coming back."

Somewhere, off behind the live-oaks that stood dry and bulging and dusty in the hot air, Milton could hear a cow-bell. It went *tank tank; tank tank*. Once there was a great scuffling plunge and a splash in the brook that ran hidden beneath foliage in the tiny gulch behind the next fence, and he wondered how many cows were over there. Bert was saying:

"Of course, it's been all right in the house so far But just you wait until they start disciplining the freshmen. Say," he exclaimed, raising himself on one elbow and peering at Milton, "were you ever tubbed?"

"No." The buzzard was making wider sweeps now.

"Well, you've got something coming to you then," Bert stated.

Milton only said: "Mmmm." Far away, down beyond the campus, a clock was sounding: he tried, half-asleep, to count the strokes. Something was sticking into the small of his back, but he was too comfortable to move.

"It'll be all right to have Tom Gresham in the house," Bert said. "I like that fellow.

Milton replied once more "Mmmmmm." He liked to close his eyes and then open them and let the sunlight trickle from his lashes and stretch out between them into changing golden patterns that snapped and formed again and snapped. The cow-bell was tankling more softly. The hot air enclosed his body and seemed to press him onto the warm ground. At last he noticed that Bert Hudson was standing beside him, and he heard him say:

"Come on, Milt, let's be starting back. It's nearly twelve-thirty." Slowly, lazily, he rose to his feet and stretched his arms upward, hearing the flies again brumming in the air. Then he said:

"All right, Bert, let's go."

VII

THE UPPER ROOM

There was only one customer now in the Minerva Café, an unshaven student wearing a sombrero who was seated under the white electric light on a high stool before the counter, having coffee and snails. He had on corduroy trousers, a gray flannel shirt, and an old blue coat hanging open around him. George Towne could see him plainly from where he stood washing dishes near the sink just inside the kitchen door, but he could not hear what he was saying, between swallows of coffee and bites of snail, to the bushy-haired, sleepy waiter who leaned near by, moving a toothpick in the corner of his mouth and nodding his head frequently. Beyond them, near the door, Pete himself, dark, sleek, dressed in clothes that always looked new, was busy over the cash register. Outside on Shattuck Avenue, George heard a Key Route train whistle.

"That must be the last Key," he said to the fat cook with the greasy mustache who was rolling down his sleeves.

He expected no answer and received none, only a kind of rumble that came from behind the dirty shirt over the cook's paunch: and he slid another stack of plates into the heavy water before speaking again.

"Going?" he asked.

The cook nodded, lifted a moist, chewed cigar-end from the stove and inserted it between his teeth.

"Mmmmmmm. No one else cahm."

"No. It's almost one o'clock."

George could feel a film of grease close around his wrists as he plunged both hands among the dishes. Bits of macaroni floated on the soapy water, and the smell of soaked cabbage rose toward the dirty ceiling with steam from the dish-pan.

At noon, when he awoke, he had received a letter from his sister in Wyoming in which she said that his father was ill, that the hotel was making no money, and that Jerry and Art were on their way home from Coblenz. He had read the letter through twice, for his understanding was slow (he had been on a "party" the night before with Tuppy Smith, Dan Wilkens and others) and then he had refolded it thoughtfully, remorseful suddenly at his neglect of study. The semester was more than half gone, and what had he accomplished? If his father were ill, he ought to get down and work; he'd been loafing enough. All afternoon, in spite of a headache, he read the text-book in botany, a course he had entered to fulfil science requirements, and arrived three minutes early at Pete's.

He felt a tap on his shoulder and turned around. The cook, gnawing his cigar, jerked a black thumb over his shoulder.

"Summon to see you."

"Huh?" said George, his dripping hands above the water.

"Summon to see you," the cook repeated.

Burton with his gray hat on stood in the doorway, looking stout in the dark blue overcoat that hung bell-like nearly to his ankles. Surprised, a trifle annoyed at the instructor's persistence (this was the fourth night he had come during the week,) George muttered: "Hello, how are you?" and added without warmth, reaching for a towel: "Glad to see you."

"I just got back from the city and thought I'd see if you were still here. Will you be finished soon?" At the end of his question Burton glanced at the cook, who was putting on an old derby hat, and nodded to him vaguely. Then he said to George in his slow way: "Go ahead. Don't let me stop you."

Moodily, George lowered more dishes into the water, and began to rub furiously at stubborn macaroni, thinking: "Oh, well, if he likes to hang around, what the hell do I care?" Until a week before he had suspected nothing behind Burton's kindly presence; but when he heard the rumors abroad concerning his tendencies in love (it was whispered that he had made advances to a freshman whom he had invited to his rooms) he began to think back over the period of their acquaintanceship, in search of confirmation. As he leaned now over the sink, he felt sure that the instructor's eyes were upon him.

"Good night," said the cook, walking out into the restaurant.

George answered: "Good night."

It was not that he cared especially. Such things were, and he lifted his shoulders. But he feared the smiles of his companions when Burton appeared. Yet what business was it of theirs? Suddenly independent, he asked:

"Have a good time in the city?"

"Oh, fair. I went to a chamber-music concert in Scottish Rite Hall. Not bad at all. They played some Mozart."

"Oh, yes."

"Slevin was with me."

"Who?"

"Slevin, in the psychology department."

"Oh, yes."

The unshaven student was no longer in the restaurant, and Pete had left the cash register and was coming toward the kitchen. When he stood in the doorway, after a respectful little nod toward Burton, he asked:

"Almost done, George?"

"Yeah, damn near."

"I don't know when he gets any sleep," he said to Burton with his slight foreign accent. "He'll go home and play poker now for the rest of the night."

I guess I'll have to take him up to live with me," Barton said. "Then I'd make him study. How about it, George? You could have the little room upstairs."

"Maybe," George answered. A few weeks before nothing would have pleased him more, but he felt uncertain now after what he had been hearing.

When he had washed the final dish, he poured the dense water into the sink, and having watched it gurgle slowly away through a bank of refuse, removed his damp apron and put on his coat and cap.

"All ready," he said to Burton, taking a cigarette from a crumpled package. "Let's go."

Outside on Shattuck Avenue, Burton said, turning south: "I'll walk down to your place with you. The Iast car has gone and I'll have to climb the hill any way. You don't mind, do you?"

"No, come along," George replied. "But I won't ask you up to the room, because I gotta study for an ex that comes tomorrow." Burton was silent.

For several days George endeavored to study, in accordance with his new resolution, going to bed as soon as the Minerva Café had closed, and arising even before ten; and he avoided his friends, who would only hinder him, and locked the battered door of his room from the inside. Wearing over his undershirt a torn gray sweater and lower down his one shiny pair of trousers with the frayed cuffs, he sat before his table and tried to make up the back reading for a course that covered the literature of the seventeenth and eighteenth centuries in England. He read *Pilgrim's Progress*, a bit of Dryden, then *Gulliver's Travels*. Whenever any one knocked on the door, he remained perfectly still, breathing as quietly as possible, until they had clumped off down the hall. Then he would grumble: "What the hell do they want around here?" or, "I haven't got any time now." One afternoon, about three o'clock, after a knocking more gentle than usual, he heard a scraping near the threshold, and when the visitor had walked away, saw on the floor, almost touching the edge of the carpet, a card that had been pushed into the room. He left his work. On it was *Mr. Philip Burton*, and two crossed lines had been drawn through the Mister.

He regretted for a moment that he had not admitted the instructor. Burton could have told him about other poems of Dryden and all of Pope that he would not have time to read before the examination on Thursday He felt like running downstairs to call him back, and he unlocked the door and stood in the hallway, uncertain what to do. He did not like to be seen with Burton after all he had heard; yet those stories were probably lies, and he would be doing harm to himself by avoiding a man from whom he could learn so much. Three years before, in Lander, Wyoming, the man who taught in the Sunday School he was forced to attend had approached him; but that fellow had a squeaky voice, plucked his eyebrows, and always had his left palm against his hip. Burton was not effeminate. "He's not that way," George thought, standing on his threshold. The English instructor's voice very soft, not at all squeaky; he rarely touched any one he knew, and frequently kept his eyes averted and seemed almost cold. "Naw," George thought, "he's not queer. All that stuff's the bunk." But he did not go after Burton: there was no use being seen with him too publicly.

Before he returned into his room, the door on the first floor closed with a great noise, and many footsteps thudded on the stairs. "The whole damn gang," thought George, rather pleased at the interruption of his studies. "What in hell do they want to come here for?" Somber, leaning there, blonde hair disheveled, he waited. Tuppy Smith's torn gray cap and freckled face rose above the banisters: then came Dan Wil kens, tall, undulating, dark. Carrying books and laughing, they stamped into George's room and fell into chairs.

"We met your lah-de-dah friend outside," Tuppy Smith said, reaching toward an open box of cigarettes that lay among ashes on the table. "He said he'd just been up here and that you weren't in."

"I was studying. I didn't answer."

Tuppy laughed. "Yes, we knew damn well you were here. Burton said you might live with him."

"The hell he did!" George exclaimed, his back against the closed door.

Dan Wilkens cackled in his broken voice. "I guess you're elected, George. I guess you're elected."

"He was worried about you," Tuppy Smith con tinued, making his voice precise and shrill. "He thought you were wasting your time."

George sat down on the bed. "Aw, what's the matter with you guys anyway?"

"When are you going to move up, George?" Tuppy asked.

Looking obstinate, both hands in pockets, George sat on the bed. "I don't know," he answered. Damn those fellows anyway. What business was it of theirs?

An interminable argument began soon afterward concerning the date of a certain "party," and the voices of Tuppy and Dan became loud and raucous, and they kept saying over and over: "The hell it was. Why, look here. Don't you remember that day?" or, "Aw, you're cuckoo. Where d'ye get that stuff?" or, "Naw. Why, for Christ's sake, listen here." George lay on the bed, which was not yet made up, one arm across his eyes and his feet on the floor, and felt angry, hearing his friends talk, because they had interrupted his studies. If he should live with Burton, at least they could not be running in every day. "And I wouldn't have any rent to pay," he thought, "and often I'd eat up there for nothing."

So Burton had thought he was wasting his time? Or else those two fellows had lied about him, Tuppy because he disliked Burton, Dan Wilkens because Burton had severely criticized the story written for the *Occident*. He had not been wasting his time. Yesterday, he had read botany for five hours, until he could name all the parts of a flower; and today he had read large portions of *Gulliver's Travels*, skipping a little here and there, of course, but learning what it was about. He felt certain that he would receive a good mark in the examination. If Burton should tell him about Alexander Pope, so that he would know what his poetry was like, he would have spent two full and profitable days, and tomorrow night he could play poker. Suppose he went now and found Burton, who would probably be in his office. They might take a walk, and Burton could tell him all he wanted to know.

He got up after a while and put on his shirt and coat. When he was looking around the room for his cap, Tuppy said: "Where are you going, George?"

"Just to the library," he answered. "You two stay here. I'll be back before long. Don't mind me."

He did not see why he should tell them he was going to visit Burton. There was his cap under the washstand. Pulling it over his head, he went away, hearing the argument swell behind him.

A number of students were in Burton's office when George entered, most of them girls, and Burton only nodded and went on discussing papers that lay on the flat desk before him. George sat down in a chair, leaned on the wide arm, and examined the other people in the room, none of whom he knew; and then, tilting his chair sideways, dabbed with his right hand at a book on the desk, until one of the students, a girl with dark hair, pushed it toward him.

"Oh, thanks," he said, settling back.

She was looking away again through the window, holding a black note-book under her left arm. Now and then she glanced at Burton, and when there were only two students left before her, she unfolded a paper and prepared to show it to him.

Opening the book (it was a copy of Beowulf,) George slid down in his chair and tried to read; but he had not yet taken any of Burton's courses in Old English and could decipher nothing. He turned back to the introduction, read a few paragraphs, then yawned and began to contemplate Burton, who was leaning forward over his desk, marking papers with a blue pencil. The instructor's voice, as he made comments, seemed more drawling and guttural than usual: a bit of sarcasm was there, making it sound frequently like a snarl (he spoke often from one side of his mouth;) but the words themselves were polite, and now and then he peered up toward the student with a tentative smile, and touched his brown mustache a moment before going on.

"Naturally, Miss Caruthers. Yes, you've done it very well. Oh, indeed?"

George yawned again and shifted around in his chair. He knew all the books Burton had in his office, mostly texts for use in schools and colleges. It was nearly four o'clock: the students were going one by one; he could not see the picture over there behind Burton, because the sunlight blurred the glass, but he knew what it was, a reproduction of Titian's *Man with the Glove*. The dark-haired girl was laying her paper on the desk, and he heard Burton say: "Oh, yes, Miss Davis, I'll look this over. You needn't wait." He could almost make out the head in the picture now. The girl was going; the gray door, with its pane of ground glass, closed softly behind her: there were only the two of them in the room now. After a moment, Burton said:

"She has brains, that girl."

"What's her name?"

"Ethel Davis. Graduate student. She ought to get her Ph.D. next year, if she doesn't get married, that is. She's engaged to a friend of mine, a fellow named Gresham. He's in business in San Francisco, and I guess he's making quite a lot of money, so that if she married him she'd probably leave the university. Well," he added, stretching his arms, "I'd like to take a walk. How about it?"

"All right," said George.

They left Wheeler Hall, crossed the old football field to the edge of the campus, turned north for a block on Shattuck, and then followed University Avenue, a long street that runs westward between wooden houses increasingly shabby, down to the municipal wharf and the bay. Burton walked with his shoulders back and his head raised, and now and then took off his gray hat and carried it for a while his right hand. All the way from Wheeler Hall, he had been talking about the students who came to him during office hours. He said now, drawling slightly:

"But let's forget about them until tomorrow. See that pepper tree over there. The trunk seems full of sunlight. There are certain trees, such as the eucalyptus, the live-oak, and the pepper tree, that seem to absorb heat and sunlight. They are the ones I always miss when I leave California. The rubber plant, too," he added. "You know, with the big shiny leaves."

"Oh, yes," George replied, slightly mystified.

"And the sky," exclaimed Burton, throwing back his head, "so rich and thick and blue. Other skies never seem quite so dense."

"No," said George. He was going to ask about Pope, but Burton went on:

"Something will happen around this bay some time. In the arts, I mean. It's so beautiful."

"Yeah," said George. Then: "By the way, Burton, can you tell me anything about Pope? I gotta have him down cold for that ex Thursday."

Burton hesitated. "Well—yes. What to know? You've read him, haven't you?"

"Oh, yes," answered George. "Some." (He had not read a word.) "He wrote a lot of stuff in that heroic couplet, didn't he?"

Burton smiled.

"I like the heroic couplet, you know," he murmured.

George did not answer, expecting Burton to continue, but nothing more came forth, and they walked in silence along a row of fat palms that drooped their leaves over the sidewalk. Finally, the instructor said:

"We'll take the car back, and transfer onto the Euclid Avenue line, and go out to my place and have some tea. I'll read you a few passages and tell you about him. You've read some of the other eighteenth century people, haven't you?"

"*Gulliver's Travels.*"

"But how much does your ex cover?"

"Oh, I don't know. The whole damn century, I guess."

"Ridiculous," said Burton. Then: "By the way, have you thought any more about taking that upper room of mine?"

"Well, no, not a helluva lot." He felt that his answer was too abrupt. Burton glanced at him.

"I'd like to have you with me. You might just as well live out there and save rent. The room is empty."

"Well, you see, I—well, I've been studying a lot these last few days. I got a letter from home saying that my father was sick, and I decided I ought to get down to work."

"You couldn't find a quieter place than out where I live."

"No," said George, "that's true."

They went on for a block without a word. George was wondering what Tuppy Smith and Dan Wilkens and the rest of the gang would say if he should live with Burton. He could tell them that he knew damn well what he was doing, and that he was willing to try anything once, especially when he could get a room for nothing. Besides, Burton was a nice fellow; all those rumors were probably false; he almost answered that he would take the room. But, as the words were entering his mouth, Burton laughed and said:

"Have you heard all the scandal that's going around about me?"

"Ah—uh—you mean—no, what? I haven't heard anything."

Burton laughed again. George thought he seemed strangely amused, considering what the scandal was.

"Well, you see," the instructor explained, "some people have started the idea that I'm having a violent affair with Alice Manning."

"The hell!" exclaimed George, grinning.

"Of course, it's all damn nonsense. Those people at the Faculty Club gossip like old women. Alice and I have gone around together a lot, but why shouldn't we? We're both instructors in the same department."

"Why, sure," said George.

"I told Alice about it last night. She laughed."

"How do you suppose the rumor got going?"

"Oh," answered Burton, "those things get started. Some damn fool."

They halted on a corner to let a truck rumble by. As they were crossing the street, Burton said:

"There's something else I might as well tell you as long as we're going to live together. I may get married next year."

"Oh," said George, and repeated: "The hell."

Burton looked toward him.

"You won't tell anybody, will you? I don't want it to get noised around."

"Oh, no," said George. The next time he saw Tuppy or Dan Wilkens he would say: "All that stuff's the bunk. Burton isn't queer. Why he's going to get married next summer."

"I think you'd like her. I met her first in New York four years ago. We corresponded all the time I was abroad, and then she lived up here nearly six months after I came back from France. All last spring and summer."

George was beginning to think he would be a fool not to take the room. With no rent to pay, he could begin to clear away his debts. He wanted to say something now concerning Burton's marriage, but could think of no fitting remark. Finally he said:

"We're nearly to the Santa Fe tracks."

"Yes," answered Burton, "getting tired?"

"Oh, no."

"I thought we might go right down to the edge of the water and sit for a while on the dock. We can find a warm place in the sun. It will be beautiful. See how clear Tamalpais is. By the way, is Dan Wilkens angry with me for criticizing his—ah—story the way did?" Burton watches George's face until the boy I answered:

"Well, I guess he was a little sore at first. But he's got over it now."

"Awful stuff," said Burton, looking toward the bay. "Why does he write like that?"

"Oh, he thinks he's modern." "You know," Burton said, and then walked on for a while in silence, peering down at the sidewalk and kicking away an occasional leaf.

"What?" asked George.

Burton shrugged his shoulders. "Well, I was thinking," he went on at last, "that you'd be much better off if you saw less of that gang."

"Why?"

"They're all right, of course. Nice fellows and all that. But they keep you from doing any work. Take Dan Wilkens, for instance."

George felt immediately the worthlessness of all his friends. He replied:

"Well, maybe."

"They wouldn't come out to my place to sec you very often, would they?" Burton asked after a moment.

"Oh, no. They wouldn't walk that far, and they never have money for car-fare."

Burton added: "They're all right. I hope they do come out now and then. The trouble with them is they have an idea they must be Bohemian and stay up all night and drink ten cups of coffee a day. That's all so silly. I'll bet Dan's people are Methodists."

"Yes," answered George, without adding that his were too.

Burton smiled. "I know the type," he said. "Escaped Methodists."

A few minutes later, when they reached the end of University Avenue and the muddy rim of the bay, George felt sure that Burton was right in his con demnation of his friends. They stood near a pile of boards.

"It stinks here, doesn't it?" said Burton. "Let's go up the line a way and sit down in that green place."

When they had stretched themselves on the grass, and were looking across the bay toward San Francisco, Burton filled his square-bowled pipe and said, having tossed away a match:

"When do you think you'll move up?"

"Oh," answered George, "next Monday, I guess. My rent is paid until then."

VIII

CONVERSATION

Mabel Richards glanced toward the kitchen stove to make certain the gas was no longer burning, then stepped into the hallway and closed her apartment door. In the elevator she thought once more of Carl glowering that afternoon on the sofa. He should not have left her so brutally. "I've got to study, don't you see, Mabel? I've got to study. Since you've been living in Berkeley I haven't opened a book. Not for more than two months." "Well, Carl, it isn't my fault. I'm sure I don't want to keep you from studying." She watched the yellow wall of the shaft glide upward; the elevator stopped, and she went out over the soft carpet into the street, gray under the evening fog. The Nolans, with whom she was dining, lived near by on Dwight Way. She walked south, preoccupied.

On the doorstep of their low wooden house she waited sadly until Mrs. Nolan appeared.

"Come right in, Mrs. Richards. I'm so glad to see you. Yes, put your things down there. This is my husband, Mr. Nolan. And you know Mr. Burton."

The husband was a pleasant-looking, rather stout man, a little bald, who gripped her hand, saying:

"Glad to know you, Mrs. Richards."

Mr. Burton, after bowing slightly in what Mabel thought a foreign way, said:

"Come near the fire and get warm. It's cold outside, isn't it?"

"Chilly," answered Mabel, extending her hands toward the flame. "This fog."

"Peter says it was simply freezing on the bay," exclaimed Mrs. Nolan. "Wasn't it, dear?"

"Mmmm," answered her husband, nodding. "I should say so."

While they talked, Mabel wondered if Mr. Burton had corrected the paper she had turned in the day before. He sat near the table, touching his brown mustache occasionally and speaking in his slow, nearly snarling manner. She feared that he would answer sarcastically were she to ask what mark he had given. Yet he seemed gentle enough now, and she felt sure that he must have an awfully good heart beneath his cynical exterior. One of the girls in the advanced writing course had told her that Mr. Burton had had a tragic love affair.

"I haven't read that batch of papers," he replied, after she had dared.

"Oh, you'll get a high mark, don't worry," exclaimed Mrs. Nolan, contracting her thin little face as she always did when smiling. "Much higher than mine. You write beautifully. Don't you think she ought to begin trying to market her stories, Mr. Burton?"

"In time," answered the instructor, regarding the flames. "I loved the way you criticized that boy's story yesterday," said Mrs. Nolan, leaning toward Burton. "Didn't you, Mrs. Richards?"

"Oh, yes," cried Mabel with a smile. Burton lifted his shoulders.

"Awful stuff," he said.

The living-room in which they were sitting occupied the width of the small house, and to Mabel, glancing around from time to time, it seemed all brown in the fire-light. A large table littered with books stood near a window; over a piano in one corner drooped a yellow cloth; and as the daylight outside faded, shadows moved upon the walls.

When they went into the dining-room, Mabel said:

"I simply love your house. Have you lived here long?"

"Ages," exclaimed Mrs. Nolan. "It is nice, isn't it? But Peter wants to move over to San Francisco."

"Oh, he doesn't!"

"It's the commuting, you see, Mrs. Richards," explained Peter. "Twice a day I have to make that long trip."

"Oh, but it's so lovely here," cried Mabel. "And then Mrs. Nolan's courses. She'd have to take the ferry twice a day."

The memory of Carl returned suddenly, and she looked down at her plate, barely hearing Mr. Burton's voice as he talked of a friend who had moved recently to San Francisco. How sarcastic he would be if he knew that she was suffering because of a young man! In his class, he never mentioned the word *love* without an ironical emphasis. One afternoon, when they had only known each other a few days, Mrs. Nolan said (they were emerging from class:) "Did you agree with what Mr. Burton said about my story? I don't think he knows anything about love. They say he never looks at a woman." "Oh, do they?" Mabel had answered, remembering what the other student had told her. She looked up now and said to him in a low voice:

"Mrs. Nolan didn't agree with what you said about one of her stories. She thinks you know nothing about love."

"Why, Mrs. Richards! I never said that." The little woman was flushing.

"Oh, doesn't she?" Mr. Burton said in the cynical way that Mabel liked so much. "Oh, doesn't she?"

"I never said that, Mr. Burton."

"You wanta look out," broke in Mr. Nolan, smiling upon them. "You wanta look out, or you'll all get flunked. Eh, Burton?"

Mabel wondered during the meal if Mrs. Nolan always had a servant or if the girl who was waiting on the table had only come for the evening. Mr. Burton was saying:

"As a rule I see little of my students outside of class,—unless, of course, they are mature and intelligent like you and Mrs. Richards. The boys especially—what have I to say to them? Youth is much overrated."

"Some young men are such fools," Mabel broke in, looking up toward Burton. Her voice trembled. Mrs. Nolan said: "Did you see that table of statistics in the Cal.? The girls are far ahead of the boys in scholarship."

"Of course," said Burton, "a great many more boys work their way through, and that takes so much time that they can't get such high marks as they would if yhey were free. I know a student, for example, who works as a dishwasher—"

"Why, I think there are just as many girls who work their way along," interrupted Mrs. Nolan.

"Oh, do you?" cried Mabel, who wanted to take part in the conversation. "Why, I had no idea."

Mrs. Nolan nodded rapidly, both elbows on the table and hands folded beneath her chin.

"Why, there are hundreds. They do everything. And besides, the boys and girls who work their way through college always get the highest marks. They are the most serious-minded. Always."

"I have a friend," said Mabel, "who is receiving a pension or something from the government. He was wounded during the war, or not wounded exactly, but he's been having all sorts of trouble with his stomach."

"The boy I was speaking of," Burton continued, "who works as a dishwasher, finds it very difficult to give the best he has in him to his studies. I often think he doesn't get enough sleep."

"Isn't that awful," said Mabel. "I always feel so sorry for a boy who really wants to succeed and is awfully poor. Especially when you see so many rich men's sons. Often I don't blame the socialists."

Mrs. Nolan smiled. "Oh, socialism. It's a religion, and a very beautiful one."

"Oh, I know," said Mabel.

"Let me give you another piece of meat, Mrs. Richards," suggested Mr. Nolan, raising a slice on the flat of the carving knife and smiling toward Mabel.

"Oh, no, I couldn't."

Mrs. Nolan turned from Burton, who was talking.

"Yes, Mrs. Richards, you must. You haven't eaten a thing. And we're not going to have very much more. Agnes, pass Mrs. Richard's plate."

"Of course," said Mabel, yielding, "if they should divide up everything, a few men would get it all again after a few years."

"But, my dear," Mrs. Nolan exclaimed, once more abandoning Mr. Burton, that isn't what socialism is." "Oh, isn't it?" Mabel regarded Burton and added:

"That's what you said it was."

"I?" Burton flushed. "When did I say that?"

"She's only teasing you," said Mrs. Nolan.

They all laughed for a while, Mabel more than the others, tossing back her head and giving way almost hysterically to a rage against Carl that made her hate Burton sitting there with a grin on his broad face. She wanted suddenly to throw a glass at him. She said:

"I read the book you lent me, Mrs. Richards. I simply love Tagore. He's perfectly wonderful."

Mrs. Nolan smiled in her pinched way. "I felt you would like it."

"Have you tried *Pollyanna*, Mrs. Richards?" asked Burton slyly.

"Now he's angry with you for teasing him." Mrs. Nolan shook her finger at the instructor. "You mustn't say things like that."

"Like what?" He looked surprised. "I didn't say anything. I merely asked Mrs. Richards if she liked *Pollyanna*. Why shouldn't she? It's a very good book. Many people like it."

"Oh, you never can tell what he means," cried Mabel. Then her voice rose like a boy's as she went on: "I don't care. Say what you please about *Pollyanna*. But it has brought a great deal of happiness into the world and I think that's a lot. Don't you, Mr. Nolan?"

"I thought it was a good story," he murmured confidentially.

"There," said Mabel.

Mrs. Nolan smiled. "Poor Peter. He's always so unhappy when we talk about books. Aren't you, dear?"

"I? Not at all."

"Well, that's what you get for having an intellectual wife," said Mabel. Then she put her hand on his sleeve and cooed: "We'll just let them have their high-brow conversation and we'll have a good time together, won't we?"

"Absolutely," responded Mr. Nolan. "Absolutely. Ha! Ha! Did you hear that, Janie?"

At that moment the telephone bell rang in the living room. Mr. Nolan pushed back his chair, but his wife motioned him to remain still.

"Agnes will go," she said. Mabel smiled.

When the maid returned, Mr. Nolan again prepared to rise, his napkin bunched in his right hand and his face lifted expectantly. "For me, Agnes?"

"No, it's for Mrs. Nolan."

"You can't have all the telephone calls," Mabel whispered to him, as his wife left the table.

"I'm expecting a long distance from Sacramento. Business."

"Oh," exclaimed Mabel. "Always business."

She felt like patting his cheek, but instead, she remarked to Burton, whom she still hated because the memory of Carl made her unhappy:

"I wish I knew what you were thinking about. You look so mysterious over there."

"What do you want to know for?"

"He's thinking of two girls who won't get by his course," said Mr. Nolan with a great laugh.

"Well, he'd better not."

The conversation dwindled. Mabel wondered what Carl would do if she went to Los Angeles. All at once, she had begun to loathe the university and Burton and her apartment, and she thought Mrs. Nolan a little fool.

Her hostess returned.

"Mrs. Faraday," she explained. "She won't be able to preside Tuesday."

"Oh, then you'll have to," cried Mabel. "You knew she was acting vice-president, didn't you, Mr. Burton?"

"I thought she was president," he answered.

Mrs. Nolan shook her head. "Oh, no. Mrs. Faraday has been president of the Western Writers' League for three years."

"But you do all the work," said Mabel.

"Why don't you let some one else preside?" Mr. Nolan protested. "Why do you tire yourself out ?"

"Oh, it doesn't tire me at all."

Carl was a pig. What did he mean by saying that she prevented him from studying? He was a selfish, mean pig. Going away like that. Mabel imagined herself strangling him and spitting in his face and pulling his hair. She looked up quickly:

"What did you say? Oh, I'm awfully sorry, Mr. Burton. I'm so absent-minded."

"She was thinking up a story to write for you, Burton," said Mr. Nolan with another laugh. "Tell it to us, Mrs. Richards."

Burton smiled. "I asked you how long you were in Paris."

"Oh, a long time. I don't know. Six months. Oh, more than that."

"Mr. Burton lived in Paris two years, you know," said Mrs. Nolan, turning to Mabel.

"Oh, did he? Don't you just love Paris, Mr. Burton?"

"Gay Paree," exclaimed Mr. Nolan. Then: "Say, Janie, why don't we have our coffee in the other room?"

"Oh, yes," cried Mabel. "Let's."

If Carl did not come to see her, their friendship would end: she would not telephone him. As she stood up, saying: "I simply love this little dining-room. Isn't it sweet, Mr. Burton?" she thought that perhaps Carl might have gone this evening to her apartment, ready to say: "Aw, hell, Mabel, I didn't mean that. Come on, don't get sore at me." She could hear the words and see him there, somber, looking down. But he knew that she was coming here for dinner: besides, she must not think what might happen, for what one thought never came to pass. Carl. She hated him.

In the living room, while Mr. Nolan poked up the fire, she peered into a book to conceal the tears in her eyes, and said: "Is this good, Mrs. Nolan?"

"Splendid. Don't you like Wells, Mr. Burton?"

He did not seem to hear. Across the room, he was gazing through the dark window. Finally, he wandered toward them. Mrs. Nolan repeated her question, and he looked up, melancholy, still remote, and replied:

"Sometimes he's very amusing."

Mabel felt his thoughts were far away.

"Say, Janie," put in Mr. Nolan, "what do you say we break out the bottle of Benedictine? There's just about enough to go around."

"Oh, how wonderful!" cried Mabel.

Burton stood with his back to the fireplace, smoking. Mabel went to him and said:

"I heard some of the nicest things about you the other day."

"Oh, yes?"

"A girl told me she simply loved your class in Old English. She said you made it so interesting and that you were so nice and that everything—oh, well, she just loves it."

Burton smiled.

"Really? I'm glad some one likes it."

Mabel felt a rapid sympathy for this sad man before her. Perhaps he was in love. Why had she thought him once so cold? She asked:

"Isn't it wonderful to have Benedictine?"

"The first I've had for a long time," he answered, taking a glass from the tray Agnes held toward him. Mabel exclaimed:

"I love all kind of liqueurs."

Carl always drank cointreau. She remembered how she watched his mouth when he sipped from the small glass, and how she used to keep him from having more than two at once. She felt unhappy.

"Here's looking at you, Mrs. Richards," said Mr. Nolan.

"Oh, thanks," she answered, "and here's to you and Mrs. Nolan and your business and her work and everything, and here's to you, Mr. Burton."

"Thanks."

She and Carl used to touch glasses and smile.

"Oh, how delicious!" she cried. "Why, my dear, it's perfectly wonderful! Mmmmmm."

The telephone bell rang.

"It's for me," said Mrs. Nolan, putting down her glass and rustling across the room. again, probably."

"Mrs. Faraday, Mr. Nolan lifted his shoulders. "Why can't they leave her alone?"

"Hello? Yes. Yes, she's here. It's for you, dear," said Mrs. Nolan, turning to Mabel.

When she lifted the receiver and said: "Hello?"

Carl answered: "Is that you, Mabel?"

"Yes."

She was trembling.

"I left a book at your apartment. I have to have it tonight for a class early in the morning. I thought I might drop around later. When'll you be home?"

"Why, I don't know," Mabel replied, trying to make her voice commonplace. "I really don't know. It may be there. The Nolans and Burton might be listening. Of course they were.

"Will you be home by twelve?" Carl asked.

"Oh, yes."

"All right. I'll be up."

"Yes," said Mabel, "if you don't mind."

"So long, Mabe." "Good-by."

She hung up the receiver and walked back to the fireplace.

"One of the students in history," she explained. "He borrowed my notes the other day, and wanted to know if I had to have them back this evening. I said no. I really don't need them." She picked up her half-empty glass. "Oh, I still have more to drink. Don't you wish you had some more, Mr. Burton?"

"But how did he know you were here?" asked Mrs. Nolan.

Mabel paused. "That is curious, isn't it?" she said, the glass near her lips. Then: "Oh, I know. I guess I mentioned it to Mrs. Jasper when I was going out. She runs the apartment house. She must have told him."

"Oh, I see."

Mabel wanted to sing.

"Here's to you, Mr. Burton," she cried. "Here's to you. Here's to you."

What a nice man the instructor was! Then, having emptied her glass, she sank into an armchair and, stretching out both legs and crossing her ankles, exclaimed:

"Oh, Mrs. Nolan. I should think you'd be too happy for words in this adorable little house!"

IX

ORDEAL

O ne Sunday, more than six weeks after Milton's initiation, his Aunt Caroline, who was spending some time in San Francisco, came over for midday dinner at the Alpha Chi Delta house. Shortly afterwards, she returned to the city, taking Milton with her, and he remained at the Fairmont Hotel until evening. When he left, about nine o'clock, she walked to the elevator and said, as he entered the car:

"Do see more of young Jarvis Smith."

He was the only one of the fellows in the house she liked. Emerging from the hotel onto California Street, Milton turned toward the ferry. He felt free once more in the cool night with the mist over his head dimming and then revealing the stars. Stubby cable cars with the thin *ting-ting* of bells trickled by him down the hill. His footfalls sounded loud. To the eastward, beyond the intervening darkness of the bay, he could see the subtle glitter of Oakland and Berkeley. He breathed in the damp air.

Aunt Caroline had found most of his friends common and crude. Wendell, the tennis-player, had a fearful twang; Hawkins had been in his shirt-sleeves when she arrived, even wearing his vest, and had remained talking with her for a quarter of an hour before going upstairs for his coat; Tom Gresham, who sat next her

at table, used repeatedly the word *folks* (Milton heard his aunt snort each time it came forth;) Paul Drummond had been wholly dumb when confronting her

Milton laughed and walked more rapidly, squeezing under his arm the book he had carried with him to read going home on the ferry. She had even disapproved of that.

"What are you reading, Milton?"

"Tolstoy's *Resurrection*."

"Humph! One of those radical Russians."

Yet she had given him, before he went away, twenty-five dollars, and had said:

"Go and have a good time, you and Jarvis Smith. He's a gentleman. But be careful." She threw back her long head. "There are all kinds of women in San Francisco and a boy may ruin his life for just a few minutes of pleasure."

"Oh, for heaven's sake, Aunt Caroline, don't worry."

"Tut, tut. I know what young men do after a few glasses of wine, and you're no different from the rest of em. At least," she added, "I hope you're not."

He laughed again. Crossing Grant Avenue, he paused on the corner near St. Mary's, and watched a Chinese girl walk by. She wore light blue pyjama-like garments and carried a glossy, patent-leather bag, and her black, tightly-drawn hair shone on her head. For a moment he wanted to follow her along the street and mingle with other Chinamen and smell the incense drifting from shop-doors, and hear more clearly the brazen music that was clanging somewhere half a block away; but inertia made him continue along California Street, across Kearny, and then between tall office buildings somber now and empty.

Aunt Caroline would return to Santa Barbara tomorrow. She was driving down with some friends, and Milton felt glad that she was going, although he liked her, and, before she arrived, had looked forward to her visit. She was wrong about the men in the fraternity house. Tom Gresham, for example, was all right: he had been in the army two years and had had lots of experience (Milton glanced up at signs on the dark buildings to see if Morton, Dunlop & Company, where Tom had been working, might not be along here,) and Aunt Caroline had no right to condemn him in that ridiculous way, just because he said "folks." Every one in the house was more interesting than the fellows he had known at school the year before, all of whom, by the way, Aunt Caroline had found "nice."

"They're a fine bunch," he muttered, adopting half-consciously a traditional slogan. And as he emerged onto Market Street, and saw the Ferry Tower, illuminated and high, he repeated: "A fine bunch"

There was only time to buy a ticket and hurry on board. Inside, on the lower deck, he sat down on one of the curving varnished benches near a tall cuspidor and opened his book, trying to remember just how far he had got in the trial scene. By instinct, he found his place and began to read.

Some one exclaimed: "Hello, Milt."

He looked up. Near him sat Aaron Berg, the young Jew, who was in the same section of freshman English.

"Hello there, Berg,"

He closed his book and moved over, liking Berg's naive and eager smile. Aunt Caroline would snort at a Jewish friend.

"Have you done that paper for English yet?" he asked.

Aaron Berk shook his head.

"Not a line. Have you?"

"No. I don't know what to write about."

As a matter of fact, Milton's paper was nearly finished, twelve pages of it, all piled carefully on his table; but he felt a pretense of stupidity and laziness to be more manly, and so he added: "I can't write papers for the life of me"

"Oh," said Aaron, "once I get started I'm all right. I tore off the other in the hour before class. And I got a one."

"Hopkins gave me a two," said Milton. "Say, he's a good scout, isn't he?"

Again Berg smiled.

"Yeah, he certainly is. I met him out in the hills last Sunday. He was walking with another English instructor, a fellow named Burton. They asked me to come along."

"Do you go out in the hills often?"

"Three or four times a week."

"So do I. We'll have to go together some time."

"Fine."

"You see," Milton went on, drawing out a package of cigarettes, "the fellows in the house don't like to walk, and I usually go out alone. Cigarette?"

"No, thanks."

Berg was silent for a moment, while Milton lighted his cigarette. The engine of the ferry-boat continued its thumping churn. At last he said:

"Why do you put that rotten stuff into your lungs?"

"What?" asked Milton, surprised.

"Tobacco smoke."

"I don't know. I guess it doesn't do much harm."

An expression of scorn passed over Berg's face.

"Wait and see," he said.

For a while, until the boat drew near the mole, they were silent, Milton inhaling obstinately; but when the first people began to leave their seats and go toward the door, they followed them and went forth onto the deck and stood in the cool air. Reflected lights in the black water.

"The slip always looks so friendly, doesn't it?" said Aaron, "with those red and green lights, and the yellow building behind it like a big shell."

"Yes," said Milton, liking Aaron again. He wanted to talk lyrically of the hills beyond, somber against the sky pitted with stars, and the soft noise of the water against the piles of the wharf; but he seemed able only to clear his throat and say: "Wonderful night, isn't it?"

When they were seated in the electric train, Aaron said: "What are you reading?" and, when Milton showed him the book, he went on: "What did you ever join a fraternity for anyway?"

Milton pondered.

"I don't know. Just did. They're a fine bunch."

Aaron was silent. Troubled, Milton continued:

"It's a good place to live. Nice house and all that."

He dared not speak of the sacred bond of friendship that united the brothers of Alpha Chi Delta, nor the mysterious value of freshman discipline to which he submitted with earnest resignation, nor the hidden glory of the *ogoura*. For a moment he became aware that Aaron was a Jew. Lest he reveal his indignation, he enumerated further material advantages. "They have a fine sleeping porch and showers with all the hot water you want."

"And jazz music," Aaron said. "How do you stand the jazz music? It almost drives me mad every time I go by a frat house."

"Why, I don't know. I—" Milton shuddered at the word *frat*. He nearly exclaimed: "We have a fine orchestra this year," for the idea had been planted hitherto unquestioned in his soul; but he remembered that several times he had found the music disturbing when he was trying to study and the window-panes quivered and buzzed from the tumult of drums, cymbals, and dancing. And he replied:

"It is a bit noisy."

"Terrible," said Aaron. "Oh, I can't stand it. I love good music so. The kind that carries you away into a wonderful friendly world where everything is soft and, oh, I don't know. Music like—like—the overture from *William Tell*, and Beethoven, and *Trovatore*, and Wagner, and *Cavalleria Rusticana* and Mendelssohn, don't you?"

"Well, yes," said Milton, a trifle embarrassed by the rapturous expression in Aaron's eyes. "Of course, I don't know anything about music, but I like it just the same."

"We'll go to the Symphony Concerts together when they begin, shall we? There'll be one every Sunday."

"All right."

The train left the mole, dipped rapidly under the Southern Pacific tracks, and turned northward. Milton said:

"Do you get off at South Berkeley?"

"No, I go on to the end."

"Listen," said Milton, all at once sympathetic.

"Let's make a date for a walk in the hills some time soon."

"All right. Let's see. How about Tuesday afternoon? That's day after tomorrow."

Milton thought over his classes and gymnasium period.

"All right. Come on down to the house about three thirty. We can start from there. It's close to the hills."

A few minutes later, when he got off the train and walked over to the Alcatraz car waiting to carry him down College Avenue, he felt that he was going to like Aaron. During months they had sat in the same classroom without once opening up to each other, and now, after a chance meeting, they were friends. It was too bad Aaron had those silly ideas about fraternities; oh, well, he would have him around to the house and show him what a fine bunch of fellows the Alpha Chi's were. Leaning back in a corner of the smoking compartment, he wondered which path in the hills they would follow on Tuesday. Aunt Caroline was leaving tomorrow. She liked Jarvis Smith because he had been to school in England. But Jarvis Smith was only a parlor-snake who spent his afternoons hanging around sorority houses. As the car rattled onward, Milton decided to invite Aaron to help spend the twenty-five dollars his aunt had given him.

He did not see Aaron the following day. In the evening, after meeting was over, Dick Folger ordered the freshmen to go to their rooms. They walked upstairs slowly, muttering to one another.

"They're going to put us in the tub," Bert Hudson whispered to Milton on the second floor. "I'll be damned if I'll stand for it."

"What makes you think so?"

"Aw, I know they are. I heard the sophomores talking."

Milton went to his room on the third floor, closed the door, sat down before his desk, and tried to read; but he heard voices and slamming doors beneath him, and finally he stepped out into the hallway and listened. On the floor below some one called out (he thought it was Hawkins, the junior:) "I'm going now," and some one else answered: "Oh, wait till we finish. Come on, Hawk. Stick around and watch."

"Finish what?" Milton thought, hesitating with one hand on the banisters. Then he heard water running into the second floor bath-tub, and Wendell shouted:

"Hurry up, Dick, let's get started. I want to go to the library."

Returning into his room, Milton sat on the edge of the bed and waited. He found it reassuring that Wendell was going to the library afterward, for nothing much could happen if life were go on in the same banal fashion. Like the initiation, which he had dreaded, tubbing was nothing to fear: just a momentary dip into cold water and all would be done; perhaps only his imagination and Bert Hudson's had conceived the idea of it, and when Wendell shouted: "Hurry up, Dick, let's get started," he meant something entirely different.

But his door opened, and one of the sophomores thrust in his head and ordered: "Take off your clothes, Milt."

Suddenly cold, he undressed. After a few minutes, while he was standing with only a bathrobe around him, the sophomores again opened his door and called:

"Come on down-stairs."

In the second floor hallway he met Tony Barragan, also in a bathrobe, but with his hair and face dripping. Tony shook his head and grinned, and Milton, who was trembling, grinned also, and walked on, trying to look as if he did not care what might happen. Around the bathroom door stood Wendell and two or three of the juniors, hands in pockets; there was water splashed on the hall carpet. Dick Folger appeared, naked, broad, and hairy, "like a butcher," thought Milton rapidly. Some one pulled off his bathrobe. Other naked forms were around him. Dick cried: "All right." And Milton abandoned himself.

He did not feel the cold of the water when it covered his head. There was a greenish light and something pressing him down. He thought: "This isn't bad. I'll hold my breath." Tony Barragan grinning in the hall. Funny green light. He remembered that he had noticed for a second that a towel was wrapped around the faucets. Now he wanted to breathe. He thought: "Enough! Enough!" and began to kick, but some one was holding his legs, and when he tried to raise his head, the weight was upon it so that he let himself go limp, knowing that if he moved again he would open his mouth or his nose and breathe in the green light. It was a wall of iron against his breathing. Tight. Tight. Tight. Oh, let me up! Let me up! Tight. Tight. Now he was going to breathe. He had to breathe. He had to breathe. The wall of iron. Heavy. Something opened.

He was gasping in the air surrounded by grinning faces. Legs still in the water, he leaned on the edge of the tub and coughed for a long time, but finally they helped him out, threw the bathrobe around him and told him to go to his room. He climbed the stairs slowly, feeling dizzy. When he had closed his door behind him, he sprawled onto the bed and lay there face down.

But what was that noise below? There was a thump ing, a shout, and then more thumping. Milton lay barely hearing, conscious only of a tumult. Water trickled along his body and one of his ankles felt chilled, protruding damp from under the bathrobe.

Thump. Thump. Several voices were shouting now. Nearby, on the third floor, some one called: "What the hell's the matter?" and then the fellow ran downstairs, and Milton heard a cracking of wood and another thump. He stood up, feeling clear-headed once more.

For a few seconds he dared not open his door and go downstairs to see what was happening. They might seize him and throw him once more into the tub. But at last he gathered his bathrobe around him and hurried to the second floor. Another shivering freshman stood wet in the hallway. Milton passed by. Near the bathroom he saw Dick Folger pushing some one against the wall: other naked bodies strained forward. Bert Hudson was behind them: for an instant, Milton saw his face, distorted and red, and then Dick Folger's head jerked back, and Milton saw blood dripping from his nose.

"You little son of a bitch," Dick muttered.

The mass of bodies vanished into the bathroom and Milton heard another shout and then splashing, and after that silence, until Dick's voice cried: "Hold his legs. What's the matter with you?"

A few minutes later Dick appeared, still bleeding. Some one called: "He's passed out." Milton went to the bathroom door and saw Bert Hudson lying face down on the wet floor, a trickle of blood moving away from his brow. Some one rolled him over. "Naw, not that way. Leave him on his face. What the hell's the matter with you? See? Pump him up and down. Like this."

As they raised and lowered the limp body, the knees and elbows knocked on the floor. Milton crouched down and took Bert's head to prevent the brow from being scraped.

"Jesus, how he pukes water! Are you all right now, Bert?" The sophomore who was pumping leaned forward.

"Guess he broke Dick's nose."

A junior in the hallway cried:

"Is it broken?"

"Yeah, he's going to the infirmary."

"Damn little fool."

Suddenly, Bert stiffened his body, and with his arms thrust away the pumping sophomore.

"Aw, he's all right."

"Come on, Bert, get up."

"How the hell did his head get cut?"

"The goddam towel slipped off the spout."

"Jesus, he bleeds!"

A quarter of an hour later, Bert lay with eyes closed on his bed, and Milton, beside him, was washing the cut on his forehead. It was very slight. As he prepared a bandage, he asked:

"Does your head ache, Bert?"

"No, not much."

Milton hated the idiots walking to and fro outside, slamming doors and talking.

"Let me get your pyjamas for you," he said. "Where are they?"

"Closet."

When Bert sat on the edge of the bed, said that he felt dizzy, and for a long time remained with head lowered against his hands. Milton pulled the bathrobe around him.

He lay awake that night and heard the clock in the Deaf and Dumb Asylum strike two and then three, while his roommate snored evenly in the other bed. Thoughts crowded into his mind. After he turned out Bert Hudson's light and went away, he descended into the living-room, still in his bathrobe, and stood for a while near the dying fire, listening to the fellows who were talking there. All of them condemned Bert, and one said that he ought to be tubbed regularly each week. "Dick may not be able to play in the Big Game," muttered Hawkins, looking around at the awed faces. Lying in his bed, sweating and then feeling cold, Milton remembered Tom Gresham's serious voice and slowly nodding head. "It's too damn bad," the alumnus said, "I thought we might make something out of that fellow, but I'm afraid he's a bad egg. He's out chasing almost every night, isn't he?" No one had spoken in Bert's favor, not even Milton, who had stood dumbly in his bathrobe, and he loathed himself now for having remained silent, and imagined that be had defended Bert Hudson, and that the brothers had expelled them both from the fraternity. He remembered Bert sprawling limp on the bathroom floor, and he knew that he loved him, and he hated Dick Folger and Wendell and the whole gang with all their talk about ideals and making good and college spirit, and he felt a need of exile in common with Bert Hudson, so that their friendship might grow stronger in suffering. What would he say to those idiots tomorrow? Aunt Caroline had not liked them, but the reasons she gave were stupid, and, in this case, she would probably be on their side, and consider Bert Hudson merely a poor sport who deserved whatever punishment the brothers chose to give him. Again and again Milton remembered Bert limp and naked on the bathroom floor, and each time he felt once more the surge of friendship that had made him lift his head and push back the yellow hair from the cut in his brow. Aunt Caroline would hate Bert Hudson. Oh, to hell with everybody. The bed clothes were too damn hot. He sat up, heart pounding. Somewhere out in the damp, silent night a clock was striking.

He must have gone to sleep shortly after that, for the next thing he knew was his roommate before the mirror, brushing his hair. He felt calm and tired, with a stuffy headache, and he took a shower and dressed, and ate breakfast silently at the lower end of the table.

The brothers were all cheerful, for Dick Folger's nose had not been broken, and he would be able to practice that very afternoon; and when Bert Hudson appeared, rather sheepish, the bandage still on his forehead, they all laughed, after a constrained moment, and soon were talking with him as though the evening before had never been. After breakfast, as Milton was leaving the house for an early class, Bert came to him and said:

"Thanks, Milt."

"Oh, hell, that's all right."

"I don't know what got into me. I just sorta hit out."

"Sure," replied Milton. "I don't blame you."

A few hours later he repeated to Aaron Berg, to whom he had narrated the entire affair (they were climbing the long yellow slope toward the highest ridg of the hills:) "I don't blame him. After all, that tub bing's damn nonsense."

"They're a lot of swine!" exclaimed Aaron, halting on the pathway and turning back toward Milton.

"Why did you ever stand for it? I'll be damned if I would."

"Oh, well, I don't know. It's a custom. I suppose I could have found out about it before I joined the fraternity, and if I didn't like it, I could have kept away."

They walked on for a while under the blue sky. Milton thought the hills around them looked like crumpled yellow robes. Aaron said:

"All the intellectual life in the university goes on outside the fraternities."

"Well, maybe," agreed Milton, rather uncertain just what intellectual life meant. They were passing some eucalyptus trees, and he wondered how he could describe the leaves, somber and drooping, yet glinting now and then as they turned slowly in the breeze; and he paused and rested his hands for a moment on one tattered trunk, and heard the leaves rattling above him like thin slabs of wood. When he walked on, Aaron was standing on a dry hillock, awaiting him.

"It's a good thing he broke that fellow's nose," he said, when Milton came up with him.

"It wasn't broken. They only thought so for a time."

"Oh," said Aaron, running a hand through his dark, curly hair. "I understood you to say it was. He gave him a good wallop anyway. What's his name?"

"Bert Hudson."

"No, the big fellow."

"Oh, that's Dick Folger. He's the football man, you know. Played two years in the Big Game."

"No, I didn't know."

The path grew steeper. They climbed in silence for a while, the slope rising on their right, on the other side dropping far down to a valley darkened with trees. Odor of sage-brush was in the air. Milton remembered the twenty-five dollars and exclaimed:

"Oh, by the way, my aunt gave me some money to go out with some evening. Want to come along? We can have dinner in the city and go to show afterward."

"Just the two of us, you mean?" said Aaron, after

"Yes, just ourselves." When Aaron did not reply, he added: "Perhaps you know of some theater that's good?"

"Well, there's not much in San Francisco now." He glanced back toward Milton. "Wouldn't it be wonderful if there were a light opera like *The Chocolate Soldier* or *The Spring Maid*? I love light opera, don't you? Last year Ferris Hartman revived a lot of the old ones."

"Oh, yes," answered Milton, "I do too. I saw most of them in New York when I was a kid. But there must be something in town. How about next Saturday night?"

"All right. In the afternoon I have to go out and see the old man. I do that every month or so. Then we can meet somewhere down town before dinner."

They decided upon the hour and place of meeting, and arrived, still talking and rather breathless, on the ridge from which they could see down a valley descending between round hills to the Tunnel Road; and because the air was warm and resounding with the brum of flies, they sat on the yellow grass and looked back over Berkeley, many-roofed under haze, to the bay and San Francisco beyond, with its white, squarely cut buildings along the hills. Pointed Tamalpais was growing violet among the lesser mountains of Marin County; far to the south, beyond the buildings of Oakland, the lower bay, tiny and flat, shone brightly; and all along, from San Jose to the yellow fields around Vallejo to the north (they seemed like mist,) layers of gray smoke, vanishing on the edges into the blue sky, peacefully extended; and the bells and whistles and rumble of the towns rose through them.

"Look," cried Aaron, stretching out his arm. See the ferry-boat. It's like a water beetle."

For a long time they were silent. Milton glanced at Aaron's dark eyes and skin and felt that he liked him more than ever. He wondered where, beneath the Slm of smoke, the Alpha Chi Delta house was standing, and he tried to find it by commencing at the pale Campanile and running his eyes southward over the foot-ball field and the pointed roofs.

Aaron said: "When everything's so peaceful and quiet and friendly down there, it doesn't seem possible that things like that tubbing could happen."

Milton had nearly forgotten the affair. "No, that's true," he answered.

"I should think you'd hate to go on living in the house when you know they do that. Why do you, anyway?"

Milton pondered. "Well, I'm there now. Besides, it isn't bad."

"Don't they make you do all sorts of things? Clean up the house and so forth?"

"Yes. Freshman duty. Everybody goes through that."

Aaron turned onto his elbow and stroked the dry grass.

"But why do you do it?"

After a while Milton answered:

"Damned if I know."

Faintly, the long grunt of a steamer whistle reached them. Aaron lay back and crossed both arms over his face.

"I wouldn't stand for it," he said.

Milton was silent.

"I left the old man when I was sixteen because he tried to beat me with a strap. He runs a second-hand furniture store out on McCallister Street. I'll never forget that day. It was the first time I ever stood up against him. You don't know what that meant to Resist the old man. No one had ever questioned him before. When he saw he couldn't do anything with me, he tried to hit my kid brother. I grabbed the strap from him. He foamed at the mouth and kicked the door and pounded the wall with both fists."

Milton waited, filled with wonder. Aaron went on:

"The old man's the type I call a regular pawn-shop Jew." Then: "I guess your old man never beat you, did he?"

"No. He died when I was a baby."

"I never knew my mother," said Aaron. "She died when I was about two. Perhaps things might have been different if she'd lived. Of course, I can't find out much about her. The old man won't tell me anything, and the cousins I have in New York haven't written much either. They just said she was unhappy. You know, I don't think the old man treated her right. He married again shortly after she died. She was a Pole and I think she wasn't Jewish. The old man's from I Vienna."

They lay there in the warmth until the sun went lower down above San Francisco and the outlines of Tamalpais became clear-cut. Aaron told more of his early life Once he said:

"After all, a friend's a person you know everything about, isn't he?"

"Yes," replied Milton. "Absolutely."

Soon a chill came into the air, when the sun was nearly touching the rim of hills. They arose and stood for a while looking at the colors growing around. Gradually, the sun flattened itself upon the horizon. All around them the sky became like tinted china.

"Well," said Aaron, glancing at Milton with the same naïve and eager smile he had liked so much at first. "I guess we'd better be going down."

X

RETURN

All that December day Tom Gresham had been absent-minded. He could not think of the papers before him. Other men in Morton, Dunlop & Company, toward the late afternoon, said to him: "Well, Tom, you're leaving us. Good luck, old man," or "Drop in and see us some time, Tommy." He knew that several of them disapproved of his plan to reënter the university in January, and that they spoke of him among themselves with amusement. But he did not care. He was turning back from this world where everything had seemed so futile and resisting, and was going home. He would be once more in the fraternity house, just as if he were an undergraduate.

When he left the office, it was raining. Carrying his bag (he was to dine with Ethel and to sleep that night at the Alpha Chi house,) he boarded a car bound for the ferry. He wished that the whole period of moving were gone by, and that Ethel had more enthusiasm for the change. She rarely mentioned it. But once she had said: "Better ask Mr. Dunlop if he'll take you back. You never know. Perhaps after a few months you might—" "Oh, he'd take me back all right," Tom had interrupted. "But I'd never go." On the ferry-boat, which rolled slightly in the early winter storm, he believed that Jessie in her cautious and elderly way had been denouncing him.

He was surprised at her cordiality when she opened the door.

"Dinner's all ready, Tom. Come right in. Isn't it raining, though! Why, your coat's sopping wet. Ill bet you're happy now that you've finished selling bonds. Ethel's in the kitchen."

Tom waited before the fire until Ethel appeared. She wore the gray apron. He felt guilty, having finally leit Morton, Dunlop & Company, and expected to hear in her voice disapproval or uncertainty. But she kissed him and exclaimed: "Isn't it wonderful, Tom, that you're all finished?"

When they sat down at the table, she said:

"I had a long talk about you with Mr. Burton this afternoon."

Tom felt happy in this familiar dining-room with the sewing-machine in one corner and the wall bed opposite. Smiling, he asked:

"What did Phil Burton have to say for himself?"

"He was very surprised that you were coming back to college. He thought you liked selling bonds."

"What did you tell him?"

Ethel described the conversation. Tom thought that her eyes had even deeper shadows under them than usual, and he feared she had been working too hard. But he reassured himself by remembering that she always seemed weary, and that the face under the black hair parted in the middle was usually pale.

"I asked him to come down here some evening, and he said he would, after the examinations were over." She added: "I like Burton very much."

"Why is he always so sad?" asked Jessie, laying down her spoon and folding her stout arms. always looks as if he were bored to death."

Ethel smiled. "Perhaps he is, poor man."

"Why, Phil Burton isn't sad!" exclaimed Tom. He thought that women were strange to have such ideas. "You ought to see him when he gets a little liquor under his belt. He's a good scout."

"He's cold as a fish," said Jessie.

Elbel shook her head. "No, I shouldn't say that. He's not cold, whatever that may mean. I think he really is bored out here. He finds very few people who are congenial. And then only one or two of his classes interest him. I'm sure he feels that he's in a rut in Berkeley."

It had never occurred to Tom that Phil Burton, whom he had always considered "literary," was not quite happy in the university where there were other "liter myary" people with whom he could talk about books. Whenever he met Phil, he always tried himself to talk about them. He would say: "I read a book a while ago." (It had usually been months before.) "By this fellow, Anatole France. Some story. Let's see now, what was it called? About a woman in Egypt and a sort of priest. You know." When Phil answered: "*Thaïs*," Tom would nod and think: "That guy's read everything."

He looked up from his plate now and said:

"Aw, that's just the way he is. I remember in the army. Often he used to wander around without saying much, but he never meant anything by it. Naw, he's all right."

Ethel examined him in that thoughtful manner of hers, one elbow on the table and chin resting in her palm. Uncomfortable under her scrutiny, he went on:

"I'm going to have him around to the house one of these days. There's a fellow there I want him to meet, one of the freshmen, Milton Granger. He's literary too. Last month he wrote a poem that they're going to put in the *Occident*."

Jessie pushed back her chair and got up, breathing heavily, and carried the plates into the kitchen, while Tom continued about Milton Granger, telling that he had been to school in Europe and that his "folks" were rich. When Jessie had brought in the meat and placed it on the table, she said:

"I've seen Burton three or four times on the ferry. He's always with some young fellow. He introduced him to me once, but I've forgotten his name."

"That was George Towne," said Ethel. "He's living with Mr. Burton."

Tom thought immediately that George Towne must be some one very literary. When Jessie added: "I guess he's a fine student. Mr. Burton wouldn't like him so much unless there was something to him," he nodded and muttered: "No, he wouldn't."

"That doesn't necessarily follow," Ethel said, beginning to eat.

The rain brushed on the windows. Tom thought how pleasant it would be on these winter evenings to sit by the fire in the Alpha Chi house. He would no longer be alone in his room on Taylor Street, hearing faintly the bell of a cable-car. And when he awoke in the morning, he would not have to hurry down town and eat his breakfast before that white counter and go to the office.

"Say," he exclaimed, "it's great to have finished up in the city."

"Have you left your room?" asked Jessie.

"Yeah. They got my trunk this morning. It's already at the house. I telephoned over to make sure."

"Well, Tom," said Jessie, "I only hope this is a wise move."

Ethel lifted her shoulders. "It's done now."

"Anyway," Jessie went on, "I'm mighty glad it's law you're going to study. That'll always help you in your business."

Tom wished his friends would not always be saying: "Anyway," or "Well, it's done now," and looking so gloomy about his return to college. Why couldn't they let him alone? His father had written from Los Angeles a long letter in which there had been such phrases as "a good start in business," "the realities of life," "your responsibilities," "drifting from one thing to another." But his father belonged to a generation that had never been in the war (Tom always explained his discontent by the war,) and could no more understand why he hated bond-selling than Jessie over there, sitting fat and kindly before her meat.

Ethel was talking now about her home in Monterey, where she was going in a few days to spend her Christmas holidays with her uncle. She added:

"There's a teaching position down there my uncle wrote me about. It's in a private school for girls, and I think I'd prefer it to a high school for a year or two anyway."

Tom flushed.

"In Monterey," he exclaimed. "Why, Ethel, that's so far. You could find something around the bay. And then next year—"

"You can't expect her to wait around Oakland while you're in college," said Jessie, becoming red. Both women were excited. Tom, feeling pained, stared from one to the other, wondering what really lay behind all this. One could never tell with women. Why couldn't Ethel accept her engagement to him as he did, as something quiet and natural that was arranged once and for all? In time they would get married. Meanwhile, it was so foolish of her to have all these little storms and to be impatient because he wanted to delay their wedding for a year or two. She was a funny girl.

He said slowly:

"Aw, you don't want to live down in Monterey, Ethel. What would I do without you?"

He left early that evening, anxious to find some of the brothers still around the fire in the Alpha Chi Delta house, and walked in the rain over shining asphalt to Broadway, where the Berkeley car passed by. The subject of teaching in Monterey next year had not reëntered the conversation. While the two women washed the dishes, Tom had strolled to and fro in the living-room, smoking a cigarette and opening one of Ethel's books from time to time. He always wanted to take an interest in what she was reading. And when they came from the kitchen and sat down, they had talked of the Big Game, which California had won, and the Junior Farce, given during the Thanksgiving vacation; and Tom had spoken of the freshman class at the house, and said that all the men were good save Bert Hudson, who would probably flunk out.

He walked slowly in the damp air. Ethel had not seemed angry when she said good-by to him at the door, and Jessie had been noisily cordial. He was accustomed to these little disturbances. Before the war, when he was a senior and Ethel a freshman, and later on, during his service abroad, Ethel had frequently, as he put it, "gone up in the air"; sometimes she had even threatened to break with him, and once, during undergraduate days, they had not seen each other for two months. But she had always been the one to make peace, coming to him in that docile and sad way of hers.

"Aw, she'll come around all right," he thought now in the rainy night, feeling, as he often did, brutal toward her, as if by his bodily strength he could force her to do whatever he wished.

On the car going toward Berkeley, as he walked into the smoking compartment, he heard some one exclaim: "Hello there, Tom," and he saw Burton, in his gray hat and dark blue overcoat, smoking a cigarette in a corner.

"Well, Phil, how the hell are you? Say, that's funny. Ethel and I were talking about you this evening."

"Really?—I saw Miss Davis today. She looks tired. Must be working hard. Have a cigarette? Here, take a light from this one." Then, after a while, he asked: "Are you really coming back to the university?"

On the defensive, Tom answered: "Yeah, abso lutely." He tried to make his voice sound jovial and assured. Soon Burton asked:

"Why?"

Tom puffed on his cigarette before answering. He was going to give the same reasons he had given to his father and to Ethel and the fellow in Morton, Dunlop & Company; but he saw Burton watching him with that half amused and sympathetic expres sion, and he remembered all at once how well they had known each other in the army.

"Damned if I know, Phil," he answered.

For a while they were both silent. Tom waited for Burton to speak, and when the instructor said noth ing, he began:

"Everything seemed so futile. What was I accomplishing over there? Why should I sell bonds? Why should I—?" He paused, not daring to tell of the confused ideas that often filled him about God and service to humanity. Often leaving his room, he had walked out Taylor Street to the top of Russian Hill and stood there looking down across the tall buildings of the city, lit dimly, and the dark bay. "What was I accomplishing over there?" he repeated.

"As much as any of us, I guess," Burton answered.

"I was making good money and all that," Tom went on, "but I don't know, I—" He lifted his shoulders.

Burton asked: "What does Ethel—ah—Miss Davis think about it? Rather hard on her, isn't it?"

"Hard?" Tom turned his head slowly. "How do you mean?"

Burton hesitated. "Didn't you plan to get married this year?" he finally asked.

"Well, yes. But Ethel doesn't mind waiting a bit longer."

"No, I suppose not."

The car moved rapidly along the empty, wet street. "The boys ought to have a good fire going, Tom was thinking, eager to drive away this suggestion of Burton's that troubled him. Of course it wasn't hard on Ethel.

Burton said: "I met Mrs.—ah—what's-her-name on the ferry the other day. Ethel's cousin."

"Oh, yes, Mrs. Schmidt. She told me she had seen you. You were with some fellow. A student."

Burton nodded. "George Towne."

"The one who's living with you?" Tom said, anxious to keep the talk away from Ethel and himself. After a silence, Burton replied:

"Well, yes, he's staying up at my place for a while. I—I happened to have an extra room, and I—ah—put him up." Then, with a sigh, he continued: "I've been horribly busy lately. Correcting examination papers."

Tom nearly said: "Oh, yes, Ethel told me you were busy." But he feared this might cause Burton again to say: "Rather hard on Ethel, isn't it?" And so be exclaimed:

"By the way, Phil, there's a boy at the house I want you to meet. A freshman named Milton Granger. He's going to write, and he's a literary sort of fellow." Tom noticed that Burton was listening with interest. He hurried on: "He's going to have a poem in the *Occident*. He was educated in Europe and speaks French. I thought I might bring you around to the house to eat some day. Next semester, I mean, when you're not so busy. Anyway, Milt's going down to Santa Barbara in a few days for the vacation."

Burton was thoughtful, and Tom decided that he had not, after all, been listening: for why should he care about young boys, when he had so many in his classes? But the instructor murmured:

"Granger Milton Granger. I've heard that name somewhere. He isn't in one of my sections of freshman English by any chance, is he?"

"No, I know he isn't. I asked him. He's taking English from that fellow Hopkins."

Burton nodded. "Perhaps Hoppy mentioned him to me. What does he look like?

"Oh, I don't know. Tom tried without success to remember Milton's appearance. "Sorta brown hair. Not very tall."

"Well, I'd like very much to meet him," said Burton. "I suppose there wouldn't be time this semester? You say he's going south. I happen to be free tomorrow, if you would be, and young Granger. I'd like to meet him very much."

"I heard him say he has two exes tomorrow, and he's going to the city in the evening with some other freshmen. The next morning he goes south."

"Oh, well," said Burton, "I guess we'll have to wait."

There was a petulant note in his voice that Tom had heard occasionally before, once or twice in the army when Burton had been disappointed. For a time, in the swaying car, he could think of nothing to say (Burton was staring through the black, glistening window,) but finally he grinned and exclaimed in his heavy and good-natured voice:

"Well, Phil, I expect you'll be getting married one of these days."

Burton raised his head and laughed.

"Oh, no. I guess not. I'm a confirmed bachelor I'll need more than an instructor's salary to get married on." He removed his gray hat and drew a hand over his short brown hair. "Besides, I haven't found the girl yet."

Tom grinned again. "Oh, there ought to be plenty of 'em in your classes." He was about to go on with the subject and to speak of "a lot of little Burtons running around," but a tall, dark fellow entered the smoking compartment, and Burton said:

"Hello there, Werner. Sit down."

In a moment Tom was shaking hands with the newcomer, and Burton was saying: "Mr. Gresham—Mr. Werner." Then the instructor went on:

"How's Mrs. Richards?"

"All right."

"I guess she's studying pretty hard now."

Werner nodded earnestly. "She sure is."

While they conversed, Tom thought of Ethel and suddenly began to feel that perhaps it might be hard for her to go on waiting month after month. He had never thought of the affair in that way before. Peacefully and surely they had been engaged, and he had taken it for granted that she was content to postpone the marriage as long as he desired, especially when she was still working for her doctor's degree. Perhaps there had been resentment beneath the smiles of the two women this evening. No longer aware of the conversation beside him, he sank into a reverie, eyes lowered to the floor.

Then Burton exclaimed: "Isn't this where you get off, Tom?"

"Eh? Eh?" He jumped to his feet. "What? Is this Durant?"

The gate on the forward platform was open, and two or three people were descending.

"Good night," he cried, plunging forward.

On the wet pavement he waved at Burton seated in the car. Then he crossed College Avenue, passed beneath a misty lamp against which he could see rain falling in tiny particles, and walked along Durant Avenue, his collar turned up.

"Maybe I ought to ask her," he thought. For a moment he felt unhappy, but when he had gone half way down the block, he saw the lower windows of the Alpha Chi Delta house all aglow and knew that some of the brothers were sitting before the hearth.

"Say," he muttered in the rain, "the fire will feel good."

EPISODE TWO

XI

ETHEL DAVIS

The wooden house in Monterey which Ethel's grandfather had built in the seventies was painted white and surrounded by a box-hedge that was becoming worn. Here and there, on both sides of the small gate, gray twigs were visible: one could peer through holes into the front yard (the old swing that all four of the Davis boys had used still rotted there;) and one could see a few bits of colored glass left on the front door shining in the afternoon when no fog covered the western sun. In the old days Joe Davis, fat and bald-headed, used to sit on the porch in his shirt-sleeves, one rheumatic leg established on a kitchen chair; and not far away against the white wall his rifle would always be leaning; for certain men in town had sworn that they would get him, and he often said in his wheezing voice: "There ain't no use takin' chances." But old Joe Davis had died quietly at the age of seventy, and the house had gone on decaying after him, standing large among low adobes, its two pointed cupolas against the blue sky.

Only two of the boys were left in Monterey when the old man died in nineteen-hundred. Sixteen years before, the second son, Frank, had been thrown from a bucking horse during a Fourth of July rodeo and his skull crushed against the edge of the grandstand; and John Davis, the eldest, was running a saloon on Turk Street in San Francisco. And so Robert and his wife, Jane, and the kid, Ethel, and Ted Davis, the youngest of the four brothers, went on living in the old house, behind the box hedge that was more solid in those days. That worked in the bank (he had begun when he was seventeen) and Robert managed the estate and lost some of it every year, and then died of pneumonia when his child was six or seven. Ethel barely remembered her father. He was a tall, dark man who smelt of whiskey: she was always afraid of him, and spent her time with Jessie Schmidt, the fat cousin who had come down from San Francisco after her own husband's death. The child felt that the big man disliked her, and as her mother, even before she went to the hospital. brooded more and more in her room facing the hills, Ethel was alone or with Jessie, and her parents were never more in her life than shadows.

So many memories of her childhood in this silent house awoke whenever she returned there. Long ago she had wandered among the big rooms and paused timidly in the kitchen door to watch Sing at work over the stove. The Chinese cook had been with the family for thirty years. He would shuffle toward her, stooping a trifle, a dead scrap of a cigarette hanging like a limp fang from his mouth, and hold out a cake and say: "Likee?" One morning they found him dead in the stuffy shack behind the house, lying on a low cot among his pipes and dirty playing cards, and for several years after that, until they could no longer afford a servant, a fat Portuguese woman, with a pock-marked face, widow of a fisherman, did the cooking. When ever Ethel came home, she remembered the Chinaman, although the shack where he lived had long since been transformed into a shed for garden tools.

The past seemed more than ever to revive in her mind during this Christmas vacation. She had left Berkeley angry with Tom Gresham for giving up his position in the bond-house and reëntering the university, and all the way down in the train, between the brown hills of the Santa Clara Valley, melancholy beside the fat Jessie, she had wondered if he were indeed the refuge she had imagined, and if this solid, normal, rather stupid man with boyish crudeness (she could not help smiling as she thought of him) might fail her. Often, embracing him, she pressed her face against his rough coat, afraid to be alone. She had so many feelings that terrified her: he was safe, strong, sane: he would never understand what went on inside her,—but neither did she for that matter—all those strange impulses that frightened her so. And now, in the old house, walking through the still, musty rooms, many of these feelings of her childhood came to life again, and she would find Jessie and sit with her, looking through the window at blue Monterey Bay, flat and glinting under the sun.

Her uncle Ted went every day, immediately after breakfast, to the bank, where he was now assistant-cashier. He was becoming very gray, and seemed this winter more remote than ever. Frequently he did not return for dinner. Ethel and Jessie would eat in the kitchen near the stove and would pass the evening there, Ethel reading. She wondered why her uncle Ted was always so anxious for her to spend the holidays in Monterey: he saw her rarely, and yet if she did not come, he would be hurt and for weeks more gloomy than usual. One rainy evening, a few days after Christmas, she glanced up from her book and said:

"I wonder where he's gone tonight."

Jessie held up by two corners a cloth she was hemming and examined it.

"Oh, to the Elks, I guess. This is the night for it."

Ethel nodded. The rain sounded on the windows.

"Yesterday he was at that church committee or whatever it was, and the evening before that there was something else. I've forgotten what."

"The Commercial Club smoker," said Jessie, after biting some thread in two.

Ethel laid her book on the table and stared at a faded calendar for nineteen-ten that hung on the yellow wall. Finally she asked:

"But why does he go to all those things? He doesn't enjoy them. He's not like other men. He's like a ghost. Do you suppose he ever says anything while he's there?"

"How should I know?" replied Jessie. She added, without looking up: "He has to do something, poor man."

The rain sounded on the windows. Ethel took a cigarette from a box nearby, and the act of lighting it and blowing out the smoke made her feel better, and she looked curiously at Jessie, sewing with bowed head. She had never before thought of her uncle as "poor man." He had always been some one in authority over her from whom she had to escape, and yet he was lonely, unsuccessful, ill: why could she not have seen him as Jessie did? She hated herself all at once for being self-centered. Putting ashes slowly into a plate on the table, she said:

"I suppose he gets into the habit of eating downtown."

"Oh," exclaimed Jessie, "don't worry about him. He's all right."

Ethel leaned back in her chair and heard the rain outside and watched the flush on the stove gradually fading and leaving the iron a rusty brown. They would burn one more shovelful of coal before they went to bed, but she would not put it in until her cigarette was finished. Perhaps, in Berkeley, with this same rain falling. Tom was comfortable before the fire in the Alpha Chi Delta house, telling his heavy stories to one or two of the boys who had remained there over Christmas. Jessie's rocking chair creaked regularly, and then, with a sudden rush of wind, came a great rattling of rain upon the windows, and somewhere upstairs a door slammed, and Ethel saw the electric light that hung by a cord from the ceiling sway gently.

She remembered an evening like this during the Christmas vacation five years before, when she had returned to Monterey after her first semester at the university. The big storm of the season had arrived that year also between Christmas and New Year's; some of the fishing boats had been blown ashore; all afternoon, during a pause in the rain, she had walked near the bay, watching the men at work saving their boats, and farther around the coast, tumultuous waves piling forward upon rocks and casting spray even to the gnarled cypress trees above. And when she reached home, warm from the exercise and hungry, just as the rain was beginning again, she found awaiting her a letter from Tom Gresham, whom she had met two months before.

How different he had seemed to her then! She had read the letter through several times, trembling near the stove. Jessie had been sewing in that same chair. Jessie had not changed since that time, as she had. She thought how naive she must have been, a melancholy, self-centered child, coming from this old house where she had grown up in silence; and she remembered how Tom had appeared to her like some figure from the poems she had read, blonde and conquering. She pressed out her cigarette against the plate on the table. He was not blonde and conquering now. There had been two years, before he joined the army, when she thought she loved him for his kindness and his strength, and then, during the war, she had loved him because he seemed once more, in absence, to become blonde and conquering, and she felt that he would be deepened by the suffering he saw and experienced, and she had awaited him silently. But the war did not change him; he became only coarser and more stolid, and during the past year she had told herself that she loved him again because he was strong and sane, and because somehow, if she clung to him, he would keep her away from this old house and her uncle and all the dark thoughts and memories that crowded her mind whenever she returned to Monterey. But what would happen now? She felt that he was slipping backward. Perhaps he was not strong.

Jessie's chair was no longer creaking.

If she were to get this teaching position in Monterey, she would come back to the old house. If she remained alone, she would come back. Why hadn't she held Tom by both his arms and cried to him:

"Don't give up, Tom. Don't. Don't. That's what you're doing, giving up. You have nothing to go back to college for. You're giving up, giving up."

Why had she not spoken to him like that?

Jessie said: "I think I'll put another shovelful of coal on the fire. It's too early to go to bed, and soon we'll be feeling cold."

"Let me do it," said Ethel, rising.

Half an hour later Jessie folded her sewing into a basket, and, after rocking for a while, went upstairs to bed and left Ethel in the kitchen. She lit another cigarette. The wind outside had fallen, but the rain poured steadily, and she could hear intermittent spattering beneath the window, and a trickling gutter somewhere else, and over everything a prolonged drum ming and rustling that came from the roof, the ground, the big trees in the yard.

What if she broke her engagement with Tom Gresham? She closed her eyes and then opened them and watched the cigarette smoke, broken a faint draught, turning and separating in the air. She was like that, blown and divided. So often she felt that she could return to the old house and teach school in Monterey, and live here with her uncle and Jessie, and grow old quietly. But she remembered the last whole year she had spent here, just after leaving high school, that lonely year in which she wandered along the roads around Monterey and read for hours in her room on the top floor and peered again and again along the shelves of the public library. No, no, she could not return.

About midnight her uncle came home. She heard him hang his coat in the hallway and take off his rubbers. For a while he remained there, and then walked quietly into the kitchen and held out his thin hands to the stove.

"Sleepy?" he finally asked.

She shook her head.

"Not a bit. The storm keeps me awake. I guess ashore."

He lifted his shoulders.

"Perhaps they have. The wind has dropped now. But it's still pouring."

She knew she could never live with this cadaverous man. She must escape from Monterey and not slide back, as Tom Gresham was sliding back.

"Did you have a pleasant evening?" she asked.

He nodded, without a change of expression. His collar was much too big for him and the gold stud was visible above the sagging tie.

"Shot a few games of pool. Most of the boys weren't there tonight." He grinned. "Guess they were afraid of the weather."

Ethel wondered why he grinned like that. There was nothing funny in what he had said. She leaned back in her chair. The rain sounded on the windows.

After a time her uncle muttered: "I'm sorta hungry."

She watched him go with his stiff walk to the pantry and saw him reaching aimlessly from one shelf to another, and heard the clink of a china lid that he set back into place. Then he reappeared, smiling vaguely.

"Nothing there, I guess."

For the first time he seemed like some one younger than herself. She sprang up.

"I'll get you some bread and butter and jam. Sit down by the fire."

Having laid the food beside him, she sat down in the rocking-chair that Jessie had left and lit another cigarette. His hand trembled as he held the bread. She thought: "Poor man."

"You know, Ethel," he began, in the midst of his chewing, "I saw Bradley this evening and spoke to him about that teaching job for you. I guess it's a sure thing if you want it."

She nearly cried: "I don't want it. I don't want it."

But she thought again: "Poor man," and replied in a low voice: "Oh, thank you, Uncle Ted, for speaking to him."

He nodded several times. She waited.

There had been a time in his life, which she remembered clearly, when he had been a dapper man with shiny black hair, who wore knee-breeches and played golf at Del Monte with people from Burlingame and San Francisco.

He chewed on, crackling the dry bread.

"I'll be awfully glad to have you and Jessie back here. It gets kinda lonesome in the house. We could have some games of cribbage, couldn't we, Ethel?"

"Yes, Uncle Ted."

His voice went on:

"None of the fellows here like to play cribbage. They'd rather play dominos or bridge or poker. But I like cribbage. Just the other day I was looking at the board. We used to have some good games when you were here."

"Yes, Uncle Ted."

"My father always liked cribbage too. I can see him now sitting on the porch playing with John John always beat him. Your grandfather was a big man, Ethel He did big things. He helped make the town what it is today." He paused for a moment to take another slice of bread. Then be asked: "You don't see John often, do you?"

"No, I don't."

He nodded slowly

"I hear he's been trying to get rid of his bar now. There's no use having a bar when you can't sell anything but soft drinks, eh? Is there, Ethel?"

"No, Uncle Ted."

She arose and walked over to the window. Along the black pane drops of water were running. She heard her uncle crackling the dry bread.

"No," he repeated, "no use having a bar now when you can't sell anything but soft drinks."

Finally she said: "I suppose I had better talk with Mr. Bradley."

"Yes, Ethel, yes. Talk with Bradley. Yes, yes."

He was eager. In the wet, black pane, very dimly, she could see him reflected, turning around in his chair. Again she thought: "Poor man."

In other days he had paid little attention to her. She had feared him. Now she wanted to go to him and straighten his tie and smooth down his gray hair.

He was saying:

"Oh, it'll be so nice to have you and Jessie back here. I guess it won't be until next fall, though. You have to stay all the spring at the university, eh?"

"Yes.

"Then there'll be the money too. It will be a great help. You see, Ethel," his voice became low, "you see, I've been kinda unlucky. Your father was unlucky too." After a pause he added: "I don't know what your grandfather would say if he came back now. I shouldn't want to face him. No, Ethel, I shouldn't want to face him."

She was thinking that her life here would go on quietly with Jessie and her uncle. It was only right that she should help her uncle. Yet she remembered how she had determined, years ago, during that final unhappy period in Monterey, before she entered the university, to live elsewhere, free, free, in love and beauty."

Uncle Ted muttered: "There was something hard about your grandfather."

Trembling, Ethel said: "I may not be able to come back. I may get married this spring."

He was silent. Then, in the glossy window-pane, she saw him turn.

"I thought Jessie said it was postponed again."

She did not answer.

"Isn't it postponed again, Ethel?"

"I don't know, Uncle Ted. It may be and it may not be. I don't know. I don't know."

He sighed.

"I'd be awfully sorry if you didn't come back."

"Jessie would come back."

She tried not to think: "Poor man." After a while she said:

"Listen, Uncle Ted, the rain is slackening up."

He nodded. She left the window and do in her rocking chair. The flush was disappearing from the walls of the stove. She would not slide back.

Uncle Ted, looking down, shook his head slowly.

"No, Ethel," he said. "I shouldn't want to face your grandfather now. He'd not like the way things have been going. He'd not like it at all."

"We don't need any more coal, do we, Uncle Ted?" She was thinking: "Perhaps this is my life here. Perhaps everything out there will give way under me as I go forward."

Her uncle's hand trembled as he drew out his watch. She looked away.

"Good heavens, no. We don't need any more coal. Why, it's nearly one o'clock. I must go to bed."

He stood up. "Are you coming, Ethel"

"Soon," she replied.

Hearing the low rustle outside of the slackening rain, she sat there until her uncle had closed the door of his room on the second floor (he had taken a long time in climbing the stairs,) and then she got up and went over to the window and raised the sash. The cool, damp air swept into the hot kitchen. She leaned out.

How often she had smelt the odor of the sea and the wet earth! Overhead, her uncle was moving to and fro. The floor of the old house creaked: she saw on some bushes outside the glow from his lighted room, which made the surrounding night even darker.

She knelt down and rested her chin and arms on the low sill. Where would she be a year from now? Here? She would not be here. She would not be here. And yet the perfume of wet trees and the smell of the sea and her uncle's footsteps above her and this old kitchen were all so familiar: she felt that life would pass by easily among them.

"I will not slide back," she thought.

Soon her uncle's light above went out.

Ethel still remained before the window. Then she too went upstairs to bed, turning out the light in the kitchen. And, after a while, the house of old Joe Davis was dark under the rain.

XII

Jimmie Scott

All along the Pacific Coast rain fell for nearly a week after New Year's, but the day on which Milton Granger returned to Berkeley was clear and sparkling, with a blue sky swept clean by north wind, and an odor of spring in the air. The hills already were becoming green; they rose inviting behind the town, and Milton thought that he would go among them, under the warm sunlight, as soon as possible. He wanted to climb the steep path when the bushes were still glistening, and hear meadow-larks dropping their broken notes on the damp fields beyond the first ridge. Even the sidewalk, as he left the car on College Avenue, seemed newly touched with pale gold. Carrying his bag, he followed Durant Avenue to the Alpha Chi Delta house and saw that some of the wooden roofs were still wet from yesterday's rain. And he moved slowly and paused for a while on the doorstep, unwilling to enter.

He found the brothers occupied with rushing. Most of them were back, and five or six timid freshmen, who were entering for the second half year, hesitated silently in the living-room. He felt sorry that Bert Hudson was not there: Bert was the only one in the house who had flunked out; and Milton, as he went upstairs to his room, wished that it had been some one else. Soon Wendell appeared, more earnest than ever.

"We'll have to get on our toes," he exclaimed, "if we're going to pledge any one."

"Yes," Milton replied. Fraternity affairs somehow were outside him and made him weary, and Wendell seemed rather foolish with his sharp red face and snapping eyes. Yet, in Santa Barbara, wandering bored around the house while rain fell, he had longed for Berkeley. Wendell was saying:

"Have a good time at home

"Oh, yes. I didn't do very much. It rained most of the time."

"I know it. I couldn't get any tennis in at all. I suppose you wrote some more poetry?"

"Oh, a few lines."

"Yeah?" Wendell looked upon him with amused wonder. "Say, that's great. You'll be a literary genius one of these days." Then: "I wanted to talk to you about the rushing. We've got four or five good men lined up. There's one in particular we want to get. Say, he's a good boy. Jimmie Scott his name is. He'll be here for lunch and you can see him. His dad runs a paper in Seattle."

Warm air entered through the open window and sunlight trembled on the carpet. Milton thought of a boy named Frank Scott whom he had hated in school the year before. Wendell said:

"I'd like to have you stick around with him this afternoon and evening. You see, you freshmen have to think about these new men. You'll be the ones to live with them for four years."

"All right."

Wendell hesitated. His face grew earnest again.

"There's one other thing I wanted to talk about, Milt. Of course, I don't want to butt in. You know what you like and all that. But I've often wondered if you mix enough with fellows outside the house. I've often thought it would be good for you to go out for some campus activity, just to get out and meet some of the men in your class."

"Perhaps," Milton answered.

"Of course if you keep on writing you'll meet some of the literary crowd. Had you thought of going out for the *Occident* or the *Pelican*?"

"Well, I might. I hadn't thought much about it "

"It would be a good thing for you, and all that helps to bring the house before the public. Do you think you'll be a writer or newspaper man or something when you leave college?"

"Oh, I don't know. Maybe—"

"There's good money in it. I have a friend who's a writer. At first he wrote ads over in the city and now he's writing travel booklets for the Western Pacific. I guess he makes a lot of money. Don't know how much, but I've seen him driving around in a Stutz and looking like a million dollars. I'll introduce you to him some time. He might give you a few tips on the writing game."

"Yes," said Milton vaguely, "I'd like to meet him."

As Wendell was going, he turned suddenly and exclaimed: "By the way, Jimmie Scott's dad might give you a job on his newspaper after you leave college. We want to do our damnedest to get that boy."

Milton heard him run downstairs. Unpacking his valise, he thought with a certain dread of "going out for something," and a feeling of despair came over him, Vjust as it had when his mother and Aunt

Caroline asked what he was going to do after he finished college. He had answered them: "I don't know. Business, I guess." And Aunt Caroline said: "A man must do something, you know," and all evening he had been gloomy, feeling that there was nothing he could do, and that the life which he enjoyed so much, of reading and walking and friendships, would end abruptly within a few years, and that he would go forth into the inconceivable existence he heard spoken of as the "business world." To succeed in life a man must make a certain very large quantity of money. There would be little time for reading and writing and walking if he were to do that. Oh, well, he still had three and a half years. As usual, he drove away the thought of what he would do after graduation; and, when his clothes were put away and his valise thrust under the bed for the next four months, he lit a cigarette and walked downstairs.

Against the living-room table a tall boy with a round pink face and light hair was laughing amid a group that leaned toward him. Some one said:

"Mr. Scott, meet Mr. Granger."

With a remnant of laughter still on his face the boy shook hands with Milton and said in a reassuring tone: "Glad to know you, Granger," and then resumed his monologue. "I tell you, Dick, there's a lot of money in song-writing. If I can get that little waltz of mine published—" Dick Folger was nodding. Milton knew that the great Jimmie Scott was before him.

A few minutes later Tom Gresham drew him aside.

"We want to get that fellow," said the alumnus.

"He's a wonder. Plays the piano and composes. You ought to hear the waltz he's written. But we've got to snap it up because three or four other houses are after him too."

During the remainder of the day Milton tried to follow the rushing with enthusiasm. For a while Jimmie Scott played bridge, and late in the afternoon two of the freshmen took him for a walk through the campus in order to point out buildings where he would have courses. Milton heard his talk of song-writing; he nodded and replied sufficiently (they were strolling below the Greek Theater near eucalyptus trees,) but he kept glancing westward toward San Francisco, beyond which the winter sun was already low, and thinking that the great Jimmie Scott was an awful ass. Somehow he recalled the Frank Scott of the year before.

A few hours later, in a San Francisco Italian restaurant, he leaned back in his chair, smoking a pipe, and watched Jimmie dance with a short dark-haired girl who said that she did covers for fashion magazines. Jimmie moved over the floor with his mouth open and his rump protruding, taller than most of the dancers and talking more loudly than they. Milton was thinking again of Santa Barbara and wondering why he had felt so detached there, as if his real life were in Berkeley, and why, after returning to Berkeley, he felt no more a part of the rushing and the noisy living-room with the jazz orchestra or this restaurant here with paintings on the walls than he had of the life his mother and Aunt Caroline were leading in the white villa among pepper trees and palms and eucalyptus, standing there on the warm slope overlooking the ocean under the blue sky.

During the holidays he had read constantly. Aunt Caroline said: "Why don't you go out with the other young people and learn to play a good game of tennis instead of sitting around with those morbid novels? What's come over you, Milton? You never were this way before. But his mother turned her remote eyes upon the scene and exclaimed: "Let him read if he wants to, Caroline. Tolstoy was a great soul and saw more deeply into life than most people. And while the two women argued, Milton carried the volume to a bench at the foot of the garden and read there, hearing the surf below the cliff.

"Aren't you going to dance, Milt?" asked Jimmie Scott. He stood near the table and wiped the sweat from his forehead. "Say, the music's great. Come on, why don't you dance? Ask any of these girls."

"I shall soon," replied Milton

He was always happy looking on at things. Now he preferred to smoke another pipe and watch the couples rise one by one from the cluttered tables when the piano and drum began. The other fellows from the house were all dancing. Wendell slid forward with his narrow head thrust over the girl's shoulder; Dick Folger danced heavily, leaning back; Tony Barragan, though stocky, was light on his feet. Milton tried to think of a word to describe Jimmie Scott's emerging rump, and he sat there with the music around him, feeling outside of it all, somehow removed from the fraternity that he had a few months before enjoyed so intensely, just as he had felt during the holidays that something had changed in him and taken him away from his mother and aunt.

Going home on the ferry-boat, he escaped from thebothers, who talked inside, and stood alone on the after- deck, watching the dim lights of San Francisco recede into the mist.

Aaron Berg came to the house the following afternoon, and Milton read him the verse he had written in Santa Barbara. When he had finished, Aaron was silent for a moment, sitting on the bed and leaning back against the plaster wall. Finally he said:

"It's all right, I guess, but what's it all about?"

When Milton hesitated, Aaron continued:

"It's good description and all that. But is there any meaning? Is there any idea behind it?"

"Well," said Milton, "perhaps not."

"Take that one about the eucalyptus tree. It gives a good picture of an eucalyptus tree in moonlight, but one must have something more than that in a poem."

"But what sort of idea do you mean?"

"Why—why—an idea. You could have the eucalyptus tree represent something else or be a symbol, or you could draw a conclusion of some kind. You've read a lot of Keats, haven't you?"

"Yes."

"I thought you would like him, because your verse is full of sense impressions. But he put an idea into his work. Take *The Ode on a Grecian Urn*. Well, that's a great poem because he comes to a definite conclusion. You remember. Beauty is truth, truth beauty and so on. He didn't just describe an urn. He had a message to put over."

Milton felt discouraged. He could write only when impressions were strong enough to trouble him until he found words for them. In Santa Barbara he often walked in the evening along the beach, watching the dark waves crumble into foam; and he felt better after discovering adjectives for the water or the sand or the trees upon the sky. He strode home more happy than he had ever been, and wrote down what he had composed, and the next day, having spent an hour in revision, kneading the sentences as if they were clay, copied the poems into a notebook and thrust it beneath papers in a drawer, safe from Aunt Caroline. But he could never begin with an idea.

"I don't seem to have any ideas," he said, tossing the notebook aside.

"Oh, I do," said Aaron, "plenty of them. We ought to combine."

"Yes," Milton replied, without enthusiasm. He knew that he could never write of a subject that did not come naturally from inside himself.

"You were reading Tolstoy last semester," said Aaron. "Well, his books are important because of his ideas. He wrote them to bring out certain big ideas. They're not just stories."

"Oh, I know. But everything with him is so natural. The descriptions are so good and the people are all so real. I'm halfway through *War and Peace* now, but I've had no time to read since I came back. We've been so busy rushing." Milton hesitated. "We wanted one or two more men. We're after one fellow in par ticular. His name is Jimmie Scott."

"What do you want him for?"

Milton felt he must defend the fraternity.

"Oh, he's a good scout. Plays the piano and composes. He'll be a fine man to have."

"By the way," said Aaron, "did that other freshman come back? You know. The one they held in the tub?"

"Bert Hudson. No. He flunked out. I haven't seen him since I came north."

"Guess he's glad to be out of the place." Again Milton felt on the defensive. Yet simultaneously he wanted to say: "Yes, he's damn glad to be out. I wish I were too. I'm sick of the whole gang, and this silly rushing, and Jimmie Scott's a terrible ass." But, instead of that, he muttered:

"No, I think he's all broken up about flunking out. He's living with a cousin in San Francisco. I haven't seen him,"

Aaron leaned back among pillows on the bed.

"When are we going out in the hills, Milt? It would be wonderful this afternoon. It's like spring."

"I can't go this afternoon. In about an hour some of us are taking Jimmie Scott over to the city. I wish I could. But I promised Tom Gresham I'd go along on the party."

"I had some good walks this vacation," Aaron said. "I went out with that fellow Burton in the English department. You know him, don't you?"

"No, I don't. I've never seen him. But I've heard Tom Gresham speak of him. They were in France together."

"I happened to meet him up on Grizzly one day. We walked down together, and he asked me to his house. He lives out on Euclid Avenue. Since then I've seen him several times. He's all right. I thought at first he was a rather commonplace type, but when you get to know him, he's better. He's very friendly."

"I'd like to meet him," said Milton.

"Yes, we'll go out some evening. I often go. Once Phil asked me to spend the night, but the folks expected me home and I couldn't."

"Oh, you lived with your family?"

"Yes, I went back to the old man for a few days. Burton has some fellow living with him out there. I've seen him around the campus. George Towne, his name is. He seems like a commonplace American type. don't know what Phil can see in him."

Milton thought for a moment. Then he exclaimed:

"George Towne. I know him. A blonde fellow, isn't he? Yes, he was in my German class for a while last fall, and he waited on the table here for a few days."

He remembered the interest he had felt in him. Since the early autumn he had barely seen George Towne, who had dropped from the German course. Once or twice, months before, he had noticed him in the gymnasium locker-room or on the ferry-boat going to San Francisco, but he had never spoken more than two or three words with him, and he doubted if George Towne even knew his name.

Aaron was talking about a weekly paper to be published on the campus, a "journal of protest," as he called it, to be named *The Hornet*, for which he had written a satirical article upon military training. He said eagerly:

"Bill Watkins is running it. He liked my article. Said it would be the best thing in the first number. Of course, I do think it's pretty good. Bill was all excited about it. He said: 'Aaron, that's great stuff.'"

"You'll bring me a copy of it when it's out?

"Oh, absolutely."

Milton watched Aaron's face light up in that same naïve way as he talked, and he thought there was something pleasant and amusing in his vanity. It was childish and exuberant. Aaron blurted out in a refreshing manner what was in his mind, his dark eyes shining. Milton remembered how Odysseus boasted before Alcinoüs; and thought that, after all, reticence and modesty were conventions in a certain narrow tradition only. He liked his friend all the more, after explaining to himself this petty weakness. For a time he forgot his growing discontent with the fraternity, and the imminent rushing party with Jimmie Scott. But when Aaron left, half an hour later, the feeling of bored detachment swept over him again.

It became intense during the fraternity meeting next evening, in the stuffy *ogoura*, where the brothers solemnly wore their green robes. Dick Folger's heavy face looked more round and yellow than ever under the cylindrical cap: he stood wearily behind the green altar, shifting from one foot to the other, and uttered with hesitation the words of the opening ceremony. During the roll-call his eyelids drooped, and twice he yawned behind hand. From his place on the fresh man bench next to Tony Barragan, Milton looked around at the brothers.

The sophomores were opposite him, and farther to the left, against the same wall, was a row of juniors, three or four of them, whispering together. On the bench along the end of the room, facing the altar, sat and Tom Gresham. Alert, eyes snapping, dell motioned the juniors to be silent; and when they did not obey, he leaned forward and touched one on the knee and said: "Key down, will you?" Beside him, Tom Gresham grinned broadly. The alumnus, who was now a graduate student, leaned against the wall, his arms folded and legs crossed; he recently had his hair cut short: Milton could see whitish bristles above his ears, and, when he turned his head, along the back of his neck. He remembered suddenly that distant evening when he and Tom Gresham had walked together through the soft-colored twilight from the boarding-house on Euclid Avenue to the Alpha Chi Delta house. He wondered what would have happened if he had never met Tom Gresham on the train coming north from Santa Barbara. A chance word in the dining-car had led to his membership in Alpha Chi Delta, and that would lead to something else in the future. The green light was strong enough to make a gold tooth shine in Gresham's face. He was grinning once more, when Wendell shook his head again at the whispering juniors. Milton thought that Tom Gresham must have a very strong character to give up his position in San Francisco and return to the university: probably he would be a great lawyer someday, for he had the powerful lower jaw of a successful man. Milton admired Tom.

The roll-call was finished now and the chairman of the rushing committee was called upon to report. Hawkins arose and coughed and began to speak and immediately the name of Mr. James Scott was introduced.

"It seems to me," Hawkins said, "that it's about time we bid him. We've had him out on several parties, and I guess all the brothers know him. He's a good man all right, and it seems to me that it's about time we bid him. I don't know whether any of the brothers have something to say. I—I," he paused, "guess you all know he's a good man, and I—it seems to me—" His speech dwindled away, and he sat down, both hands pressing his robe between his knees, his face turned toward Dick Folger.

The president cleared his throat. Then he asked:

"Is there anyone against Mr. Scott?" In the silence of the green *ogoura* the brothers glanced at one another. Impulsively, Milton raised his hand.

After a moment Dick Folger said: "Have you something to say, Brother Granger?"

Milton stood up, ideas and images crowding into his mind. He knew that he hated Jimmie Scott, yet he could think of no reason for his hatred. He thought of Santa Barbara and Aunt Caroline and decided that his mother would hate Jimmie Scott, and he remembered the conversation he had had the preceding afternoon with Aaron Berg, who was able to tell him what was good and bad in his poetry, and who liked to walk in the hills. He felt suddenly how uncongenial all these fellows in the *ogoura* were, and how brutal and stupid Dick Folger had looked the night they put Bert Hudson in the tub. And so, because he felt antagonistic to them and because the *ogoura* was too warm, he answered:

"Most Supreme Master-Brother, I don't like him." Standing there before the altar, he tried to think of something else to say But nothing came, and so he sat down.

At the end of the room, Wendell was bending forward, snapping his fingers.

"Brother Wendell," said Dick Folger, and nodded permission.

"It seems to me," exclaimed Wendell, rapidly on his feet, "that Brother Granger ought to have some reason for turning down a man like Jimmie Scott. He's not the kind of fellow you find every day. I—I—" His face was red, and he spoke slightly through his nose, Well, I think it's damn foolishness to turn him down."

Several brothers wrapped the benches with their knuckles. In silence, Milton knew that he hated Jimmie Scott.

Wendell sat down, his breathing hurried. Dick Folger cleared his throat.

"Well," he said, "there's no use taking a vote unless Brother Granger changes his mind."

No one spoke. Milton felt Tony Barragan nudge him. What did that mean?

At last Tom Gresham rose slowly and said:

"Most Supreme Master-Brother."

"Brother Gresham."

"Ahhhh—" Tom's deep voice got ponderously under way. "Aahhh—I think it would be a good plan to take the vote. Brother Granger might reconsider. Aahhh. It will do no harm to take the vote—ahh—" Several of the brothers were nodding. Tom looked at Wendell and said: "Don't you think so?" and then sat down, a trifle red, and drew his robe closely around him. Milton lowered his eyes.

He heard a rattling of marbles against wood. Each of the brothers would take a marble from the compartment of the box presented him and drop it through a hole in the cover. If a black ball were found among them, when all had voted, the candidate would be dismissed. As the marbles clicked one by one against the wood, Milton kept his eyes on the open floor.

He hated Jimmie Scott. Yet suppose he were wrong? Tony Barragan nudged him again. He imagined that he heard Aaron Berg say: "Jimmie Scott's a very commonplace American type." Aaron had a curious snobbishness. The brother held the box out toward him Knowing that his mother would hate Jimmie Scott, he dropped a black marble through the hole. He scarcely heard what went on during the rest of the meeting.

As he was walking downstairs, half an hour later, Tony Barragan said: "Good work, Milt. That fellow Scott's an awful ass."

In the living-room Hawkins muttered: "I sort o' think you were right about Jimmie Scott. He's too damn fresh."

Milton felt free. All at once he began to like the fraternity again. They were a fine bunch. Tom Gresham grinned at him and nodded, and soon Wendell came up and said: "Well, Milt, you're the doctor. You freshmen are the ones who have to live with these new men for four years."

As he went upstairs to his room he began to think: "Perhaps I was wrong. Perhaps Jimmie Scott isn't so bad." But the affair was ended. He shrugged his shoulders and sat down at the table. In a few minutes Aaron Berg would come over to hear some more poetry: this would make a good story to tell him.

XIII

BURTON AND GEORGE

Burton lived beyond the end of the car-line on Euclid Avenue, a street that winds north into the hills. One end of his cottage was attached to a larger house; a eucalyptus tree stood near the other and shed on the roof scrolls of dried bark; along the front, parallel to the sidewalk and a step below it, ran a narrow verandah, upon which the door opened. Entering the house, one came into a large room with a single long window extending across the western wall, and through it one saw the bay and San Francisco and Tamalpais, and on clear days the Pacific Ocean. There was a fireplace opposite the window, a table between them, and bookcases around the walls. And Burton's piano was in a corner near the door that opened into his bedroom.

George Towne slept above in a low room under the roof. Lying in bed, he could hear the eucalyptus leaves rattling upon the shingles. In the morning he heard Burton moving about downstairs, preparing to go to the university for an eight o'clock class; and he closed his eyes and turned over and tried to sleep for an hour or two longer. It was usually ten or eleven before he got up. Burton had helped him to get a small job in the library that required barely two hours a day, from twelve until two, and so he did not have to hurry. Unfortunately, he received only twenty-five dollars a month, which was not enough to buy all his food. But he was able to borrow whatever he needed from Burton.

He liked to smoke a first cigarette in the silent living-room. Already the noon sun would be falling through the bedroom windows in the south end of the house. He would sprawl in Burton's morris-chair, feet toward the empty fireplace, cigarette in a drooping hand, hair still unbrushed, and think of the poker game of the night before, or of the book he must read sometime, or merely watch a bit of sunlight in the bedroom doorway. Dead cinders usually lay on the hearth (Burton read before the fire almost every evening;) and on a small table nearby would be a cup with a little cold tea in the bottom, and a teapot beside it, and a sugar-bowl; and near them a book and a jar of tobacco and, dribbling ashes, a small briar pipe with a square bowl and straight stem.

Sometimes George reached out, without turning his head, and lifted the book that Burton had been reading and opened it with languor. Frequently, it was a volume of the *Thousand and One Nights*, which Burton reread constantly; and George would follow a series of adventures until he noticed, by the clock on the mantelpiece, that it was nearly twelve. Then he would put aside the book, stretch his arms upward, yawn, sliding down in the chair, and arise and go into Burton's room and use his comb and brush (he had left his own at Tuppy's and kept forgetting to bring them up;) and finally run from the house, slamming the door behind him, and catch a Euclid Avenue car that would bring him to the north gate of the campus. He usually reached the library ten or fifteen minutes late.

He enjoyed this tranquil existence. Most of the classes he attended occurred in the afternoon. In the evening, if he did not return up the hill with Burton, whom he sometimes met at dinner, he would go to Tuppy's room and play poker with his friends. He slept more and worked less than before, and as he walked occasionally up the hill from the university, he began to look fresh and clear-eyed.

Burton himself played small part in his mind. Sometimes in the morning, before he left the house, and while George was still half asleep, the instructor would come fully dressed into the upper room and stand looking down at him with a preoccupied air and ask him if he had slept well. George usually murmured an indistinct reply. He wondered if Burton were going to start something, for the suspicions he had entertained reawoke from time to time. Now and then, to see what would happen, he threw back the covers and exposed his bare arms. If Burton wanted anything, he would not refuse: a surrender of that sort would free him from any monetary obligation. But Burton never did more than sit on the edge of the bed, and George little by little assumed that nothing more would happen.

At the beginning of the semester Burton's mother arrived from New York, where she had been with her brother and his family, and went to live at Cloyne Court, a small hotel on the north side of the campus. Burton spent many evenings with her. Sometimes, as he walked up Euclid Avenue, George met them coming slowly together down the hill. Mrs. Burton was rather stout and resembled her son, and George always felt slightly embarrassed in her presence, though she seemed to like him, He was glad when he was able to leave them and continue homeward.

One evening he entered the cottage about nine o'clock and found a letter from his sister in Wyoming Before reading it he built a fire and settled himself the morris-chair with a package of cigarettes at his elbow. The warmth felt good on this February night, Emma had written that Jerry and Art were home from Coblenz, but that neither of them had found work, though Art had agreed to act as horse-wrangler for a dude-ranch the following summer. She went on to say that both the boys were looking well and that they did not seem to worry over their inactivity. "Father is no better," she wrote. "He hopes all the time that the boys will take hold of the hotel and keep it going. But they don't seem to take any interest in it."

There were a few details about the cold weather in Lander (Emma had gone up there from Cheyenne for the Christmas holidays,) an anecdote about a Shoshone buck who had got drunk on bootleg whiskey and killed two men over at Fort Washakie, and an account of a play she had put on in the high school. In closing she said: "I know, George, that you are studying hard, and that you will make a big name for yourself some day. Please write me all about California. How wonderful it must be to have roses in the middle of winter! The snow is now three feet deep outside my window, and I can hear sleigh-bells going by along the street."

Before a crackling piece of eucalyptus, George tried to imagine the life they must all be leading in Wyoming, Emma teaching school in Cheyenne, the rest of the family living in the old wooden hotel in Lander which his father had opened back in the 'eighties. The new brick Hotel Central took most of the best trade now. George remembered how his father used to tell him stories of the days before the railroad, when Chief Washakie was a power in the country. The impressions of the past year in California had temporarily covered his boyhood life, as if all of it had befallen someone else. But memories revived now: hot summer rides along roads rimmed with sage-brush, Indian dances over at Fort Washakie, flat-topped buttes rising upon the sky, white winter storms, people he had known, Mrs. Brown, who taught Sunday School, Margaret, the girl he had gone with through high school, Dick Steele, who had been, before he was killed one day in an automobile accident, broncho-buster with an outfit down south of Lander. And then there was Joe Farley. Sitting comfortably before the fire, George felt ashamed: all this year he had not been to see Joe Farley who was still in Alcatraz.

He wondered just what Emma meant when she hoped that he would make a big name for himself. Two years before, when he announced that he was going to California, his father and mother had both opposed him, and had asked what he expected to gain from a college education. At random, for he did not know himself, he answered that he would study law, and that had seemed practical to his father, who nodded and spoke of Joe Miller and his office in the new brick building. And when Emma returned from Cheyenne, she had backed him up, urging him to go; and he had come West on freight-trains, uncertain what he would study, desirous vaguely of finding an atmosphere to appease his discontent. Emma would be disappointed if she knew he were accomplishing nothing. He watched the flames. She was the only person save Joe Farley who had ever comprehended why he read books now and then, or why he wanted to go somewhere else Doubtless, she imagined that he would be a great lawyer.

He yawned, feeling sleepy, and mused about the poker-game going on in Tuppy Smith's room. For several evenings he was able to remain up the hill reading in a comfortable chair, or hearing Burton play Bach and Mozart; but he always had to return to the fellows he knew and among whom he felt at home. He would go there tomorrow evening. Meanwhile, he might as well sit here in the warmth until Burton came home. He considered Burton a curious person, always preoccupied, and of late more than ever, since his mother's arrival. Yet he admired him, in a way, and thought him fortunate to have his position in the university.

The instructor returned about eleven-thirty. He removed his dark blue coat and gray hat and laid them on a chair beside the door. Then he sat down near the fire and stuffed his square-bowled pipe. After a while, when the tobacco was burning, he asked in his slow, half-sneering voice:

"By the way, George, do you know a freshman named Milton Granger?"

George pondered.

"It seems he does some writing," Burton drawled.

"A friend of mine, Tom Gresham, spoke to me about him last semester." When George did not answer im mediately, he added: "I—ah—I just thought you might have happened to meet him."

Finally George nodded. "Yes, I know him. He was in a German class with me last fall, and then he's in that fraternity house where I slung hash. Why, what about him?"

"Oh, nothing in particular. Tom Gresham seemed to think he was intelligent. I saw a poem of his in the *Occident* this month. He has a very good sense of color and describes well. He transposes all his impressions into the visual plane. Overdoes it a bit, I guess. Mixes up sound and colors."

"I always thought he was a typical fraternity man," George said.

"One thing I like about his stuff is that he doesn't try to make it mean something else. He's satisfied merely to present. There's one in there about a eucalyptus tree in the moonlight. Most people would have made the tree a symbol. He didn't."

George thrust the poker into the fire. After a few minutes of silence, during which Burton drew on his square-bowled pipe that clicked softly, George said, leaning the poker against the side of the fireplace:

"I got a letter from my sister today."

"Any news?"

"Oh, no, not a helluva lot. The old man's still sick, and my two brothers have got back from Germany."

He told what Emma had written, and while talking tried to recall who Tom Gresham was. Burton had several friends in San Francisco who came now and then to the house. George felt sure that two of them were queer. Perhaps Tom Gresham, whoever he might be, was that way too. He was saying:

"Jerry and Art don't know what they're going to do. I guess they're like most of the fellows who were in the army. Don't give a damn any more."

Soon Burton asked: "Think you'll ever go back to Wyoming?"

George moved his shoulders. "Damned if I know. Oh, sure, I'll go back some day to see the folks." He paused. Then: "It's not bad. I think about it now and then."

Slowly, Burton said: "I'll never go back to the place where I used to live." He shuddered. "A little town in Kansas. It was something like Lander, I suppose. Flat all around, a few hills in the distance, sagebrush, and a single track running off to the main line fifty miles away."

George nodded. "Of course there are the Indians near Lander. You see, the Shoshones and Arapahoes are on a reservation over by Fort Washakie. That makes it more interesting, because they have dances and rodeos and things like that."

"There was nothing in Kansas," muttered Burton. "Just flat."

George glanced at him and felt, for the first time, that Burton's youth had not been altogether unlike his own. Hitherto he had never regarded him as some one who had had the same problems as himself.

He had always been an instructor, some one much older, beyond the age of problems, who had been to London and Paris.

"I've often wondered," Burton continued, "how boys get started in places like that. Everything is against them. What makes them leave their homes and go to universities all over the country? What happens to them afterward?"

"Oh, I guess they just go away because they want to."

They followed the subject no further. George leaned back, joined his hands behind his head, and closed his eyes. A slight wind was rising and he could hear eucalyptus leaves patter on the roof.

Burton said: "You've never told me much about your mother. Doesn't she ever write to you?"

"Not often. She's too busy around the hotel. Then she has the kids to look after."

"How old are they?"

"Let's see. Billy is ten and Jack is twelve—no, thirteen."

"You came along somewhere in the middle of the family."

George nodded, without opening his eyes. Burton asked:

"What is your mother like?"

George tried to visualize her—a stout person with blonde hair nearly untouched by gray, who wore an apron during the daytime and went to church on Sunday. But he could think of nothing definite to tell Burton. He opened his eyes, bent forward and took hold of the poker.

"Aw, hell, I don't know. She's all right. She's raised a big family."

He glanced at Burton, who was smoking his pipe silently, and wondered if it were not almost time to go to bed. The eucalyptus log was nearly consumed, but the instructor looked solid in his chair, eyes thoughtful. At last, removing his pipe, Burton said:

"Of course, I'm awfully glad to have my mother out here, and I'm very fond of her, but sometimes I think everything is better when we're apart."

George did not answer. After a while Burton went on:

"We're so very much alike. I think that's what the trouble is. Often we get on each other's nerves. Always about such little things too."

He knocked out his pipe against an andiron, and began slowly to refill it from the jar of tobacco on the floor near the hearth.

"But I always want to be with her when she's away."

George handled the poker idly. He had always believed Burton so fixed, so self-assured, so urbane. Yet there had been such uncertainty in his voice during this last sentence, as if a little boy had uttered the words. Was it of things like that Burton thought when he wandered silently around the room?

"Is she going to be out here long?" he asked, be cause he wanted to say something.

When the tobacco in his pipe was alight, Burton threw the match into the fire and answered:

"She probably will stay out here permanently. Anyway, that was the plan when she left New York." He paused, and then proceeded in his slow voice: "She has been living there with my uncle Edward and his family. He's her brother, one of them, that is, because there were several children. But the climate out here is better for her."

George nodded. He felt sleepy again and wanted to go to bed, but the instructor went on:

"She feels that she has lost contact with all her old friends in the East. She came from New England originally, and then she married my father and they went to live in Kansas. I guess it was hard for her to begin with. At that time the town was fifty miles from the railroad."

George let the poker dangle between his knees. Burton asked:

"Did your parents come from the East originally?"

"No, they were born in the West. Father in Ne braska and my mother in Colorado. They met in Lander, I think."

"My father was a lawyer," said Burton. "He didn't do very well in Kansas. He died when I was about fourteen."

"Yeah?"

"About a year after that," Burton said, "we came to Los Angeles. I finished high school there."

Only a single narrow flame survived around the charred wood. It danced hither and thither, vanished occasionally and then darted forth with a tiny pop. Eucalyptus leaves pattered on the roof. George rose, stretched his arms, and yawned.

"It's getting late," he said.

In the black window across the room he could see the moving, golden fire reflected. Burton said:

"I think we'll probably take an apartment together. I don't know."

"I thought you were going to get married."

Burton lifted his shoulders. "Oh, I'm afraid that's all off."

"The hell," George muttered. He began to go toward the narrow staircase near the kitchen door. For a moment he waited on the bottom step to give Burton, if he desired, a chance to say more. But the instructor was silent.

In bed, George thought: "He's a funny one, and determined, as sleep was coming over him, to look more closely at Burton's mother the next time be saw her.

The room she had in Cloyne Court was on the second floor, and the window opened to the south on a garden beyond which, above the wooden roofs of fraternity houses, she could see the tops of tall trees on the campus. It was pleasant on these warm mornings to sit near the window, with the sunlight pouring around her, and to look down at the grass already green, and to see, when she raised her head, over a corner of the Beta Theta Pi house, a bit of green hill rounded upon the blue sky. Often she went into the garden about eleven and sat there with a book for an hour before lunch. Birds would be singing, birds newly come with the spring; and she would read a few pages, until the sunlight fell across her page, and then watch some boys playing tennis in the court nearby, and think it was almost time for Philip to return from the university for lunch. Her nephew, Wayne, who had been graduated from Williams the year before, was starting in the exporting business with a friend of his father's. She hoped the boy had got over the bad cold he had when she left, and that he would not catch another in the subway. Edward had written her that Alice, who was a year younger than Wayne, had been on the go every minute during the holidays. She must write the child a letter, and send, pressed between two sheets of paper, a golden poppy, one of the first of the season, which she had found growing in a vacant lot on Euclid Avenue,

Philip nearly always came to lunch. He would come into the garden, stoop over and kiss her, and sit near by on a wicker chair and place his gray hat on the ground beside him. It was good to be with her son once more. Ever since he first left her to go to college, she had seen little of him: there had been four years at the university, then two years abroad on a scholarship, and, following close upon that, the longer and more terrible absence of the war, when he had been lieutenant in the artillery. Usually, while they were inside at lunch, she would say:

"Did everything go all right today?"

"Oh, yes," he would answer, "nothing out of the ordinary happened."

When she first came to Berkeley, he had been, for a few minutes, nearly a stranger to her. Feeling that he had important affairs of his own into which she must only penetrate with delicacy, she had spoken sometimes with hesitation, and there had been silences between them. But she soon discovered that he was not far different from the youngster she had known; he had the same melancholy, the same sudden and unexplained gaiety, the same irritability (in some ways he resembled his father;) and she tried to recognize the qualities that had not changed, and to see again the boy of thirteen or fourteen. When he was in college or abroad in the army, she often thought that the period of his late boyhood had been the best; they were such constant companions then, during the years immediately before her husband's death; she had in a way formed him to be her companion, for there was no one else in the town who loved music or who read books; and he, in turn, by what he read and thought, awoke portions of her that had been dormant for years, ever since she had left her home in Pittsfield and came West with Frank Burton. During that last horrible year before her husband's death Philip had been her only reason to live. Now she looked forward to being always near him in Berkeley; perhaps they would take an apartment together; he was well established in the university; somehow, she felt that the struggle was over and that the remainder of her life would be calm.

She often wondered if Philip would get married. He must be sometimes lonely, living as he did. At present he would be unable to afford marriage, but promotion would be certain before long (he had his doctor's degree,) and then he would be far more happy with a wife to keep house for him. Frequently, she thought over the friends of his that she had met to see if he might be interested in any one of them. There was Alice Manning, who was also an instructor in the English department: she was a nice enough girl, but Sarah Burton felt sure that Alice Manning and Philip were good friends and nothing more; and as for that young widow—what was her name?—Mrs. Richards, who seemed to be so interested in him, why she hadn't the intelligence of a rabbit, and Philip wouldn't look twice at her. There were no other unmarried women among his acquaintances. Yet he went out frequently and saw many people. There were the Cramers (Mr. Cramer was in the department of Romance Languages) and the Nolans and Mr. Slevin, the psychologist, and then that nice Mr. Hopkins who was also in the English department.

She could think of no other friends. Now and then, when he was at home, he perhaps saw that boy to whom he rented the little room upstairs, but he was too young to be congenial in any way. On the whole, Philip did not seem to have many friends. Sarah could not help feeling a little glad that this was so, for he would turn to her for companionship, and a period that resembled the old days might begin.

When she heard him mention Ethel Davis, she felt a momentary antagonism. Without looking up (they were seated at lunch,) she asked:

"Is she a nice girl, Philip?"

"Yes, very intelligent. I've known her for some time. She's engaged to a friend of mine."

She was silent. He went on:

"She's taking her doctor's degree, and I'm helping her out a bit. The man she's engaged to gave up a good position in San Francisco and came back to college as a graduate student. I think he's a fool to do it, but Ethel doesn't say much. I don't know why he did it. Perhaps she wanted him to. One never can tell. One never can tell about anything," he added, the same petulance in his voice that his mother had heard so often when he was a small boy.

"Oh, well," she said, "perhaps it's all for the best."

She had felt suddenly, for no reason that she could give herself, that Philip was in love with this Ethel Davis. If only he would confide in her.

"They won't be getting married right away then?"

He shook his head and replied: "No, mother."

Again he resembled the little boy who remained moodily with her while his companions were playthinh.

"I haven't met this Mr. Gresham, have I, dear?"

"No, he doesn't go around very much, I guess he's studying pretty hard. He lives in a fraternity house on the other side of the campus."

When he had gone back to his office in Wheeler she went up to her room and sat in the sunlight with an open book in her lap. Birds were singing outside the green hill was fresh upon the sky; there was springtime smell in the air. She felt sad because Philip did not come to her, as he would have long ago, and tell her what was causing him pain. The afternoon gradually faded and about four o'clock, little by little mist came eastward from the ocean. She could set drifting over the sun. Then completely, in the early evening, fog covered the town.

XIV

The Changing Heart

Meanwhile, Ethel Davis was doing the reading necessary for her doctor's thesis. She lived quietly in the apartment with Jessie Schmidt. Every morning Jessie rose first and made the coffee, and they ate breakfast in the small dining-room, near the window from which they could look eastward toward the hills. Ethel loved these spring mornings, so filled with light (the rains were stopping early that year, and the green hills were soft,) and she lingered at the table, with sunlight around her, putting off the moment when she must take the car and go to Berkeley and shut herself up to read for several hours in a seminar room. The air seemed richer than usual that spring, and the sky a deeper blue. Yet she was listless and melancholy in the midst of the warmth and the colors.

Frequently, she met Tom Gresham at noon, and they would eat in the Specialty Shop, a small restaurant on Telegraph Avenue near Sather Gate. He would sit opposite her, moving heavily on the slender chair, both arms on the varnished table-top among knives and forks and glasses and paper napkins, and would relate with happy grins what had taken place in the courses he had had during the morning. Around them were chiefly girl students, all talking. Two young men, assistants in philosophy, always ate at the same small table near the window. Ethel rarely saw any one she knew, though Mrs. Richards, a friend of Burton's, now and then came in and sat by herself in a corner Tom talked throughout the meal, and Ethel listened to him.

He seemed happy, yet she wondered just why he was here, among all these students so much younger than himself, thinking the same thoughts as they, but some how more clumsily. Once she felt that Tom in college resembled Uncle Ted at the Elks' Club in Monterey; they both seemed outsiders living in a world that was not their own. Yet there were many older graduate students: why should not Tom be here? And as for Uncle Ted, he had lived in Monterey all his life, and was as much a part of the town as any one. Looking up from her plate, she smiled in answer to what Tom was saying (girls and men were passing along Telegraph Avenue on the other side of the tall plate glass window) and drove away the thought, and watched his broad, reddish face. After all, she had never seen him so jovial; he knew all the men that came in; and, if they were near enough the window, he was forever tapping on it to attract the attention of some fellow who was going by.

At other times she met him on the street, surrounded by friends. He walked among them laughing, head back, eyes lighted up, arms swinging. When he lifted his hat there was something triumphant in his greeting: she felt momentary resentment, for he seemed apart from her, no longer the rather weary Tom Gresham who would come to see her after a hard business day in the city, and to whom she would say:

"You're awfully tired, aren't you, Tom? Sit down by the fire and smoke your pipe."

Jessie said when Ethel spoke of him "Just you wait. It will turn out all right. I always think everything works out for the best if you give it time."

But Ethel felt there was something grotesque about Tom living once more the lazy fraternity-house life among all these youngsters, and she could not believe that he was taking his law courses seriously. One afternoon she met Burton coming from Wheeler Hall, and they walked a few steps together through Sather Gate and along Telegraph Avenue among students in caps and sombreros and corduroy trousers. When Burton asked about Tom Gresham, Ethel replied that he seemed to be getting along very well, and then suddenly, after a pause, she said: "Oh, don't you think it was foolish of him to come back?"

"Well," Burton answered slowly, "one never can tell." Finally he glanced at her and asked: "You didn't want him to do it then?"

"I? Want him to give up his good job? Oh, no."

She felt that Burton was surprised. He strolled on without speaking. After a moment he laughed and said:

"So he came back of his own accord to study law?"

"Why, yes."

They were passing a restaurant in which waffles were sold and sandwiches and doughnuts coated with chocolate, and Ethel wondered if Tom were inside, eating and talking. She heard Burton say:

"I know Tom pretty well. We were in the same outfit in the army for more than a year. I confess I see no reason why he should be in the university. He always seemed made for business of some kind. What was the matter? Didn't he like the work he was doing in San Francisco?"

"No. He kept saying that it was futile, that he wasn't accomplishing anything, that he wasn't producing,"

"I guess he just wanted a change," said Burton.

They crossed Bancroft Way (the yellow car ready to carry passengers to the Key Route train was standing there) and walked by the Smoke Shop. Ethel glanced in to see if Tom were shaking dice over the counter. But he was not there, and she said to Burton:

"He's probably playing bridge at the fraternity house now. He does that by the hour."

She tried to banish any note of complaint from her voice. Before Sather Gate Book-shop Burton halted and said: "I've got to go in here and order some books. You know," he went on, as she was turning away, "you seem to be worried about Tom." He smiled and his voice became more drawling. A band of coeds went by laughing. "Well, there's no reason why you should be. Give him time to find himself. He's like everyone else—a bit lazy; and he wants to do something different now and then."

She almost cried out: "He gave up over in the city. Don't you see? He gave up just because the work was a bit unpleasant for him."

But she did not say it, and she was glad afterward that she had been silent, for she began to think that perhaps she was regarding the matter too seriously. And the next day, when she saw Burton again (carrying a stack of blue-books, he was climbing the stairs between the third and fourth floors of Wheeler Hall,) she tried to appear more cheerful, and, talking of her work, she accompanied him along the hallway to the door of his office. Standing with his hand on the knob, he said:

"I saw Tom for a minute this morning outside Bolt Hall. The change seems to have agreed with him. He's growing fatter already."

"Oh, it agrees with him all right," replied Ethel. "*He's* enjoying himself."

Burton looked at her for a moment, with a smile, in a way that she did not understand, opening his office door slowly. Then he said:

"But how about you?"

"Oh, that doesn't worry Tom," she answered, laughing and angry.

S he told Jessie about her conversation with Burton.

"Well, I think he ought to know what's best," said her cousin, raising the cloth she was sewing and regarding it. "He's a professor, and he wouldn't say it was all right unless he knew."

"No," Ethel answered, "I suppose not."

In this way she found the situation, when reflected in Burton's mind, less disturbing, and she began to see him more often, waiting for him occasionally after class, or going to his office on some pretext or other to converse with him for half an hour. She talked to him of her uncle in Monterey and the old house and the teaching position that she might accept for the following year. He understood her reluctance to live at home and the somber desire that pushed her there; and told her something of his boyhood in Kansas, of his father's death, and of his struggles to break away from all the ideas that had surrounded him. One afternoon they were strolling along the road that led past the Greek Theater up Strawberry Canyon; they emerged from the grove of eucalyptus and walked beneath a green hillside on which meadow larks were singing. When he stopped talking, she looked at him and said:

"I didn't know you had been through all that."

He laughed and answered: "Why, everyone has a few things of the sort to clear up. One gropes for a while. Tom Gresham is doing that now."

Burton went on about Tom. Beneath them, on their right, a brook swollen after the rains ran along under foliage. Ethel was thinking that Burton was intelligent and sympathetic, and that it was pleasant to have him to talk with. She glanced at him beside her: he was walking with his hat in one hand, his face a little sun-burned (he spent every weekend on the slopes of Tamalpais) and his head tossed back as he laughed now and then. But he seemed remote; there was something impersonal in everything he said; she felt Tom's presence, not his, as if Burton were merely a window through which she could see Tom Gresham; and she thought how strong and dear a fellow Tom was, and, for a moment there on the yellow road in the sunlight, wanted to be with him.

When she did see him that evening, and told him of her walk, he seemed a bit gloomy, and she felt that something had gone wrong in his classes. But they went to a moving-picture show together, and he became more cheerful. On the way home he exclaimed: "Say, Burton's a good scout, isn't he?" She agreed with him. A few minutes later, as he left her before her apartment building, she thought it would be better if Tom could come in too, and if they did not have to separate every evening. She stood with the door half open, watching him walk away down the dark street, and it seemed to her that she loved him as much as ever.

A few days after that she went with him one afternoon up to Burton's house on Euclid Avenue (the instructor had asked them both for tea). There she met Mrs. Burton, who was sitting in the curved window-seat when they arrived, looking off to the westward over the bay and toward the hills beyond. Ethel stood beside her. Burton came from the kitchen and offered them cigarettes. Ethel thought how much he resembled his mother and how agreeable it was for him to have her out here. A kind of bitterness flowed through her when she remembered her own home in Monterey, and Uncle Ted, silent and frail, shuffling around the house. But she said:

"Isn't it wonderful to have the sun pouring in all the afternoon?"

"I just received a letter from New York," said Mrs. Burton. "My brother wrote that it snowed all week. You'd hardly believe it, would you?"

Ethel found her way of speaking much like her son's; she had nearly the same drawl. Sitting down in a rocking-chair, she said:

"It's perfectly amazing how much you resemble Mr. Burton. Don't you think so, Tom?"

"Yeah, I certainly do."

He was smoking a cigarette before the empty fireplace, looking bulky beside the instructor who stood near. Suddenly the thought crossed Ethel's mind that they would be married and that they would have friends like Burton and his mother and houses like theirs to come to, and that all this would form a screen between herself and Monterey.

"In every way," she went on, "your voice is just like his, and you look like him too. Of course, lots of people must have told you that."

She noticed the books on the table, several volumes of the *Thousand and One Nights*, and the piano over in the corner near the bedroom door. Burton had told her that he played two or three hours a day. Somehow she felt glad that Tom Gresham did not play the piano and read books. Standing there against the mantelpiece, he looked so strong and solid in comparison with Burton, who was bending forward over the table, arranging cups and saucers. Facing Mrs. Burton, she began to talk with her about the early spring and the flowers on the hills and the table at Cloyne Court. And she could hear Burton ask Tom how the classes were going.

"Oh, all right," Tom answered.

He did not go on talking about his work. Holding in his left hand the cup Burton gave him, he went over to the wall near the kitchen door and examined the pictures hanging there. Ethel wondered what he really was thinking about, for she knew he was not interested in etchings. While conversing with Mrs. Burton, she watched him and saw him glance over his shoulder several times at Burton, who was pouring hot water into the tea-pot.

At that moment George Towne came in and tossed his books and cap on a sofa.

After he had been introduced, he sat down near the window, silently. Ethel thought him rather sullen and loutish. Why did Mr. Burton have him around? He sat in a straw chair, leaning back heavily, with his legs stretched out before him, and shook his head without uttering a sound when Burton offered him some tea. To Ethel he seemed out of place in this sunny room that was so delicately furnished. Tom was talking to him now: she could not hear what he was saying, for she had to face Mrs. Burton, who was telling of her nephew and niece in New York.

The old lady's voice continued:

"I do wish Wayne would come out West and go into business in San Francisco. The climate's so much better. He has colds all the time in New York."

Burton said: "I didn't know Tom took an interest in etchings."

He stood near the window-seat. She looked up and answered: "He doesn't. Why?"

Burton moved his head to indicate Tom Gresham, once more peering at the wall. Ethel thought Burton was making fun of him; momentarily she felt angry and replied:

"Perhaps he does. A little."

Again she loved Tom. Slouching in the straw chair, George Towne yawned. Mrs. Burton was stirring her tea, and her spoon clicked against the side of her cup. Burton said:

"There's an interesting exhibition over in the print rooms this week. How would you like to go over tomorrow afternoon?"

"Why, yes. I'd like to. Let's see. I think I have no classes."

Rapidly, Tom Gresham turned from the wall and exclaimed:

"That's the afternoon we were going with Jessie to Oakland,"

He stood there, lowering. Instinctively, without hesitation, Ethel said:

"No, Tom, Jessie told me she couldn't go tomorrow." Then: "What time shall we start over, Mr. Burton."

"Oh, about two. I'll come to your seminar room in the library."

She nodded and stirred her tea, and watched Tom Gresham prowl across the room and stand, a trifle red, before the empty fireplace. She wanted to burst out laughing. Poor Tom. Glancing up at Burton, she said:

"I'll be so glad to have you to explain them to me "

Then she remembered how she had heard that young widow, Mrs. Richards, speak to Burton one day in that same tone of voice, and that she had been amused and had made fun of her later to Tom, imitating her speech. George Towne yawned again over in the straw chair. Mrs. Burton once more was speaking of Wayne. Disregarding Tom, who remained silent and flushed across the room, Ethel listened to her.

On the way home in the Euclid Avenue car, Ethel talked of Burton's house, his mother, the view from the living-room window, that boy who was staying with him, and the interesting books he had in the cases on both sides of the fireplace.

"I didn't know whether you noticed them or not," she said to Tom, who sat beside her, face turned toward the window. He replied:

"No, I didn't."

She thought again: "Poor Tom," and she loved him more than ever, sitting beside her, dumb in his stupid jealousy. But another feeling came through her that made her say:

"I think I'll ask him to lend me a volume of the *Thousand and One Nights*. I haven't read them for years. When I was a child, I loved them."

"Um."

There had often been times when she hated Uncle Ted and wanted to make him suffer. Before she returned to Berkeley, she had said: "I doubt if I'll teach in Monterey next year, and she had watched, with a curious satisfaction that she did not understand, the almost childish expression of grief that had come over his face. Often she had been afraid of that feeling of cruelty. Now it was coming through her again She said:

"Don't you think Mr. Burton has a nice house?"

Tom nodded. "Yes. It's all right."

They were alone in the rear compartment of the car. It moved rapidly down the hill, rounding curves, between palm trees and wooden houses. Occasionally, she looked off westward toward San Francisco. The sun was low.

"Did you see much of Mr. Burton when you were in the army, Tom?"

It was nearly as if someone else were asking the question. After a while he replied:

"Yes, quite a bit."

She thought him all at once a big, stupid lout sitting there beside her.

"I suppose," she said, "that you'll go back to the fraternity house and play bridge all the evening."

He was silent. "Is that what you're going to do, Tom?"

Without turning his head, he answered: "I thought we were going to the movie, Ethel."

She almost said: "Of course we are, Tom." She loved him again: there had been such a pathetic note in his voice. But instead of that she said: "Oh, no, I have to study this evening."

"All right, Ethel."

More people were getting into the car now. She was thinking that she would go down to Shattuck Avenue and transfer to the car that ran to Oakland. Tom could do that also, as the car followed College Avenue, and go with her as far as Durant. Then she began to think that it would be nice to go to the moving-picture show tonight. Why had she refused so bruskly?

Without looking up, Tom asked: "Are you really going to San Francisco with Burton tomorrow after noon?"

"Why, yes, Tom. I want to see that exhibition. It will be very interesting. Why do you ask?"

"Oh, nothing. I—I don't know."

"Do you want to come with us?"

After a brief hesitation, Tom answered: "No, I don't want to come."

When the car reached the north gate of the campus, before it turned down Hearst Avenue toward Shattuck, Tom arose and said:

"Well, Ethel, I've got to go to the law library. So long."

She said: "But, Tom."

Without looking back, he jumped from the car and walked rapidly into the campus. As the car followed Hearst Avenue, passing below a stone parapet over which vines and flowers were drooping, Ethel wondered what she had done. "Poor Tom," she thought. Then she lifted her shoulders.

XV

Mountain Walk

E arly in March Milton decided to spend two days in Marin County, walking on Saturday from Mill Valley to Bolinas, where he would pass the night, and returning on Sunday along the road that follows the cliff above the sea. The desire to leave Berkeley had come over him suddenly one afternoon as he stood looking from his window over Durant Avenue. He felt sick of books and classes and the fraternity house. He knew that if he went downstairs now he would find Tom Gresham sitting gloomy in the brown leather morris-chair before the cold fireplace, resting one side of his head on his right hand, just as he had been doing for more than a week. Tom Gresham's melancholy suf fused all the house. Milton wanted to go away from it. And Aaron Berg was always busy in the office of the *Hornet*, or in the library preparing for the freshman-sophomore debate. There was a growing glibness about him; Milton found him less interesting, and wanted to be alone. Reading Whitman of late had something to do with his state of mind. And so one Friday night he put some lunch and a book into a canvas knap-sack (after deliberation he chose the Butcher and Lang translation of the *Odyssey*) and set his alarm-clock for six-thirty. And the next morning, while fog still covered the bay, he was on the Key Route ferry-boat going to San Francisco.

He felt chilly out on the forward deck with the fog around him. Why had he come? All day the sun might remain hidden, and he would be walking through cold mist. Perhaps it would be better to stay in San Francisco instead of crossing over in another ferry to Marin County. Shivering a little, he drew his sweater closer around his throat and watched the shadowy end of Goat Island dropping sternward in the fog. A bell was tolling there: with difficulty, only because he knew what they were, he could make out the blurred letters of the words: CABLE CROSSING. Gulls wheeled over the boat like particles of mist more solid than the rest; once or twice he heard them crying above him; the gray water rustled beneath the rails: feeling cold again and still sleepy (the coffee he had hurriedly taken had not aroused him,) he slid open the door and went inside and sat down on a curving varnished seat and listened to the thumping engines.

He thought of Tom Gresham brooding around the house. One day Aaron Berg had come, and Milton had introduced them to each other. Grinning, Tom had pulled himself heavily from the armchair and held out his hand, but Aaron had responded coldly, and Milton felt dislike in all his subsequent remarks. For a while Tom seemed unaware of any hostility, but soon he began to cast doubtful glances upon Aaron, and when he had gone, asked Milton: "Who's your snotty little friend?" Milton answered: "Oh, he's all right. I don't know what was the matter with him today."

He felt more like going to Marin County when he reached the ferry building, for he thought that the fog might go, and he did not want to wander around San Francisco all day wearing army breeches and an old coat. Throughout the crossing on the Sausalito boat, there was only the powdery white mist drifting by around him, though once a pale corner of Alcatraz Prison emerged for an instant, and he leaned back in the seat and thought sleepily of the conversation be tween Aaron Berg and Tom Gresham. They had been in the living-room, Tom sprawled in his morris-chair beneath tobacco smoke, Aaron sitting on the davenport. Burton's name had been mentioned. Tom was silent. Aaron said:

"No, I don't suppose you would have very much in common, would you?"

When he reached Mill Valley after a ride in an electric train, he saw that the mist was rolling together into great bulbs that left uncovered patches of blue sky, and as he climbed the hill opposite the railroad station, he began to feel warm, and removed his coat and slung it over the strap of the knapsack. He was glad now that he had come, for a green hilltop was visible here and there, and the round masses of fog, tumbling over slowly in the air, were shining white in the sun. He began to walk rapidly. For a while there were redwood trees on both sides of the road: the mist lurked among their somber trunks, and Milton sniffed their damp odor. Then he left the road and climbed up a path that led by a water-tank to the track of the Tamalpais railway. Standing here in the silence, he looked around at the fog that was separating. Behind him it was still dense and white, and in a valley beyond it was turning sluggishly over and over like slowly boiling gray fluid; but over his head it rolled in great white fragments, and farther on, in the direction where he would go, it was growing thinner, and behind a melting film, transparent and touched with silver, he could see, rising upward, the calm gray and green façade of Tamalpais, the top-most ridge, whenever the mist opened before it, clear-cut and hard upon the sky.

He hurried onward, commencing to sing. Petty irritations of Berkeley were falling from him. Soon he left the railroad, this time to cut across the yellow face of the mountain along a crumbling trail rimmed with sage-brush. The fog surrounded him again, and for a while he felt cold and could see nothing save the ground beneath his feet; but finally he emerged into blue glistening air (all at once a buzzard wheeled across the sunlight) and saw the white fields of the mist below him. They were swollen, sometimes moving, traversed here and there by floating wraiths, shadowed over by the mountain and flashing white elsewhere. He was far above them. They filled the valleys and lifted shining veils into the air and extended across the bay and out over the ocean and south along the coast where only the top of a gray headland appeared. Milton stood in the clear air, the sun burning down upon him. Occasionally trees came forth on a distant ridge. And once, over a hill and into a green hollow hitherto unburied, a smooth gradual cataract of gray creamily poured, and the trees grew blurred and then faded and vanished away.

The morning ripened into the heat of noon. Little by little the plains of fog heaved up in dwindling plumes, and the valleys below grew visible, and the blue floor of the ocean lay tinily fringed with white surf along the beach. As he followed the yellow trail between West Point and the Mountain Theater, a buck leaped from beside him and sprain crackling off through the brush. When he reached the grove of trees behind the theater, he halted, and, feeling languorous, leaned against the hot wooden fence and looked down into the green meadow below Rock Springs. It sloped away, damp and fresh under the blue sky. It was a place, he thought, for gods. No wind came over the ridge from the sea. Yellow poppies and blue lupin crowded the rim of the brook that moved through the grass. He went forward to the gray rocks from beneath which the spring arose, and having drunk, strolled along the soft ground over a low ridge and into another small valley, where a brook ran with peaceful sound among stones. There he lay on a warm slope and ate his lunch, and spent the hot hours of midday.

It was pleasant to lie here on the ground and look up through half-closed eyes at the sky clamped down over the still mountain, emprisoning it in warmth. Birds were hopping and twittering nearby; he could hear them among the leaves; and once in the brush farther up the hill sounded a crackling that made him raise his head and wonder if a deer were there. But he saw nothing and lay back on the ground, thinking suddenly that his mother had announced in a recent letter her intention of going to India in the spring "to study at the very feet of the master," as she had phrased it. Aunt Caroline was going abroad. She wanted him to go with her. The noise of the brook, the flutter of birds among leaves, the drone of insects, the feeling of heat, the crushing blue of the sky and the fresh greens around him: all this flowed over what he was thinking and became his mind. He was only something through which impressions were passing, no longer even himself, and Berkeley was far away. Aaron and Tom Gresham and the fraternity house were fading. He closed his eyes.

All at once he sat up, blinking in the light. The glade seemed more silent than ever; the day had over-topped its maturity and was declining into a rich and shadowed afternoon; the brook ran on with a more tranquil and resigned tone. Aaron's voice seemed to speak out in the stillness: "No, I don't suppose you would have very much in common, would you?" And the brook among pebbles echoed the words. Then he saw a man in khaki emerge from a grove of trees down the valley, and he lay back hoping that the intruder would not see him, for he felt tranquil and remote in this solitude.

It was curious that Bert Hudson never came over to the house. He was working in an automobile store on Van Ness Avenue in San Francisco, and living with a cousin out near Golden Gate Park. One Sunday Milton had gone to see him; they had walked through the park to the beach and then back to the shell-shaped band-stand where the weekly concert was going on.

He heard footsteps on the moist ground; there was a crackling and rustling of foliage. Lifting his head, Milton saw the man in khaki standing nearby, leaning on a cane, and smoking a briar pipe with a square bowl and a straight stem. For a while they were both silent (the flies hummed about them in the air;) then the man took off his cap, tossed it on the grass, and said in a drawling voice:

"I hope I didn't wake you up."

"No, I was just lying here."

The flies were humming. Mopping his face and brow, the man hesitated for a moment he had a short brown mustache,) and then sat down beside Milton and yawned and uttered a long sound as if to indicate that he was satisfied, after hard walking, to rest for a while,

"Ah," he said, "that feels good."

He stretched his legs, and, leaning on one elbow, began to knock out his square-bowled pipe against the palm of his left hand. Milton thought that he had seen him somewhere before, perhaps in Berkeley, and he felt displeased that this fellow should have come into his lonely glade, just when he was so detached from the university. While stuffing his pipe, the man said:

"Walked far today?"

"Up from Mill Valley."

"So did I." (His speech came forth slowly.) "I left there about ten o'clock, just as the fog was beginning to clear away. By Jove, it was beautiful above it on the ridge. Between West Point and the Mountain Theater I saw three deer."

While he talked, his glance kept resting for an instant on Milton's face and then darting off into the trees and toward the ground. He seemed very nervous. His eyes were penetrating and filled with uneasiness, and there was something strained and hard about them, which made them resemble polished blue stone. They reminded Milton of someone he had known long before, someone with the same restless and piercing eyes. While the stranger talked, he tried to remember who it could have been. But the memory seemed gone forever. He lay there hearing the man's voice and the whispering stream and flutter of leaves when birds sprang into the foliage, and wished that he were still alone. After a while the man asked:

"You live in San Francisco, I suppose?"

Milton nearly replied: "No, in Berkeley," but a little perversity strengthened by his displeasure at the intrusion made him say:

"No, I'm from the East. I'll only be out here a few days longer."

"Oh, yes." The intruder's voice became very drawling. "Is this your first walk up Tamalpais?"

"Yes—well—that is, no. I've been up here before. Sort of been up," he added. Then he went on quickly:

"It's a wonderful place to walk. We have nothing like it around Chicago."

"Oh, you're from Chicago?"

"Yes, I—I've lived there most of my life."

"I live across the bay, ah—in Oakland. I come over here a lot. Almost every weekend."

They said no more for a while, lying there on the warm slope. Milton again tried to recall the person whose eyes had been like this man's, but the fragment of his past remained obstinately hidden. Soon the man asked:

"Where are you going this afternoon?"

Milton wanted to be alone. He answered:

"I don't know."

The other went on:

"I'm going to drop down Cataract Gulch and hit the Fairfax road. I don't know where I'll spend the night."

"I have to meet some friends," said Milton vaguely. "Back there."

They sat for a long time without talking. Finally the man reached out and took Milton's arm and said

"You have a good tan."

Milton did not answer. The man drew his hand several times up and down his arm, fondled his wrist, and then, as if thinking of something else, nodded toward the book whose end protruded from Milton's knapsack.

"What are you reading?"

Slightly embarrassed, wanting to draw away, Milton replied:

"The Butcher and Lang translation of the *Odyssey*."

"Good," said the man in a rather agitated voice, "that's great stuff."

All at once the memory he was seeking returned to Milton. The eyes reminded him of the pale young man with yellow hair and red lips from whom, several years before, he used to take lessons in Algebra. He had had the same caressing habits.

"Yes," Milton said, "it's a wonderful book."

The hand on his arm moved up and down again. The man said:

"I'm awfully sorry you're going away so soon. I think I'd like to know you."

A kind of watery smile invaded his face. Then bruskly, he withdrew his hand, cleared his throat, and sat up and began to relight his pipe, which had gone out. Milton, unhampered now, rose and looked at his watch. It was nearly three. Perhaps he had better get started down toward Bolinas, for it would take him two or three hours, and he might have to wait a long time on the end of the sand-spit for the old man to row over and carry him back across the outlet of the lagoon.

Having stretched himself, he picked up his knapsack and slung it over his shoulder.

"Going?" asked the man, still seated on the ground.

Milton nodded. He thought again of the pale young man in Santa Barbara, and impulsively asked:

"Are you a teacher?"

The man stared for a moment. Then he replied:

"No, I work in a bank. In Oakland." And after an instant he went on: "We happen to have Saturday off this week. The—ah—vice-president died."

Milton started to move away.

"Good-by," he said.

"Good-by," the man answered in an indifferent voice.

Then he lay down on the ground and turned away his face while Milton walked back toward the Mountain Theater, below which he would strike an old wagon-road that descended Steep Ravine, among dark trees, to the sea.

And as he went down the hill, looking back now and then to see Tamalpais rising behind him, he thought again that he had seen the man some time in Berkeley. But he could not place him. Next summer the white villa at Montecito would be closed up or rented. Aunt Caroline had written: "Come abroad with me and spend a year in France and Italy. Then if you want to go back to Berkeley, all well and good. But I think you will prefer some Eastern college. He had not yet answered the letter, for he was uncertain whether he even wanted to go abroad, especially with Aunt Caroline. Somehow he felt that he was different from what he had been the year before, and he feared that his aunt's company would be stifling.

The air was cooler now among the tall trees of Steep Ravine. Through the uppermost branches the sunlight slanted in long bars and poured golden patches over the ground, and occasionally a stream dribbled down the bank on the right side of the road, soaking the black soil. As he descended, a gentle fatigue began to creep over him. He no longer felt the exuberance of the hot morning when he first broke upward through the fog. In the quiet, metallic air, with the sun going lower, he felt the arriving chill of late afternoon, and hoped he would be able to attract the attention of the old man from the end of the sand-spit.

At last he reached the open hillside above the shore. There was the ocean once more shining below him. Along the horizon a gray wall of fog stood ready to roll shoreward with the darkness. Wisps of it already floated now and then across the face of the low sun. One of them, shining silver, passed rapidly over his head, and melted gradually inland; but the greater part was still far away, and he decided, as he cut straight down the hill through a farmyard toward the first trees and houses of Willow Camp, that he would follow the beach to the end of the sand-spit and cross over to Bolinas before the fog swept toward the shore.

Small bulbs of kelp popped under his feet as he walked along the damp brown sand. When he reached the end of the sand-spit, half an hour later, he could see the old ferry-man on the pier, and he shouted, and the old man, after tying and untying a few boats, soon came toward him across the narrow outlet of the lagoon, sitting erect, and rowing with short, choppy strokes. In the cool air, sitting on an old box tossed up by the waves, calmly tired in the late afternoon, remembering the early fog, the heat of noon, the stranger on the mountain (all this seemed to have befallen someone else,) Milton waited for him.

XVI

SUCCESSION

During the events narrated in the preceding chapters, Mabel Richards was living in her apartment on the corner of Durant and Telegraph Avenue and attending classes in short-story writing and lectures on the history of painting and on domestic science. She was fairly happy in her small routine, although she had been unable to forget Carl, whom she had not seen for more than two months, not since before the Christmas vacation. Days would go by during which she did not think of him. Then a chance word or a bit of scenery or an air that some one hummed on the street would recall him. Becoming sad (or, if she were talking with a friend, silent) she would see his long face and closely cropped hair, and the same old pain would fill her again. Thoughtful, her blonde head drooping a trifle to one side, she would usually walk home and try to read (she often found comfort for what she considered her unhappy life in theosophical books;) but many times in class or with someone she could not leave, she would stare vacantly or with melancholy into the air, deaf to the professor's voice if she were in a lecture-room, or to her friend's question, if she were outside.

In her reasonable hours she knew that she would never cease thinking of Carl until there were some other young man whom she could establish in her mind and surround with all the fluctuating materials of tenderness now without aim. More than ever she had been feeling of late the futility of her existence. What was she doing in Berkeley? She had come there for Carl, and he had gone from her, and there was no one now to be the center of her days. When she was in New York, she had often thought how good it would be to say: "No, I can't do that tonight. This is the evening Carl and I go to the theater," or "Next summer I shall remain West, because Carl will be in San Francisco." She wanted to know that someone had need of her. But for a long time after Carl's defection, she felt indifferent to all men, and she would stroll melancholy and detached among the foliage of the campus, her note-book under her left arm, between the white buildings under the blue sky, turning rarely to glance at students who passed.

"You don't seem interested in anything anymore," said Mrs. Nolan one afternoon, when they were coming down Wheeler Hall stairs from Mr. Burton's short-story class. "Are you perfectly well?"

"Oh, yes," Mabel answered, looking at the ground. "Perfectly."

"You're tired," went on Mrs. Nolan. "I think you've been working too hard."

Mabel shook her head. As they entered the heavy warmth of the spring afternoon, Mrs. Nolan insisted:

"Yes, you have, Mrs. Richards. I'm sure you've been worrying about the stories you do for Mr. Burton When there's no reason to. Because you write So well. I'm sure Mr. Burton would give you two weeks extra for the long one if you asked him. He's such a dear."

They walked down Telegraph Avenue together and separated on the corner of Durant, after pausing for a few minutes to chat near the drugstore. At the end of the street the hills stood green above houses Rising in the elevator to her floor, Mabel thought that she would indeed have to ask Mr. Burton to allow her an extra fortnight for the long story, because she had not even thought of a plot. During more than a week she had not opened a book connected with her studies. There had been a languor upon her, dimming the sunlight of this early spring; and she had felt too lazy to write long stories for Mr. Burton, who never seemed to care whether the students handed their work in on time or not. He had not even given back the three stories she had written last month, having twice forgotten them. When she opened her apartment door and walked into the small living-room, which was also a sleeping-room if one lowered the bed from the wall, she noticed that the cluster of yellow poppies on the table (she had gathered them behind the Greek Theater two days before) were hanging their limp petals over the rim of the vase; and she sank down into the leather armchair before removing her hat, and heard a car going by along Telegraph Avenue, and thought that she would not care if Mr. Burton did refuse to give her an extra two weeks.

He was one of the nicest men she had met since her arrival in Berkeley. Yet she felt that she liked him for reasons entirely different from those which had drawn her first to Jim Richards, when she was twenty, then to the French officer, who had spoken to her one evening in the Nord-Sud, and finally to Carl, who had wandered on a cold day into the Red Cross canteen of the Gare St. Lazare. Burton did not attract her physically: moreover, there was something so impersonal about him, an absence of the eternal possibility of aggression that she felt in other men. She found herself talking to him without restraint, as if he were a friend of her own sex; and she often thought that the girl he married would be very fortunate, because he understood love so well.

She heard voices of students outside and lay back in her chair, thinking how demoralizing this first warm weather was, when the blue sky pressed down upon the green hills still damp from the rain. None of the books on the table appealed to her. There was a volume of Tagore and two or three paper-covered books popularizing theosophy. She yawned and wondered what to do for the long story that she must hand in to Burton within a week. She had decided to lay the scene in Paris during the war, and an opening sentence had come to her: "The Boulevard des Italiens was very crowded that evening with soldiers of every nation whose uniforms it was interesting to see," but she could think of nothing else to write, and, as she sat now in her apartment with eyes half closed, she remembered that Mrs. Nolan had said: "Oh, my dear, I have any number of plots, but I can't write them." "I never can think of a plot," Mabel had answered.

Burton's mother was a nice old lady. Mabel had met her one afternoon at the Nolans' where they had all gone for tea, but she felt that Mrs. Burton had rapidly disliked her, and she almost feared to meet her again. Other people had been there, two friends of Burton's, a man named Gresham and his fiancée, Ethel Davis. Mabel had rather liked Tom: he was big and simple, but she had been afraid of Ethel Davis, who seemed fearfully intellectual. At first she had wondered why Mr. Burton and Mr. Gresham were friends, until she learned that they had been in the army together. It was easy to see why Burton and Ethel Davis were congenial: they had the same rather sad way of looking at things. But one could never tell why people went with each other. There was that young boy who was always with Burton. Mabel had thought him rather stupid and heavy, and she never had understood why Burton had found him interesting.

It was four o'clock now, the hour when she often made herself tea. She yawned and felt she had barely strength to put water on the stove and rinse out the tea-pot. Finally, without getting up, she pulled off her hat and tossed it on the sofa against the wall; then, after a few more minutes, she left her chair and went into the kitchen and lit the gas stove. The act of tossing away the burnt match reminded her of Mrs. No Jan's kitchen, where there was a small stone jar especially for burnt matches ("If you haven't something like that," Mrs. Nolan had said, you never know where to put them;") and the kitchen in turn, because Mrs. Nolan had yesterday read aloud one of her stories there, made her think of Burton, and she thought she might give a little tea in her apartment for the Nolans and Burton and his mother and Mr. Gresham and Ethel Davis. It would be pleasant to have them in some afternoon, because they had all been so nice to her, and she felt that she wanted to pay them back. Standing about in the small kitchen, listening to the droning of the tea-kettle as it prepared to boil, she remembered similar moments when she and Carl had made tea in the afternoon, either in his apartment or in hers. What could be be doing now? A few weeks before she had met on the campus one of Carl's fraternity brothers, whom she knew slightly, and he told her that Carl had practically dropped all his classes, though he was still registered in the university in order to draw his government pension, and that he was spending his time in San Francisco, investing all the money he could get in a boot-legging scheme. The young man had added: "He's sure he's going to make twenty-five thousand the first year, but I think he's a fool to waste his money that way." Carl still had his apartment on College Avenue. One day Mabel had seen him go in, but she thought that he would probably leave Berkeley for good before long, and cross over to San Francisco. He would not remain in the university.

When the water boiled, she prepared her tea, and went back into the living-room with a cup and saucer on a straw tray. While she was sitting there, the bell rang. "Good heavens, who can that be?" She glanced at herself in the mirror before opening the door.

A young man stood there. At first Mabel did not know who he was. Then she recognized George Towne, the boy who was living with Mr. Burton in his little house out on Euclid Avenue.

"Oh, come in, Mr. Towne. You're just in time to have some tea."

He hesitated, grinning bashfully and moving about. Then he said: "I—ah—I happened to be coming down by this way and Burton asked me to leave some papers with you. They're some things he forgot to give you today in class."

"Oh, yes," cried Mabel, "my stories."

She took them from George and looked at the marks and flushed with pleasure when she saw that she had received one's and two's. Unfolding the first she noticed that Mr. Burton, in his small hand, had written several comments in the margin: she began to read, but remembered Mr. Towne and looked up and exclaimed:

"Oh, excuse me. I was so anxious to see what he had written here. Often he says the most sarcastic things."

George grinned once more.

"Well," he said, "I guess I ought to be going."

"Oh, no." Mabel laid the papers on the table. "Oh, stay and have some tea, won't you?"

She hoped he would go, as he seemed to be an awkward hulk, but he hesitated and finally said:

"Well, that does sound pretty good."

"Oh, I'm so glad. Sit right down there and I'll get you a cup."

George sprawled in the armchair and thrust his legs out before him.

"How is Mr. Burton?" asked Mabel in order to make conversation (she had come from one of the instructor's classes less than two hours before.)

"He's all right. He has taken his mother over to the city this afternoon. Otherwise he would have left the papers himself."

"She's a dear," said Mabel. "Don't you think she's too sweet for anything, Mr. Towne?"

"Yeah."

"And I think it's so nice for Mr. Burton to have her out here. I suppose he's simply delighted."

"Yeah," said George, "I guess he is."

Mabel brought in another cup and saucer and poured out the tea and sat down in a chair nearer the window. It was beginning to grow cooler now, for the first scraps of the evening fog were crossing the sky: she thought that before long she would have to close the window. George stirred his tea. Mabel noticed that his shirt and collar were dirty.

"What a lummox," she thought.

"I—ah—" said George, "I—ah—this tea is certainly good."

"I'm so glad you like it. I always have a cup in the afternoon. There's nothing rests you so when you're tired. I'm awfully sorry I haven't any lemon. Do you care for lemon? I never take it, and so I always forget to have some around."

"No, I like it plain. With sugar that is. Burton doesn't even take sugar. He says it spoils the flavor."

"Does he drink tea often?"

"Every evening before he goes to bed he makes himself some."

"Oh, I think it's too cosy for anything late at night."

They talked for a while of Burton until George's cup was empty.

Then Mabel poured him some more tea, and, because it was too strong, went into the kitchen for the hot water. With their second cups, they lit cigarettes. Mabel wondered why Mr. Burton should have this young man living with him: Mr. Burton was so polished and cosmopolitan, and George Towne seemed like a nice enough boy, but not at all the same type as the instructor. Leaning back in her chair, she examined him more closely: he was rather good-looking in a heavy blonde way, and his body was doubtless well-formed (she could see the strength of his chest and shoulders under his coat,) but those were not details that would interest Mr. Burton, who was so intellectual that he probably could not even tell what George looked like. It was certain, moreover. that George's mouth and skin were attractive and his wrists made her think of Carl's. Wishing to learn more about this boy whom the instructor found interesting, she asked:

"Where are you from, Mr. Towne?"

"Wyoming."

"Oh, really? I've always wanted to go there so much. Every time I ride through on the train I think I'd like to get right off in the desert and start walking through the sagebrush."

"You'd better not," said George, grinning, "because you'd never get anywhere."

"No, I suppose it's awfully far. Do you live anywhere near the track the Overland Limited goes along?"

"No. I used to live in the northwestern part of the state. I know that country in the south though, between Cheyenne and Evanston. My sister teaches high school in Cheyenne, and I bummed my way down there from Lander the year I came West. Then I rode to California in freight-cars."

"In freight cars! Do you mean you stole rides?"

George nodded.

"Sure," he said: "I never paid a cent of railroad fare in my life."

He told her of his summer in the Mendocino County lumber-camp, and how he had come back to San Francisco in a box-car. A quality in his halting narrative reminded her again of Carl, Rocking slightly in her chair, a cigarette smoking in her hand that hung limp beside her, she studied his face, and began to think that he had a strong chin, and that there was a lot of character in his blue eyes. A young man must have real ambition to leave home and come so far away in search of education. Memories came to her of pictures she had seen in the advertising sections of magazines wherein cleancut young men in trim business suits were toiling up long hills at the top of which were white circles (representing light) labeled *Knowledge or Success.* There was something epic in her vision of George Towne, ax in hand, among the redwood trees of Mendocino County.

"Did your father want you to come? That is ah—your father is—ah—"

"Oh, the old man didn't care. He runs a hotel back in Lander. He hasn't given me a cent."

"And you've been putting yourself through college? Isn't that wonderful!"

George told her of his job as dish-washer in the Greek restaurant on Shattuck Avenue. He said that hardly any time remained for study, and that he had flunked out the first year (Mabel thought how fine it was of him to be frank about his failure;) but he added that Burton had helped him to find a small position in the library which enabled him to study all he wished.

"Things are sorta easy this year," he concluded.

Crushing out her cigarette and lighting another, Mabel regretted that she had formed so hastily an adverse opinion concerning George Towne merely because he was a bit awkward and wore a dirty collar. "The poor boy probably is having a hard struggle," she decided, and she felt a surge of admiration for Mr. Burton, who had been keen enough to detect a sterling character beneath a crude exterior. It was so nice of the instructor to help this young man along. And especially to say nothing of it. She would tell Mrs. Nolan and all her other friends of Mr. Burton's kindness, how he had taken young Towne right in to live with him and found him a job in the library that only required a small amount of time each day. From his appearance she had considered George a husky and half-educated ranch boy, quite without manners, who was hanging around the university for no serious reason and doing just enough studying to get by.

"That just shows, she thought, watching his tanned face, that one must never judge by appearances."

The sky was gray now, for the fog had come in, and Mabel rose to shut the window. When she returned, she took a book from the table and held it out to George.

"Do you like Tagore?" she asked, leaning toward him.

He opened the book and read a few lines (she admired his thoughtful face) and then shook his head and replied:

"No, I never cared for that sort of stuff."

"What do you like?" asked Mabel.

While he was talking, she sat down again in her chair, and wanted suddenly to reach out and take one of his hands that lay on the table; but she only leaned back and listened to him, without paying great attention to his words.

Finally, she got up and walked around the room. Noticing the faded poppies in the vase, she said:

"They're all wilted, isn't it too bad?"

Her voice was unnatural, for suddenly she had imagined herself crushed in his arms, held tightly against his strong body, lifting her face slowly toward his and running her hands up along his shoulders. She trembled.

"Where'd you get 'em?" asked George. "Out on the hills?"

"Just up behind the Greek Theater."

She went over to the window and looked down to the street and noticed a man starting an automobile. The gears clashed. Then it moved away. Her heart was still beating after that first rapid impulse She was thinking: "I'd be a fool. He'd tell Burton and every one would know." But she felt herself drawn aching back to the table. She repeated:

"You don't like Tagore?"

"No," he answered.

She tried not to look at him, but her eyes wandered toward his face. She found him regarding her. All at once she felt that something would happen between them that afternoon, and she sat down in her chair, laughing, and said:

"Do you take any of Mr. Burton's courses?"

George shook his head.

"He's such a fine instructor," Mabel continued. She was thinking that he could not read her thoughts. All these ideas had been inside her: he knew nothing of them, and would go away without attempting anything, which, after all, would be better. He said:

"I had two courses with him last year."

Then he got up and walked over to the window and stood there, playing with the curtain. Mabel knew that he knew.

A sort of luxurious indolence came over her then for she felt that she could remain there and do nothing and that sooner or later he would obediently make the advances she desired. She glanced at the wilted poppies on the table and remembered how weary and discouraged she had felt an hour before, when she had come in from Burton's class; and she wanted to laugh now, because life was so rich and so interesting. It would be terrible if someone should ring the bell just at this moment. Yet who would come? She knew that Mrs. Nolan was in Alameda this afternoon, and there would be no one else.

"Do you go out for athletics?" she asked.

"No, I don't."

George prowled across the room.

"I suppose you ride horse-back beautifully. Every one in Wyoming must do that."

"Mmmm," replied George.

She lay back in her chair with one band dangling over the arm and watched him silently. He kept glancing at her, but when she spoke, he answered with out meeting her eyes. She began to feel slightly antagonistic toward him, but now and then a rush of tenderness came through her, which would remain for a while and then go, leaving watchful hostility.

At last she walked over to the window and stood beside him.

When his shoulder pressed against hers, the first impulse she had was to draw away, perhaps even to run into the kitchen and close the door. Laughing, she only moved back a few inches, feeling a delicious fear at the determined and brutal expression on his face.

"Now don't be silly," she exclaimed.

He was breathing loudly. The bristles on his face were rough. Then his mouth was against hers, pressing in.

When they passed the table, she heard the vase of poppies tip over and the water trickle to the floor. She hoped it would not leak through into the apartment below. Then she remembered to reach behind and knock her hat from the sofa before allowing herself to fall upon it.

George's arms were squeezing her against him. She smelt once more his dirty shirt. But she did not care. He was her dear, dear boy. He was big and strong. Giving a little cry, and wrapping her arms around his neck, she began multitudinously to kiss him.

XVII

COLLAPSE

Wearing a bathrobe, Tom Gresham sprawled in the brown morris-chair, his feet stretched out toward the unused fireplace (he wore slippers that fell away from his heels) and, with eyes half closed, smoked a pipe and paid no attention to the brothers who returned from morning classes and threw their note-books onto the wide table. One or two of them spoke to him: "What's the matter, Tom? Not feeling well?" or "Look at old Tom Gresham lying around all the morning when he should be working." He answered their questions, but opened no conversation, for he did not feel strong enough to rise through the black mood that oppressed him. During the past weeks, ever since those suspicions had come into his head, he had been unable to study, although he dreaded the examinations that were not far away. Languorous and suffering, he had loafed around the house or strolled through the campus, and, when he went to see Ethel, there were long silences between them, and she broke forth once or twice impatiently with: "Oh, Tom, what is the matter with you?"

He had detested Burton ever since that afternoon at tea when the savage pain had begun. Before then he had felt momentarily unhappy hearing Ethel tell of her walks with the instructor, but the feeling had gone away, and he had thought that Burton was a "good scout." Now the agony was in him like a disease, poisoning the day as soon as he awoke; and he did not want to see Burton or to think of him, although some times, lying there in the morris-chair, he felt like going to him and crying out: "Why did you butt in? Why didn't you keep away? Don't you see I can't stand it?"

A few of the brothers read newspapers around him this late morning. Now and then someone walked up or down stairs, and once the telephone bell rang, and he heard Wendell on the second floor converse for a long time about the tennis team. He knew that he should be studying, but a heavy fatigue prevented him from opening a book. The evening before he had had dinner with Ethel and Jessie Schmidt in the Oakland apartment, and both the women had spoken of Burton. Jessie had begun and Ethel had asked questions about him, and Tom had sat there dumbly, looking down at his plate. He wondered now why Jessie had talked so much about him. While they were sitting at table she had said:

"I've met Mr. Burton two or three times recently. Once in the city he was walking along Market Street with a young soldier. I don't think he saw me. It was probably a man he used to know in the army. I think it's awfully nice of him to keep up old acquaintanceships that way."

Ethel said nothing, and Tom, still regarding his plate, wondered if she had not met Burton several times. He nearly asked: "When did you see him?" But he did not speak, for he sometimes feared Ethel. During the evening she remarked: "Burton told me this," or "Burton told me so and so," and Tom would glance up at her in surprise, because her voice sounded so natural.

He thought now, sitting in the morris-chair, that Ethel and Burton must spend hours together. Doubtless they laughed at him, because he had not read all the books of which they talked. It was eleven o'clock and some of the freshmen and sophomores in uniform were hurrying off to drill. Tom heard the front door slam and their voices and footsteps diminish on the sidewalk, and he remembered how one day he had met Ethel and Burton walking along Telegraph Avenue, and how their conversation had ended abruptly when they saw him, leaving incomplete smiles on both their faces. At this time he had been happy to see them, and he had walked back with them as far as the Sather Gate Bookshop, where Burton was going to get some books he had ordered a few weeks before. But now he felt sure that Burton had merely gone into the store because he could no longer be alone with Ethel. Probably he had met her afterward, when she was again free.

Incidents of this sort had been tormenting him during the past fortnight, especially when he sat before his table with an open book. He would gaze off wearily into the air and develop them in imagination. One Monday he had seen a cluster of mountain lilac in a vase on Ethel's table, and when he asked if she had been off somewhere for them into the hills, she replied that Burton had brought them to her from Mount Tamalpais, where he had been tramping over the weekend. For a while Tom had thought nothing more of the matter, but while he was sitting in the brown morris-chair the fear suddenly came to him that Ethel had gone with Burton to Marin County, Perhaps they had spent the night together in some hotel over there. He closed his eyes: for a moment he wanted to find Burton and take him by the throat and press his head against the wall of his office and make him confess. If it were true, he would kill him. But he remembered that Ethel had gone Saturday afternoon to see this man Bradley, who happened to be up from Monterey, about the teaching position she wanted down there next year. At least she had told him that she had gone to San Francisco for that reason. But had she lied to him? Oh, he did not know. How could he know? He almost turned over and pressed his face against the leather cushion, but the screen-door slammed and a group of brothers entered the living room and tossed their books onto the table, and Tom straightened up and began to knock out his pipe against his shoe.

He felt better at lunch-time, when the chimes on the Campanile were sounding, and the underclassmen, returning from drill, were passing along the sidewalk outside or coming into the house. But he remained silent at the table, filled with anxiety. When he saw Milton Granger, hot in his uniform, talking among the other freshmen, he remembered that he had planned to bring Phil Burton around to the house in order that the two might know each other. He felt pain once more, as if the instructor himself had walked in.

But these hours of suspicion gave way occasionally to fairly long periods when he said to himself: "Aw hell, I'm crazy. There's nothing going on between them. They're good friends, that's all. And why shouldn't they be? He's helping her with her work." Sometimes he strode in high spirits through the campus, among the white buildings glaring in the sun, certain that his fears were conjured up by his own fancy, and once he met Burton and greeted him noisily and slapped him on the shoulder. But while he watched the instructor, stocky under his gray hat, go away toward Wheeler Hall, the old dread mounted through him again, like climbing water. He felt weak all over and wanted to run after him and say, humbly this time and pleading: "For God's sake, Phil, tell me the truth We've been good friends in the army. I must know. I must know."

Yet he never followed these impulses. Rather cumbersome, slouching a trifle, hands in pockets, he returned home along Telegraph Avenue and then up Durant toward College, beside palms that looked green ish gray in the heat. And when he was among the brothers he remained usually silent, though now and then he talked in his heavy voice about business conditions in California or the law courses he was no longer attending. Once he nearly told Wendell about his preoccupation, but he feared the tennis player would laugh at him, and so he said nothing.

Each time he saw Ethel (he went down to her apartment as usual three or four times a week) he came forth momentarily as if into clear air from the stuffy cavern of his suspicions. She seemed so unconcerned, so frank. During half an hour he would think that he had been a fool. But then Burton's name would enter the conversation, and he would almost break out with: "Damn Burton, why are you always talking about him?" Or, if neither of the women mentioned the instructor, he would suspect that they were avoiding his name purposely, and would imagine that he had detected a furtive glance between them. On such occasions he himself would introduce the subject, speaking in an ominous voice.

"I suppose you're going over with Burton pretty soon to look at some more etchings?"

"Not that I know of. Why? Is there another exhibition in San Francisco?"

"I don't know. I was just wondering."

Once Jessie put in:

"I think Ethel's mighty lucky to have a man like Mr. Burton explain things of that sort to her. He seems able to talk on any subject. The other day at the concert he explained all about symphonies."

Tom shuddered. His heart was pounding.

"What concert?" he asked.

For a long moment Ethel's melancholy eyes rested on his face. Then she smiled and answered:

"We went over to the concert in San Francisco Friday afternoon. Mr. Burton has season tickets."

"Oh," said Tom. Then, voice trembling a little: "You didn't tell me."

Ethel looked at him again in the sad and amused way of hers he never could understand. Finally she answered:

"Oh, didn't I? I must have forgotten."

Tom thought that Jessie turned away to hide a smile. Abruptly, he felt that all these people were playing with him. For the remainder of the evening was sulky and without words.

A few days later the weather grew even warmer and Tom began to go nearly every afternoon to the swimming pool up Strawberry Canyon, where he would on the warm pavement and dive occasionally into greenish water. Somehow he felt better under blue sky, dozing in the heat. The spring board would be thudding, there was always splashing in the puu and, when he opened his eyes, he would see lithe tanned bodies all around him, glistening with water. While he lay there, in the hollow between green hills, his unpleasant thoughts would fade and finally go away entirely, and only a blurred sequence of colors and sounds would traverse his mind, all suffused with the warmth of the concrete on which he was lying.

One afternoon he heard someone say: "Hello there, Tom," and, having opened his eyes gradually, saw Burton, in swimming trunks, standing above him. For a moment he was silent. Then he replied: "Hello Phil."

The instructor's body was burned pink. He sat down on the warm stone beside Tom.

"I didn't know you came up here often," he began, laying down a book that he had brought with him.

"I've been here several days," Tom answered.

He lowered his eyes, planning to say no more, for an abhorrence of Burton swept over him, He loathed this stocky man with the drawling voice and brown mustache who sat beside him. But half through indolence, because he could not sustain hatred, he said, even before Burton had spoken again:

"It's sorta nice to lay around in the sun."

"Oh, it's beautiful," exclaimed Burton, tossing up his head, "perfectly lovely I've often thought that this is about as much like an Athenian palestra as any- thing one could find today." He paused and added:

"And then the hills, of course, and the sky and all that."

Several boys were diving, one after the other; spray flashed in the sunlight. Tom thought that Burton was just as he used to be in the army, always talking of things no one knew about, and he felt briefly the same amused tolerance he had had for him then, He looked now at the instructor, who was staring at a tanned youth just come from the water, and nearly said: "Look here, Phil, I've had enough of this. What are you trying to do anyway?" He would plead and threaten. Burton turned to him and asked:

"How's Ethel?"

Flushing, Tom answered: "She's all right." He had nearly cried out: "You ought to know better than I."

"She's working hard, I know," Burton went on. "She ought to finish everything by May. You should make her take a good rest next summer."

The calmness of Burton's voice infuriated Tom. He rolled over on the warm pavement, away from the instructor, and looked towards the hills. Burton said:

"The sun is glaring, isn't it? Usually I bring an eye-shade up here with me. You know, one of those green celluloid things. It shades your eyes and also throws a green reflection over them that is very restful. Especially if I read I find it necessary."

Tom did not reply. Burton continued:

"Yesterday I read here for three hours and didn't even go into the water."

Tom hated him. One could never tell what was in his mind, for Burton always talked on in that unperturbed manner. No one had ever known how me women he had gone with in France: he never spoke of such things (unlike everyone else,) but Tom had always suspected that he did a lot of chasing in his quiet way. He faced him again.

"Oh, I don't mind the glare," he said, "I just turned over."

He heard a voice he recognized and saw that three or four fellows from the house, Tony Barragan, Milton Granger, and one or two others, were going into the shed to undress. Burton said:

"I want you and Ethel to come up for tea again some afternoon."

Tom finally answered: "All right."

Burton again was staring at the boy near him who lay prone, forehead resting on brown arms. At last he said:

"How's your work going, Tom?"

"Oh, all right."

He did not like to talk of the studying he had not done. It rose before him, insurmountable; he felt a sick dread. He was glad when Burton spoke of other things.

"I've been looking all over Berkeley for an apartment recently. Mother and I shall take one for next year if we can find just what we want. But there seems to be absolutely nothing. Perhaps during the summer I may find something. But I'm afraid the summer session crowds will make it just as difficult."

Tom let him talk. Lying back on the pavement, he closed his eyes and listened to the instructor's voice going on. He talked of his mother, of the books he was reading, of his classes, but he did not once return to Ethel Davis. Inwardly, Tom sneered at him. When he opened his

CLARKSON CRANE

eyes again the brilliance for a moment dazzled him,) Burton laughed and said:

"I was beginning to think you'd gone to sleep."

Tom shook his head. Perhaps Burton had spent the whole morning with Ethel and had invited her to another concert. He could never tell what might go on behind their lying masks. The pain filled him again. He said:

"No, I didn't go to sleep."

He heard Tony Barragan's voice somewhere in the pool: the fellows from the house would probably see him. He began to think that he would go away and dress, for he could not stand being near Burton.

"I have to dress pretty soon," he announced.

"Going to see Ethel this evening?" asked Burton.

"Give her my regards if you do."

Tom was silent. At that moment Milton Granger pulled himself from the water half onto the concrete bank and leaned there, dripping.

"Hello there, Tom."

"Hello, Milt."

"It's great up here, isn't it?"

"Yeah."

Sadly Tom remembered that there had been a time when he wished to introduce Milton to Phil Burton, because he thought that they would like each other, both being literary. He hoped now that Burton had not heard him say "Milt," for he might intrude. But he noticed that the instructor had suddenly turned his back toward Milton Granger. A moment longer the freshman hung there on the edge of the pool. Then he shook the water from his hair and cried: "So long Tom, see you later," and disappeared with a splash

Burton stood up.

"I think I go in and dress," he said.

Filled with sudden hatred, Tom exclaimed:

"Oh, by the way, Ethel told me about that concert you and she went to."

He thought that Burton seemed agitated. Standing there, the instructor asked:

"Who was that boy?"

Tom smiled at the fellow's attempt to change the subject.

"Milton Granger," he answered, as dryly as he could "one of the freshmen at the house. I think I mentioned him to you one day."

"Oh," Burton stood without moving. Then he said: "Well I really must go," and he walked away.

Reclining there, feeling that his remark about the concert had taken effect, slightly triumphant, and yet aching with pain, Tom Gresham watched Burton, pink and stout, follow the curve of the pool, pass behind the crIme near the springboard and, without turning his head, vanish into the dressing-room.

He tried not to think of him for the remainder of the afternoon, for a reaction to his anger had come over him as he walked down the canyon from the swimming pool; but after dinner that evening, when he had installed himself in the brown morris-chair, Milton Granger walked over and stood with his back to the empty fireplace and asked:

"By the way, Tom, who was that fellow with you at the pool this afternoon?"

Tom removed his cigarette from his mouth and replied slowly:

"Phil Burton. He's the instructor in the English Department I told you about."

For a while Milton said nothing, but soon he asked: "He never worked in a bank, did he?"

"Phil Burton?" Tom laughed at the idea. "He, work in a bank? Ha! Ha! Hell, no! What made you think that?"

"Oh, I don't know." Then: "I met him up on Mount Tamalpais one Saturday."

Tom nodded. "He walks up there a lot." Suddenly the idea occurred to him, but for a moment he dared not speak. "He was alone, wasn't he?" he at length demanded, almost with defiance.

"Oh, yes, he was alone."

Milton leaned thoughtfully against the mantelpiece and said nothing more, and Tom felt weak in his chair and closed his eyes. What if Milton had replied that he had not been alone? He suffered from thinking merely how he might have suffered. But perhaps it had been a different weekend. After hesitation, trembling a little and endeavoring to make his voice sound natural, he asked:

"Let's see, when were you up there? Phil told me something about being up there. It was two weeks ago last Saturday, wasn't it?"

Milton nodded.

"Yes, two weeks ago last Saturday."

Again Tom felt weak, but a great relief rose through him, and he opened his eyes and smiled up at Milton like a convalescent. Indeed, that was the Saturday after which Burton had given the mountain lilac to Ethel.

Suddenly more friendly toward Burton, he said:

"He's a good scout. I knew him well in the We were in the same outfit."

Milton did not answer, and Tom went on: army.

"I'll bring him around to the house one of these days. You might like to know him. I've mentioned you to him."

"Me?" Milton looked surprised.

"Yeah, he said he'd like to meet you."

Some of the fellows gathered around him just then and began to talk of the Alpha Chi Delta convention that would be held in Philadelphia the following July. Milton drifted away. Soon Tom went up to his room and sat down at his table, on which were piled the books he had not opened for several weeks. The end of the semester was approaching: he knew that he should be studying, but when he opened a volume the page stood before him like an impenetrable wall and he could not apply himself. He kept reading a solitary paragraph over and over: finally he gave up and lay back in his chair and lit a cigarette and stared through the open window into the spring night.

The fact that Ethel had not lied to him about the cluster of mountain lilac proved nothing in regard to her relations with Burton. Yet somehow he felt better, and slowly the thought came to him that he had been unjust in his suspicions. Blowing smoke toward the ceiling, he watched the curtain swell inward. Little by little a gentle calm fell over him; he wished that Ethel were there so that he might take her in his arms.

But suppose there were a cause for his jealousy? Once more the pain flowed through him, weaker this time. Crushing out his cigarette, he returned to his book and for half an hour read words that he did not understand. Then angrily he arose and began to move to and fro in the room, pausing sadly once before the bureau and once before the window through which came the dry breath of the warm night.

Something in the sound of the car-bell on College Avenue reminded him of his room on Taylor Street in San Francisco and the *ting-ting* of the stubby cable-cars that rolled to and fro on California Street not far away. Those days had not been so unpleasant. His evenings were always free: he never had incomprehensible reading to do, and, whenever he did not go to Oakland to see Ethel, he would bowl in an alley on Ellis Street, or lie on his bed reading the *Saturday Evening Post*, or merely stroll up and down Market Street, watching the crowds and feeling comfortable in the glare from the electric signs and the illuminated store windows. Sometimes, during the war, he had dreamed that he was back in school, and that he was preparing for impossible examinations. He would awake in agony. Somewhat the same feeling came over him now, a helpless dread, but this time it was true: he was back in school, and he had examinations to prepare for

On the floor above a door slammed and two of the brothers walked downstairs, talking loudly. He tried to hear where they said they were going. For the first time it occurred to him that he was not really living the same life in the house as the others; he rarely went on parties with them; his only contact with the undergraduates was a sort of good-natured bantering in which he was usually called "old Tom Gresham "the old man." He was merely an outsider.

Another whiff of warm air, fragrant from the spring drifted through the window. He sat down again in his chair and peered at the book. A great weariness came over him. He thought:

"Perhaps I made a mistake in coming back to the university."

It was like a frontier he had crossed into a new land. He felt more at ease now about not reading the book. Offspring of his idea flocked to him: "It might be better not to go on." "The fraternity house is a bad place to study." Finally, he remembered that distant evening when Burton on the car coming from Oakland had said: "Isn't it rather hard on Ethel?" Maybe it was hard on Ethel, keeping her waiting this way, month after month, for a marriage that must seem to her infinitely remote. It was only because of this delay that she was considering the teaching position in Monterey. It might be only because of this delay that she was going with Burton. He lowered his head, unhappy once more.

Last year, when he had no books to study, he used to awake every morning in his room on Taylor Street, free from all care, certain that he would pass an agreeable day at the office among good fellows, and that he would see Ethel, if he desired, in the evening. He always had breakfast before a clean white counter in an alley just off California Street. He used to have a baked apple and then shredded wheat biscuit, and after that a stack of hotcakes with a big cup of coffee. The waiter knew what he wished, and always laid the baked apple before him as soon as he sat on the high stool, Those were the good days. He wanted all at once to go back to San Francisco and to live that life again.

There were footsteps on the sidewalk outside. Some of the brothers were stamping up onto the wooden porch. All that sort of thing was good for them. But why had he come back to college, and why was he here? He had blindly followed a vague discontent. Yawning, he rested his neck on the back of his chair, and closed his eyes and felt that he could never learn enough to pass the examination.

The memory of Burton appeared to him. He shuddered. Why had that fellow come tearing into the fabric of his life? Why had he let him remain in his life? He stood up and leaned from the window. He must do something. Suddenly, he remembered that he could leave college if he wanted to and that he need not take the examinations. But what would Ethel think of that? He would talk it over with her the next time they met. It seemed natural that he should talk things over with her. But suppose she no longer took the same interest in him as before? Suppose she did not care? A sort of whimpering fear rose through his weariness.

It was only ten-thirty, still early enough to see her tonight. The idea rushed through him that he must see her. He would not be able to sleep or even to live, unless he went to her and told her that he might leave college and that he did not know what to do and that perhaps they had better get married. He would talk of Burton too. He strode toward the door.

It was Ethel who answered the telephone.

"Yes, Tom. Yes—This evening?—Why, it's so late.—It will be by the time you get to Oakland.—Well, if you want to. Is anything the matter?"

In snatching his hat from the rack near the telephone closet, be brushed against the dinner-gong and set it humming. He was beginning a new life. Several brothers stood in the hallway, but he passed by them without speaking and slammed the screen-door behind him.

XVIII

ETHEL AND TOM

W hen Tom Gresham telephoned, Ethel was reading, and Jessie, in a rocking-chair near the green box-couch that unfolded every night into a bed, was yawning and filling a round basket with her work.

"Who can that be?" she said, looking up, both her feet planted squarely on the floor.

During the conversation she did not move. When Ethel walked back into the room (the telephone stood in the narrow hallway by the front door) and announced that it was Tom and that he was coming down to Oakland, Jessie exclaimed, laying aside the basket:

"Tonight? Why, what does he want? He's crazy."

Ethel lifted her shoulders.

"Something has happened," she said. "His voice was strange."

After a pause, during which she glanced at herself in the mirror above the fireplace, she added: "Don't look so blank, Jessie. I don't know what he wants any more than you do." She laughed shortly, went to the window and stared out over the polished black street that gleamed under a lonely arc-light. An automobile went by, then a man walking. She thought that soon Tom would come striding over the smooth surface and that his shadow would bend up suddenly against that house-wall and then flatten out and extend rapidly like a shooting tongue, along the pavement.

She said: "You don't have to stay up, you know without turning around.

"I? Well, I should say not. I'm going to bed right away."

When Jessie had gone, Ethel lit a cigarette and sat down in a broad, soft armchair, and wished, rather sleepily, that Tom had chosen another evening for his late visit. Her mind had been occupied during the past week with her Uncle John in San Francisco, who had been ill, and whom she had gone to see frequently in his apartment on Union Street. He had seemed to her more vulgar than ever with his hard, smooth-shaven face and his talk of the Turk Street saloon: she came away each time with a feeling that it was absurd for her to be forced into intimacy with this man just because he was her father's brother. One afternoon she described him to Burton (they were sitting in his office.) The instructor had agreed with her that nothing was more ridiculous than family feeling between people who had not seen each other for years, and he told of false situations in which he had often found himself among distant cousins who lived in Milan and Rome.

She had mentioned her uncle's illness to Tom, but he had paid little attention, for he had been absent minded of late. "Too bad," was all he had said, walking across the room with hands in pockets and head bent forward; and Ethel, feeling no interest awake in him for her own difficulties, had talked of his studies, which seemed to be troubling him. But even that subject left him unresponsive: angry, she had turned away, flushing a trifle, and gone over to the window determined to let him alone until he came forth from his ill humor. The remainder of the evening had gone by with only Jessie's loud voice from time to time in the silence.

She could hardly believe that Tom could be stupid enough to be jealous of Burton. Half closing her eyes now in the broad armchair, she smiled and watched the smoke from her cigarette rise bending upward, reflected in the mirror. Yesterday she had told Burton that Tom was jealous: they had laughed, as if it were a great joke; and riding home on the car, she had felt a short repentance for having spoken that way of Tom with a man who was surely not a stranger, but whom she had known only a few months. She entertained now for a moment and then dismissed the idea that Burton and Tom had talked of the subject: no, no, men were not like that, at least Tom was not; she was not sure of Burton, who seemed fond of gossip. Then she thought, not without a certain quiet pleasure, that it was good for Tom to be a little jealous of her now and then. It stirred him up.

What was that? The sound of footsteps in the street? Yes, but not Tom's, for it would take him more than half an hour to come down from Berkeley. She began now to feel glad that he was coming: it would seem so homelike and pleasant for them to be sitting together, late at night, in the still living-room. She knew that even if they said little, she would be happier than when she was alone. It was this feeling, always present beneath her temporary irritation, that she could be at ease with Tom Gresham through all the intimate and unspoken ways of life, that made her, in hours of doubt, return to the thought of him with tenderness, and consider other men, like Burton for example, as surface friends, with whom she might enjoy conversation, but in whose presence she could peve with tranquillity remain silent.

Leaning back in her chair, she held her cigarette out beyond the arm and remembered the long walks she and Tom used to take together during the first year she knew him. Perhaps that had been the happiest period of her life. The future in those days, with her first unspoiled illusions about him, had appeared so easy: they would marry, when she finished college and Tom would go on with the business in which he had already started, and they would live in an apartment in San Francisco. It had seemed to her then that she would be free of her past, or would retain from it only what she desired (she would visit Uncle Ted occasionally in the old Monterey house, and Jessie might stay with them for a while in San Francisco;) and during months she had been able to live with more enthusiasm than ever before. But now, after all this time, her life seemed to be running into a sort of delta, with so many other objects beside marriage with Tom. Portions of her even fled Tom. Sometimes she feared that what remained of her affection (she knew just how suffused it was with habit and inertia) would fade wholly away were she to meet some man to whom she was strongly attracted. Their engagement had dragged on so. Yet whenever she thought of breaking with him, a tenderness would pass through her, a tenderness that was half pity, and she would think: "No, I can't do that." Then, as the feeling ebbed, she often wondered if she could be the wife of a man with whom she had no intellectual companionship whatever, and she thought of Burton, who was so congenial. But the instructor did not attract her at all; sometimes he was even physically repellent; she felt that Tom did attract her, and that only with him would intimacy be complete.

Many of these thoughts came to her now as she sat awaiting Tom Gresham. In the next room there was a click as Jessie turned out the light, and she saw that a thin golden glow no longer lay over the threshold of the door. More footsteps sounded on the pavement, and she listened, turning her head slightly, half expecting them to halt beneath the window; but they went off down the street, diminishing gradually, and she felt disappointed that it had not been he. If only they could throw off all the cluttered past and somehow begin over again. Putting out her cigarette, she closed her eyes.

He rapped softly on the door a quarter of an hour later. For a minute, in the armchair, Ethel did not move. Then she rose and went into the hallway and admitted him.

Stumbling, he exclaimed: "I didn't ring because I thought Jessie might be asleep." He dropped his hat onto the table and walked into the living-room. "She didn't wait up, did she?"

"No, she's gone to bed."

He seemed relieved.

"You know," he said, turning upon her suddenly, "I'm going to quit college."

Fear passed through her.

"Tom," she said, "what's the matter?"

Tall, blonde, a bit red, looking down, he stood there, his big hands dangling limp at his sides. Her fear went away and she wanted to laugh, for he seemed like a boy confessing something, but she controlled herself and walked over to the window and noticed again the gray polished asphalt, and said:

"Has something happened, Tom?"

Dumbly, he shook his head. She felt impatient, nearly scornful, and regarded the street-light, deter. mined to let him be silent as long as he desired. He exclaimed:

"How much longer are you and Burton going to keep this up?"

He was trembling and his face was distorted. Afraid once more, she took a step toward him, and said: "Why, Tom—"

"You and Burton," he muttered, "you and Burton."

It occurred to her that he might be mad: she thought of running across to the door of the other room and opening it to call Jessie; but something weak in him made her suddenly calm again, and she walked over to her armchair and sat down. Severely, she asked:

"Tom, what do you mean?"

He was sniffling. She waited, feeling that everything was at end between them. She would definitely accept the teaching position in Monterey and live in the old house with her Uncle Ted. She was half glad this had been decided for her. She could live in Monterey.

"You see, Ethel," he said, peering at her with hurt eyes. "I just wanted to talk this over with you. I don't seem to be getting anywhere. I know I'll never pass my exes at the end of the year. I sometimes think I don't belong in the fraternity house. More and more I think that." He rambled on, not mentioning Burton, and Ethel, bewildered, felt again he might be mad.

"You see, Ethel, I may have made a mistake in coming back. Perhaps I ought to have stayed over in the city. I was making good money there and we could have been married by this time." As if recovering himself, he straightened up and cleared his throat. "Of course," he went on, becoming red again, "I'm glad I came back. I should never have been satisfied if I hadn't tried out the university for a while, and I've learned quite a bit that will be useful to me. Yes," he repeated, in a heavier voice, looking at Ethel, "I've learned quite a bit that will be useful to me." Then, after clearing his throat again, he asked in his ordinary tone:

"What do you say we get married tomorrow, Ethel?"

Amazed, she stared at him. "Tom! What are you talking about?"

He stood before her, still flushed, scratching the side of his head now and then. Gradually his face took on a disappointed and drooping expression that filled her with a sudden rush of sympathy: he seemed so young and helpless.

She rose and walked over to him and led him to a chair and ordered: "Sit down, Tom." When he had obeyed, she returned to her own chair, thinking not without amusement how poor Jessie, lying awake in the next room, must wonder at all this talk. She felt entirely calm now. In a low voice she said:

"Jessie's trying to sleep in there." (Her head moved sideways.) "Don't talk loud."

Tom nodded.

"Now," she commanded, "tell me what's the matter."

After a pause, very slowly, he began:

"Well, I've been thinking a lot these last few days. I—ah—"

Waiting for him to go on, she felt suddenly the mockery of all her dreams, the lot of them dissolved into this warm room with a man before her stammering unintelligible words, and she laughed aloud; but when she saw the pained expression in Tom Gresham's eyes, she took pity on him and said:

"Why, Tom, if it's only about leaving college that you're so upset, for heaven's sake, why, go ahead and leave if you want to. I surely think it would be the best thing to do."

He leaned forward, his face lighting up.

"Do you, Ethel? Say, that's great. I was afraid that you'd think I was giving up or something. You see, I've been thinking a lot." He paused, then blurted out: "It isn't fair to keep you waiting this way."

She smiled. What put that idea into his head?

"Oh, Tom," she answered, rather coldly, "don't worry about that." Gradually, as he sat looking at her, his face grew red (she saw the flush creeping up to the beginning of his yellow hair) and his eyes opened more widely, just as they had when he first appeared.

Afraid, she said: "Tom."

A sound came from him. He rose and took her by the shoulders and muttered:

"You don't care, eh? You don't care, eh?" and he began to shake her to and fro. Then he raised her up and squeezed her against him, and she closed her eyes and let her face go against his coat.

A moment later he had pushed her into a chair and was over by the window, staring out. She could hear him breathing. Soon he walked back and sat down.

"You've got to tell me, Ethel; you've got to tell me. Don't you see, I've got to know. How about it with you and Burton, anyway?"

"Why, Tom, nothing—what do you mean?"

"Come on, now, tell me. Why are you always with him?"

"I'm not, Tom. I'm not always with him."

"Yes, you are, damn near."

His voice rose, and she knew that Jessie must be hearing every word, and she made a motion toward the door and shook her head. "Not so loud, Tom," she pleaded.

"Oh, what the hell do I care?"

"But, Tom—"

"See here, Ethel, I've been square with you. You've got to be on the level with me. I know I was a damn fool to leave business and I'm ready to admit that I was and go back and get my job again."

Endeavoring to make her voice as calm as possible, she said:

"Tom, listen to me, please. You're all wrong about Burton. I swear it, Tom. I promise you. Why, I don't like him at all. I laugh at him. What if I do see him now and then about my work? What if I do? That doesn't mean anything." She paused, trembling, and then a rapid impulse made her say: "I love you, Tom. I love you!"

His face softened and he grinned for an instant. Then he leaned forward and took her hand.

"Say, Ethel, I didn't mean to talk that way. I'm sorry, kiddo."

She broke away, fearing to see him humble again, and went over to the window. The pavement was still gray under the light. He said:

"Ethel."

She stamped her foot. Oh, why didn't he come to her? His chair creaked and she heard his breath.

"Tom!" she cried, turning against him. "Oh, Tom, Tom!"

He left shortly afterward. She watched him stride across the gray pavement beneath the light, and she stood there near the window long after he had vanished into the darkness down the street. When Jessie opened the door and stood fat and wide-eyed in her wrapper, Ethel exclaimed:

"Go to bed. I can't talk about it now. Go to bed."

"But, Ethel—"

"Go to bed, I say."

The door closed softly and once more she heard the click of the electric light. Taking a cigarette, she sank again into the armchair.

XIX

A New Acquaintance

April was a warm month that year; flowers in gardens and before houses seemed more abundant than ever; in the hot, quiet air, tempered by almost no fog, the grass on the hills began early to fade, so that when May arrived there were already brown patches on them, and what yellow poppies remained looked frail and desolate. Every morning, clear and golden, contained a premonition of heat; mature noon lay dead over the white buildings and polished leaves. The gray evenings had faint western colors, rising voices and footsteps along the streets, water rustling from hoses over lawns. Days followed each other tranquilly.

Milton fought against the languor of this precocious summer. His last examination would come on May tenth, and on the twelfth he would leave for Chicago, where Aunt Caroline was to meet him. Supplicating letters from both his mother and aunt had urged him to go abroad; Aaron Berg had said: "Why, you're a fool not to. Don't lose an opportunity like that," and he had agreed. He feared that something developed in himself during the past year would be destroyed by three months with Aunt Caroline. She's mid-Victorian," he thought, feeling himself modern. But often his mind withdrew from what he was reading, and exultation came over him when he remembered that he was going to Europe. For a long time he would sit idle before his table, hearing the noises from outside frequently it was still light enough for two of the brothers to play catch, and he would hear the ball striking their gloves;) and he would have to shake his head and throw off a somnolence come partly from the weather, partly from anticipation that drained the present.

One evening he climbed to his room immediately after dinner and sat down with an open book before his table, Throughout the meal the brothers had discussed the marriage of Tom Gresham and Ethel Davis, which had occurred the preceding week. Several of them thought Tom foolish to leave college so near the end of the semester (he had begun to sell insurance for a company whose main offices were in Oakland,) but Wendell said:

"Don't you worry. Old Tom Gresham knows what he's doing. Probably those fellows in Oakland made him a good proposition, and he decided he couldn't throw it down."

Milton agreed with Wendell, for he considered Tom a man of judgment and great force of character. Three weeks before, telling Milton of his marriage, Tom Gresham, standing with both hands in his pockets and speaking in his heaviest and most deliberate voice, had made his action seem one of reason,

"I feel it's the best thing to do," he said, with a slow nod of his head, "Ethel and I talked it over. I didn't seem to be getting quite what I wanted in college, and so I cut loose. Oh, yes" (his voice went deeper,) "this is much better than Morton, Dunlop & Company. More money in it."

They were married one Saturday in Oakland by a justice of the peace and went to San Rafael in Marin County for their honeymoon. The following week Tom Gresham moved from the fraternity house to the Oakland apartment.

"We'll live there for a while," he told Milton, "until Ethel finishes her work in college. Jessie Schmidt has gone back to Monterey."

Sitting before his desk, Milton thought with a certain envy of Tom Gresham, who was able to carry on his life so boldly. The alumnus would be a success in business; he would have a home and children; the fraternity would mention, as if by chance, to prospective members: "Thomas Gresham is one of our men, you know." Milton could see future banquets at which Tom would speak, a bit stouter, his coat drawn back from his vest.

Aaron Berg had shocked him by exclaiming:

"That moron! Why, he's an utter dub. What do you see out of the ordinary in him?"

Aaron would probably come around this evening. Meanwhile, he had better read over that last chapter. Leaning forward and burying both hands in his hair, he tried to study, but memories of his mother, who had passed through San Francisco the week before on her way to India, rose before him, and he saw her again in the hotel room, nervous, slightly flushed, regarding him with her vague eyes. She had taken a cigarette from the package he held toward her and had said:

"Do whatever you think best about coming back to California next year. Stay abroad if you want to. A year in Paris and Italy will do you no harm at all."

And when he had not answered immediately, she went on:

"There are certain things a young man has to be careful about, especially in Paris. There are always women, you know."

His Aunt Caroline, once before in San Francisco had used nearly the same words. Milton thought of all the adventures Bert Hudson had had, and felt himself hopelessly inexperienced in matters that seemed the constant preoccupation of his mother and aunt and all his friends. He would be nineteen in August; perhaps something would happen before that time to put an end to his chastity. All the men in the house had exclaimed with envy when Milton said he was going to Paris, and Tony Barragan had drawn him aside, his dark eyes shining, and told him of a friend of his from Chile who lived over in Montparnasse.

"I'll write him you're coming. Be sure and look him up. He goes to a café called *La Rotonde*."

The Spanish roll to the r that Tony gave to *La Rotonde* filled the café with interest, and Milton promised to go there. As he leaned now over his book, the place seemed mysteriously inaccessible.

Aaron Berg arrived half an hour later. He sat down on the bed and drew a hand through his dark hair.

"Let's go up and see Phil Burton this evening," he said. When Milton hesitated, he added:

"He'll be home, I know. He half expects me. I said I'd probably be up around eight."

"Did you tell him you might bring me?"

"No, but that makes no difference. Phil is always glad to see people. He'll be all alone up there, I'm sure, because that fellow Towne is almost always out. What's the matter, Milt? Phil won't hurt you."

"Well, I really should study, but—"

"Oh, you have plenty of time for that."

A few days before Milton had seen Burton again on the campus, but only from a distance, and he was sure the instructor had not seen him, for he had gone immediately, to avoid the man, in the opposite direction, not knowing how to explain the story he had told that Sunday on the mountain about living in Chicago. He remembered afterward that Burton's words also had been untrue. "It's about equal," he thought. And he decided to meet him face to face the next time and to talk, if the instructor recognized him, as though nothing had happened. But he remembered, with a feeling of uneasiness, as if something yet hidden in himself might emerge in answer, the strange hard look in Burton's eyes, and those caresses when the instructor had taken his arm. Perhaps he would not see him again. Yet he wanted to. He had told Aaron nothing of the incident on Tamalpais.

"All right," he finally said, pushing away his book. "Let's go. I'd like to know him. I met him once, after a fashion. But I guess he wouldn't remember me."

B urton opened the door for them and said slowly: Hello, "Aaron, come in," but, seeing Milton, he paused, his face calm, and was silent for a moment. Milton stood nervously, waiting.

"I brought Milton Granger," Aaron explained. "Mr. Burton— Mr. Granger."

The long window facing the door was open, and through it Milton could see foliage touched with light from the big house adjoining. He shook hands with Burton: the minute passed in which he might have said: "Yes, we've met before"; Burton drawled: "Glad to know you, Mr. Granger"; they walked over to the window and stood looking out into the soft darkness Momentarily, Milton wondered if this really were the man he had met on Tamalpais, and he glanced at him and knew that he had not been mistaken, and then thought he saw an amused expression cross Burton's eyes. But the instructor offered them chairs and asked Aaron how his examinations were going.

"Oh, all right. I only have two more. The 'Econ' wasn't nearly so hard as I thought it would be.

Burton walked toward the piano and turned an arm-chair about and drew it nearer them. He kept his eyes upon Aaron, who talked on, head slightly back, legs crossed and hands around one knee. Milton felt the man disliked him; ill at ease, hearing Aaron's monologue, he glanced around the long room, at the stairs going up, the door into the kitchen (he could see one edge of the sink,) the mantelpiece encumbered with photographs, the wide bookcase. On the top shell be saw two or three volumes of which duplicates existed in his mother's library: the familiar bindings recalled evenings at home when the booming and rustle of the surf came upward from beneath the cliff, and he felt briefly unhappy because the villa would be closed, or perhaps even rented to strangers. By this time his mother must have left Honolulu. The two others were no longer talking. He started.

"I beg your pardon. What did you say?"

Aaron laughed with the raucous tone that was sometimes in his voice.

"Come back to earth. We were talking about the exes. I asked when you'd be finished."

"I? Oh—ah—on the tenth. My last one comes that day in the morning."

"On the tenth!" exclaimed Burton, turning suddenly to Milton and peering at him with interest. "On the tenth! That's early, isn't it?"

"Yes," replied Milton, "two of my courses had no final examinations."

He felt he had been wrong in thinking Burton disliked him. Instinctively, he lowered his eyes.

In a soft voice Burton said:

"I—ah—saw some verse of yours in the *Occident* the other day."

Immediately embarrassed, Milton answered:

"Oh, yes, I did have something in there. Nothing much. Just a little thing." He wanted to change the subject, but Burton went on:

"I liked it very much. You managed to give the effect entirely by sense impressions without breaking into the intellectual plane and stating what you meant abstractly. I like the way you describe. You seem to hit upon the right word often. Of course, there were one or two things—" He paused and reached out a hand and took his square-bowled pipe from the table and began to knock out the ashes into a copper tray. (Milton saw him again in walking clothes on the mountain, smoking that same pipe.) Then he continued:

"I rather think you transpose sound too frequently into color and vice versa. It's being done a lot, I know, but it always seems to me a bit strained. You see, it's so very individual a process. A sound may suggest a color to one person, and an entirely different color to another. It depends upon the contents of the reader's mind, and the association of ideas that is set going. For instance, you speak of the 'gray drive of the wind.' Now—"

"Oh, I think that's all right, Phil," interrupted Aaron. "It gives the idea of fog and a cold day. Besides, it isn't exactly sound he transposes there. He says the 'drive' of the wind. I think that's pretty good."

Burton nodded slowly. "Perhaps you're right. Any criticism of this kind is so entirely a personal matter. But don't you think that 'gray drive' has a peculiarly local connotation? To one who knows the hills along this coast where the fog is so constant—" He hesitated. Then: "It sounds as if you had the Bolinas Ridge in mind when you wrote this. Didn't you?"

Milton replied: "Yes, I did," and nearly added: "I first got the idea near the place where I saw you that day," but he felt that he should make no allusion to the meeting, though he knew not exactly why. He said: "I walk over there sometimes."

Burton's sad and intent gaze made him feel uncomfortable. Finally the instructor looked away quickly (his eyes seemed to tremble for a moment) and he began to stuff his pipe, lifting stringy tobacco from a china jar, and said:

"Of course, I don't know why you shouldn't give a local connotation to your words. In fact, that was one of the things I liked about some of your other verse. You seemed to give the feeling of this coast which is not quite like any other coast. In a way, when one comes to live here, one's scheme of feeling the outside world has to be made over. The seasons are different. The colors and trees are different. So much verse written here is not quite true. It is still falsified by memories of another climate, another framework of seasons, other skies."

He paused to light his pipe, which made a small rattle when he drew in. Furtively, his eyes drifted again to Milton. Into the silent room came night noises, the tiny whistle of a Key Route train down nearer the bay, the interminable, rhythmic song of the crickets.

Looking up suddenly, Burton exclaimed:

"Hear that." He lifted a hand. "The crickets."

Milton nodded. He had so often tried to find a word to describe them. Sympathy for Burton filled him and he said:

"Isn't that a white sound? White thorns appearing and vanishing one after another."

Burton pondered.

"I have more the impression," he said, "of a shell of moonlight, or invisible strings being touched in the air."

They listened for a while in silence. Through the window Milton saw the star-covered sky curving to blackness near the horizon. On the bay a revolving light loomed periodically into a sweep of gold. Burton said:

"A poet might grow here whose verse would be the emanation of this warm coast. It would rise naturally from the colors and smells, and be as delicate and evanescent as sunlight on leaves. Something changing, light, sensuous, untroubled by ideas." He paused and then asked:

"I wonder if you happen to know the poetry of Francis Jammes? In his early verse he caught the odors and feeling of the hot south. You read French, don't you? I remember Tom Gresham once mentioned you and said you knew French."

Milton nodded.

"Yes, pretty well."

"He ought to," said Aaron. "He's been over there a lot, and he's going again this summer."

Burton's face for a moment seemed to lose its expression.

"This summer. But you're coming back to California in August, aren't you?"

"I'm not certain. I may stay abroad, or I may go to college in the East."

Burton said nothing. His pipe had gone out. He took a match from the table and relighted it.

When Milton and Aaron rose to go about half an hour later, Burton said that he would accompany them down the hill a short distance; and they set forth in the warm night, deciding to walk all the way, and followed the Euclid Avenue car-track between palms and dark houses. Aaron left them several blocks north of the campus, turning up Cedar Street where he lived in a white frame house that stood alone on a corner, and Burton went on with Milton. For a long time he was silent (Milton was flattered that the instructor should walk so far with him,) but finally Burton said:

"And so you're going away. I'm sorry. I hoped I'd see you during the summer."

The tender melancholy in the man's voice disconcerted Milton. He replied:

"Yes, I'm going with my aunt. We'll stay for a while in Paris, and then go down into Italy."

He gave a few more facts, talking rapidly. As they entered the campus and walked along the dark path beneath trees toward the library, Burton took his arm and pressed it slightly against him and seemed so much on the point of saying something that Milton turned his face and waited. But no sound came forth, and Burton, looking down, seemed preoccupied, and held Milton's arm as if he had taken it by chance, and now, thinking of other things, had forgotten to release it. The same uneasiness that he had felt before on the mountain invaded the boy. He said, as naturally as he could:

"Aaron told me that George Towne is living up with you. I know him slightly. We were in the same German class at the beginning of the year."

After a moment, Burton answered:

"Oh, yes. He's been staying with me for a while. I—ah—he couldn't find a place to live, and I let him have that little upstairs room of mine."

Silence came. Once more Milton felt that Burton, who had turned toward him, was about to speak.

After a while, Milton said:

"I hardly ever see him now."

"He thinks he may go back to Wyoming this summer," Burton remarked. Then, squeezing Milton's arm more tightly, he said in a gentle and agitated, almost broken, voice:

"You're a nice boy. I'm awfully glad I met you."

Embarrassed, Milton laughed. The sediment of innumerable jokes heard at school or in the fraternity house and long forgotten rose now from the bottom of his mind into memory, and he waited, a bit nervous, half pleased, almost understanding, for Burton to say more. But suddenly Burton dropped his arm and said in a drawling and slightly ironic manner:

"I envy you. Your trip abroad this summer. Perhaps in a year or two I'll be able to go over for a few months. But I hope you'll come back."

"I don't know. Perhaps I shall."

He was unable to say more. For a while they went on without speaking. Then Burton laughed and said:

"You may have noticed that I have the *Thousand and One Nights* up at my place. I read them all the time. It—ah—I—it has given me a rather curious habit of mind. Sometimes, when I'm off on a holiday or something of that sort, I imagine I'm someone else. I've told people strange things."

The gray façade of the library was dim before them. Milton smiled.

"Yes," he answered, somehow pleasantly disturbed. "I often do that too."

Laughing shortly, Burton took his arm again.

He accompanied him to the Alpha Chi Delta house, and said good-by rather gruffly, and walked on toward College Avenue where he would take a car. Milton watched his stocky form move away in the darkness, and then climbed slowly to his room on the third floor. His roommate was snoring lightly. Undressing, he thought that if he should return to Berkeley for another year, the instructor would be an interesting person to know.

He saw him again often during the following week, although he was busy with his examinations and had little time to himself. Once Burton took him to a theater in San Francisco, and one afternoon he went up the hill for tea and met the instructor's mother, who was sitting near the open window, watching a hummingbird touch swaying flowers on a vine. When she heard that Milton would spend a few days in New York, she exclaimed that he must go to see her brother and his family, because Wayne would be able to show him all around New York. ("He's just your age or perhaps a little older.") But her son said that Milton would be with his aunt and would be very busy, and the project crumbled away without ultimate decision.

While they were having tea, Burton drew forth reproductions of favorite pictures in the Louvre and the Italian galleries, and told Milton that he must see this one or that one, and then laughed and said that he must pay no attention to what he was saying, because the beauty of a work of art must dawn upon one gradually.

"When people tell me to see a thing, I usually dislike it," he said.

Milton found himself talking easily to Mrs. Burton. He told her of his Aunt Caroline, his mother's voyage to India, the villa in Montecito. All at once he noticed that it was six-thirty and rose to go.

"Come and have dinner with us at Cloyne Court," Mrs. Burton suggested.

"Oh, I could hardly do that. I—"

"Yes, yes," said Burton. "Come on. Just the thing."

Milton succumbed.

Days later, on the train going East, or on the steamer, as he looked back upon this last week in Berkeley, so blurred now and filled with preparations and good-bys, it seemed to Milton that Burton had been with him constantly. Several evenings the instructor dined at the fraternity house; two or three times they went together to the city; Burton helped Milton pack his trunk; he took charge of a box-load of stuff to be left behind, and had it sent out to his place on College Avenue.

"It will be safer," he explained. "If you don't come back here, I'll send it East to you. I know what fraternity houses are. There are so many fellows that no one would take the responsibility of sending it on."

"Oh, thanks, Mr. Burton, but really there's no need of your taking all that trouble."

"No trouble at all. It's done now. I've told the expressman to come. Besides, I wish you wouldn't call me Mr. Burton."

One day he brought Milton four or five books to read on the train.

"The next time you're out at my place, look through the library. If you see anything you want, take it along."

On the morning of May twelfth he went with Milton, carrying one of his bags, to the Oakland mole, and sat with him in the Pullman car until the train reached Sixteenth Street. And as he got off, he said:

"You'll write me often, won't you?" and stood on the platform looking at the car window.

Milton saw him turn away. The instructor was a nice enough man: if Milton returned to Berkeley, he would be glad to see him. But he would also be glad to see Tom Gresham and Aaron Berg and Bert Hudson and Tony Barragan. It was almost a relief to be alone again and not have Burton around: there was something so patiently attentive about him; sometimes Milton felt that Burton agreed too easily with what he had said, or approved too warmly of verse he had written. And then that caressing habit of his became a bore.

Leaning back on the green plush seat, he watched the gray water of the bay, and the brown hills on the other side of the train, and felt luxuriously idle with three days of travel before him in this car. Slowly, drowsily, his mind drifted again to Berkeley. He thought of the year he had just finished, and of the Alpha Chi Delta house, and Bert Hudson and Aaron Berg; and he wondered if he would ever return to California and see all those fellows again. Soon the porter in his white jacket came down the aisle and gave a pillow to the middle-aged woman who occupied the section opposite Milton. She laid it behind her head and leaned back, closing her eyes, her hands folded in her lap. Forward in the car a man was talking; somewhere he heard a woman's voice; then a child came swinging along on the arms of the seats. Long before the train reached the Benicia ferry, a negro in white announced that luncheon was being served in the diner: Milton glanced at his watch and decided to wait an other half hour before eating. As he sat there, the year gone by dwindled like a stream in summer, and he remembered the trip from Santa Barbara north along the coast (even the porter's face emerged) and behind that other days in Pullman cars rose up, until soon his life seemed formed of nothing else, and the periods between, each of which had been so long, became brief and un important. As a child he had traveled often from Chicago to New York or to the south. And then there were European nights in the *sleeping*, with awakenings upon some frontier, and the faces of custom house men.

But somehow this journey would be different from the others. He would see in Europe all he had not seen as a child. Months of wandering spread out before him. One by one the ties that held him to Berkeley were loosening: everything there seemed less momentous. Brown hills and fields were sweeping backward on either side of the train. He was going, going. Tomorrow he would awake in the gray desolation of Nevada: the next day he would be in another state, then another. Idly, he lay back and looked through the window. The future was bearing down upon him like a great galleon, richly laden.

XX

George Towne

An examination was going on in the big lecture room in California Hall. Three or four students had finished and had left their blue-books on the platform where the professor usually stands and gone out through the open door behind the desk. George could see them talking together on the lawn beneath trees. He turned over the pages he had written and began to read them, but the sunlight coming through the tall western windows finally reached his broad chair-arm and the paper on it, and he had to twist his shoulder around in order to create a shadow. It seemed to him that he had written enough: at least, had answered all the questions, which was far more than he had hoped to do. All around him students were leaning forward and writing abundantly. He wondered how they could find so much to say, and whether he should not have filled a second blue-book. But he raised his head confidently: during the final two weeks he had borrowed notes from a friend and had "boned up," and now he felt sure that he would pass.

The ray of sunlight spread again over his paper. On either side of him students were leaning about to escape it; a girl nearby began to make despairing gestures to someone yards away: but finally the reader in the course, a young man George knew slightly, walked down from the back of the room, pulled up the yellow shade, looked around to see if it were high enough, and, when someone still dazzled shook her head, drew it up a few inches farther, while the students uttered sounds of relief. It stood golden against the sun, and scraps of light glittered through tiny crevices.

Although he had finished, it would be difficult to leave his place, for no one in the same row had gone away, and he would have to clamber across the knees of five or six persons. He yawned and decided to wait until one of them had gone. Then he would go down to Tuppy's room on Grove Street, where he had been spending most of his time recently, and see if he could get up a poker game or a party to San Francisco. This was his last examination. He might not return up the hill for the night, for Burton of late seemed barely conscious of him, ever since he had met that other fresh man, Milton Granger, with whom he had been almost constantly during the past ten days. Even Granger's departure for the East did not arouse the instructor from his brooding.

George had detested this fellow, seeing him one day in the cottage on Euclid Avenue. What did Burton find in him? Why did he have him up to the house and go chasing around Berkeley with him? Granger was a typical fraternity man, George thought, and of the studious kind, which are the worst. Burton had some intelligence, not a large amount of course, for there was something soft about him; but he had usually been a fairly good judge of men until this recent enthusiasm. Now he seemed to think of no one but Milton Granger: there was even a change in his attitude toward George.

A few days before, when he was in the midst of examinations, he had received another letter from his sister in Wyoming. She wrote that Mr. Towne was worse, and rarely got up now, and that the hotel needed a young man to take charge, because the two other boys would be away all summer, Jerry playing baseball in Laramie and Art working as horse-wrangler for a dude-ranch in Jackson's Hole. She had written: "I often wish that you could be here during the next few months, but I know how far away you are, and how important it is for you to keep on with your studies when you are doing so well." The sentence had remained with him, for he had been thinking much of Wyoming lately (memories kept rising into his mind of the lobby of the Towne Hotel with the moth-eaten elk's head over the desk and of the gray roads leading from Lander into the sagebrush country and of the green banks of the Little Wind River over at Fort Washakie;) and one evening he had told Burton that he might go back there for the vacation, because they needed him in the hotel. After pondering for a moment, Burton had answered: "It might be a good thing to do," and George felt that Burton had given him a surface reply, thinking of something else. "I'd come West again in August," George had added. Looking up from his book, the instructor asked: "Do you really think you'd ever return to Berkeley once you were in Wyoming?" "Damned if I know," George answered.

He closed his blue-book, screwed the cap onto his fountain-pen, and stretched out his legs beneath the chair before him. Often he wished he could have Art's job as horse-wrangler for a few months; the dude-ranch would spend several weeks near Jackson's Lake: frequently, on the bare hills above the Snake River, one saw thin-limbed antelope against the sky, and across the lake the Grand Teton Mountains rose somber, hooded with glaciers. Sitting there in California Hall, he could see Mount Moran with dark streaks upon the snow of its broad summit, and he remembered how dense the fish were in the curdled water beneath the dam, and how he had spent hours there with a line trying to make one of them take the hook. Now he saw that he had forgotten to write his name on the cover of his blue-book. He took out his fountain-pen and wrote it hurriedly.

Chair-arms clattered down as students rose to toss their books among others on the platform. The blue heap swelled gradually, spilling over. George stood up and sidled out into the aisle, squeezing his way by people who still wrote, and walked down to the front of the room, left his book with the others, and went out through the door beneath the blackboard. Thick-leaved trees were motionless in the hot air. He heard voices around him: "What did you say for the third?" "Who's Stanhope, anyway?" "Oh, I didn't know he meant that." He strolled away, down over the old football field toward the path running between live-oaks and eucalyptus toward Shattuck Avenue. He felt sure that he had not failed, yet the thought gave him no pleasure, as it would have done a year before. One had only to study a very little to get by these examinations: there would be many of them, one after another, reaching ahead of him for three years; and, after that, were he to take law, many more. The prospect made him infinitely weary, for would he be any better off when he had a degree? He thought again of Jackson's Lake, long and winding beneath the mountains. Then he paused and considered if it would not be pleasant to visit Mabel's apartment on Telegraph Avenue instead of going to see Tuppy Smith as he had planned; she would give him some tea and cake, and, later on, they might have dinner together. He would ask her what she thought about his return to Wyoming. He wanted to talk to someone about it, for he could never make up his mind. But the afternoon was so hot that he did not feel like walking back up the slight hill, and so, because he had started in that direction, he went on toward Grove Street, where Tuppy lived.

Both Tuppy and Dan were at home, sprawled in chairs, reading. George walked among magazines and clothes that littered the floor. Dan said:

"All through?"

"Yeah."

"Get by all right?"

"Aw, sure, I think so."

George took off his coat, threw himself on the bed, and lit a cigarette.

The room was hot, with flies humming in and out through the open window.

"I saw What's-her-name on the street today," said Tuppy.

Dan looked up. "Who?"

"Oh, you know. That broad of George's."

"Mabel," George said, letting ashes fall on the carpet. "Yeah, that's the one. I saw her on Telegraph Avenue, walking along with some other woman."

"Mrs. Nolan, I guess," said George.

"A little thin woman with a pointed nose."

"Yeah, that's her."

Mabel had taken him to the Nolans' house one afternoon, and had introduced him as a young man who was going to be a writer. She had exclaimed, on his remonstrance:

"Yes, you are. Now don't be so modest."

Mrs. Nolan had fluttered about, making tea, and had urged him to become a member of the Western Writers' League in order to meet all the people around the bay who were "doing things."

George knocked ashes from his cigarette. If he did not return to Wyoming, he would be able to remain in Berkeley, working in the library during the two summer sessions. But then he would have to see Mabel constantly, and already he was beginning to weary of her. There was something stifling about the way she had taken possession of him; he wished to be tied to no one; he wanted to be free; and if he should remain, they would become more and more intimate. Often he wished he had not made advances to her that afternoon in her apartment. Had there not been talk about her among his friends, he never would have done so.

Tuppy asked:

"Have you decided to go home, George?"

"No, not yet. I guess maybe I will."

Tuppy would spend three months at the Davis farm (he had work to do in soil chemistry,) and Dan was going to read for two economics courses and would probably enroll in Summer Session in order to get a few extra units. George could do that also, but somehow the glamour had departed from intellectual life.

He lay on the bed while the others studied and the flies hummed in the warm air. A year ago at this time he was in the Mendocino County lumber-camp, dissatisfied because he had flunked out of college, but sure that he would reënter and find what he desired. It had seemed then only a question of honest studying. But for two semesters now he had taken courses and passed them, and he seemed to have gained nothing. He had not read the books he planned to read at the beginning of the term; he had not even been to see Joe Farley, who must be still in Alcatraz Prison. He remembered when he crossed the bay from Sausalito, coming down from the north, and how he had looked upon the white walls of Alcatraz and thought that he would visit Joe weekly. His life always ran by like that. Nothing he planned ever came about: events took hold of him and that was all; and here he was, uncertain what to do, waiting for some influence stronger than the rest to push him forward.

He closed his eyes, and memories of Wyoming came to him. It was curious how much he had of late been thinking of the past: sights, voices, odors welled up. Even before he received his sister's letter he had thought it might be good to see the old place again, and now that there was a reason for going, he felt that he could easily leave the university, where three more years piled up ahead, filling him with weariness. He could go home and help to run the hotel, and after a few months, if he wished, he could travel West again and go on with his studies. But he knew that once back there he would never again come to Berkeley. Some force in him would diminish and he would settle down.

The humming of flies, the regular breathing of the two who were studying, the warmth of the room made him sleepy, and he stood up. Perhaps he would think more clearly outside; he might be able to make a decision. Putting on his coat, he said:

"I'm going out for a while. Be back soon."

Neither of them answered. George closed the door and went downstairs. In the street, he walked toward Telegraph Avenue, but he did not think of Mabel until he saw her apartment window. Then he decided to go up.

S he opened the door, wearing an apron, and exclaimed:
"Sit down, George. I'll be with you right away. I'm washing out some handkerchiefs."

And she vanished into the bathroom. Sinking into a morris-chair, he took a magazine from the table and began to look at pictures, but Mabel asked:

"Did you pass that last one all right?"

"Yeah, I think so."

"Ob, I'm so glad. Now you're all finished, aren't you?"

"Yeah."

There came a momentary rush of water from a faucet. George closed the magazine and slid it back on the table among books. Mabel called:

"Mr. Burton gave me a one in his course."

"Good work."

"There. Now I only have two more to do. The laundry simply tears them to pieces."

It was pleasant to have a place like this to come to where he could feel at home, not a guest in the house of someone else, as he was with Burton, but in an apartment that seemed really his own, as if he were married. If he remained in Berkeley, he would spend more and more of his time with Mabel. She always did everything he wanted. And yet he did not care to be tied to any one.

A moment later she came in, without her apron, and lit a cigarette, and exclaimed, sitting down on the couch:

"Oh, I'm so glad I did that. I've been putting it off for days. Once I got started, it took no time at all."

George did not answer. Leaning forward and dabbing her cigarette against an ash-tray on the table, she asked:

"What's the matter, George? You look so sad."

"I'm thinking."

She embraced him suddenly and then dropped back against the pillows.

"Well, he just mustn't think if it hurts him so."

Annoyed, a little bored, George announced, quite suddenly:

"I guess I have to go back to Wyoming this summer."

Her eyes opened a bit wider, and the smoke from her cigarette rose quietly before her face. Finally, she said:

"Oh, George, what do you mean?"

"My old man's sick," he explained. "The hotel isn't going very well. My two brothers will be away and my sister thinks I ought to come home."

"Oh, but, George—"

"And then I haven't been there for a long time. I sorta want to see the place again." He grew serious. "Of course, I owe it to the folks not to leave them in a hole when they need me."

She nodded, her face mournful. The smoke stream from her cigarette broke in two and humped over. George felt certain that he must go to Wyoming. All at once, in a rapid motion, she curled her legs beneath her, gave a little bounce on the sofa, and smiled quickly.

"But you'd come back next August, wouldn't you?"

Heavily, he answered: "Darned if I know."

Her smile was gone. She said:

"It would be too bad to stop college now that you're doing so well."

He did not answer.

"I know Mr. Burton would be awfully disappointed."

He moved his shoulders. "Burton wouldn't care."

"Yes, he would. He's awfully fond of you, I know."

A slight antagonism to Burton came over him: he thought of that fellow Granger.

"Aw, he wouldn't care," he repented. When she did not speak, he straightened up and exclaimed: "Well, I have to go back there, anyway."

She regarded him for a while, her head on the pillow, and finally said very slowly:

"Well, I think it's awfully fine of you to do it. To sacrifice yourself that way for your family."

He blushed and looked down. "Yes, it is," she insisted, nodding vigorously, "it's—it's—noble."

Soon she asked: "But won't the trip be fearfully expensive?"

He shook his head. "Oh, no. I'll hook rides. I think I'll try the road this time. There are always lots of autos that will give a fellow a lift."

"All the way by road?"

"Why not?"

"But the desert. All across Nevada."

"Oh, if I'm lucky, I may get a car that will take me right across without stopping. I've known several fellows who travel that way. One made it all the way to New York in less than a month."

She nodded, thoughtfully. "Oh, it will be beautiful. Out in the mountains."

"Yes," he exclaimed. "Great stuff. Wonderful lakes to go swimming in Nights out in the open air. The stars look big and near."

Wide-eyed, she listened. Then: "Oh, I wish I could go with you."

"Yeah, I wish you could. You're going to stay in Berkeley, aren't you?"

"Yes, I think so. The Nolans want me to drive to Tahoe with them in July. I may go. But until then, I'll be here. What is Lander like?"

George talked of his family and the hotel and the town. He felt sure that he was going home now, and yet he wanted to less than before, when he was still uncertain For a few minutes, he almost said: "Oh, maybe I won't go after all. It would be kinda nice to stay in Berkeley all summer." Mabel was a useful woman to know: she gave him tea and cake and let him come to her apartment whenever he wished. He might have changed his mind bad she not looked at him mournfully and asked:

"Oh, George, do you really have to go to Wyoming?"

When he left her in the evening (they had dinner together in the Specialty Shop,) she put her arms around his neck and asked:

"When do you think you'll go?"

At random, he answered: "Day after tomorrow."

"Oh, so soon?"

He nodded, drawing away.

"You'll write often, won't you?"

"Sure. I guess so."

He opened the door and started to go out into the hall. Standing there beside the table, she said:

"You'll come tomorrow, won't you? Then you'd better stay here tomorrow night. I'll cook you a good breakfast in the morning, so that you can start off with a full stomach. You'll come, won't you?"

"Sure," he answered, stepping into the hall. "I'll come."

He glanced back at her over his shoulder and grinned and then ran downstairs.

He came and went away, starting early one morning, and left Mabel in her apartment, melancholy. She spent several hours arranging her books, shifting the chairs around, putting the small kitchen in order; and in the afternoon, after she had lunched in the cafeteria near her apartment on Durant Avenue, she went to see Mrs. Nolan, who had taken her last examination that day. Preoccupied with the questions she had answered, the little woman listened to her with an absent mind. When Mabel told her that George Towne had gone back to Wyoming, she said vaguely:

"Oh, yes, I suppose he wants to get some local color."

"No, his father's ill and he's going to help them with their hotel."

"Oh, really? He is an awfully nice boy, isn't he?"

Mabel nodded. Somehow, she could not talk to Mrs. Nolan today. But, making an effort, she said:

"The people are already beginning to arrive for intersession. There'll be an enormous crowd. I noticed that some of the fraternity houses are renting rooms for the summer."

"Yes, yes, I saw that." Then, with almost a wail, Mrs. Nolan exclaimed: "Oh, my dear, I knew that third question perfectly. I could have answered it. If only I had taken a little time to think. But I was so rattled."

Throughout the evening, alone in her apartment, Mabel kept thinking of George and wondering how far along he was on his journey to Lander. And once, during the night, she lay awake for a while in the darkness, trying to imagine where he must be, asleep in some village hotel, or lying near the road under the stars, wrapped in the army blanket he had carried with him. When she opened her eyes in the morning, she felt for an instant that she had a reason to be unhappy. Then she remembered that he had gone.

One by one the men to whom she surrendered herself departed. Former separations had hardened her to bear this one. She had loved Jim Richards and he had left her; the affair with the officer in Paris had lasted only two months; Carl had fled from her, as if she stifled him; and now she had lost George. Lying in bed with the fresh sunlight outside, hearing the noise of a Telegraph Avenue car, she thought that she would henceforth live alone, and not open herself again to suffering. To each one she gave too much of herself: yet it was necessary for her to love intensely, without afterthought. Though she had determined many times to hold aloof, she could not do so, and her ardor once more brought boredom into her friend's eyes.

A few days later, when intersession had begun and new crowds were on the campus, Mabel met Mr. Burton one afternoon, and they walked slowly to the head of Durant Avenue, then climbed a few steps, and followed a road that runs up a canyon between tawny hills. All at once Mabel felt sad, smelling the dusty, dry brush.

She said: "Do you think George Towne will come back next year?"

Burton removed his hat. "Perhaps," he answered, "but I doubt it."

"Oh, really?"

They strolled on while a cow-bell tankled on the hillside across the valley. Mabel glanced at Burton, wondering how much he knew about herself and George, but he moved slowly, head back, face sunburned, impenetrable, and finally said, without looking at her:

"No, I'm afraid he won't come back. There's something wrong somewhere. Of course, he's lazy. But I used to think that if he once got started, he'd go on."

"But he did very well this year, didn't he?"

He nodded. "Fairly. But he's too inert. It's as if he had used up all his energy in breaking away from his early life. There's nothing left to push him on. He'll sink back."

Mabel asked: "But what will he do back in Wyoming?"

Burton lifted his shoulders. "He'll settle down and be contented. The country is full of men like him. False beginnings. A momentary flicker. Nothing more."

"Oh, I don't think so at all," cried Mabel. "Besides, it's awfully fine of him to go home of his own accord when his family needs him. To sacrifice himself that way." She threw up her head.

"Yes," said Burton, "it is."

Then he glanced at her and smiled, and it seemed to Mabel that he knew.

After a while, looking down, he said: "No one seems to get anywhere." But, in a moment, he went on:

"I met a very interesting boy a couple of weeks ago. A freshman named Granger. Milton Granger. I wonder if you know him?"

She shook her head. "No, I don't."

Burton cleared his throat. They were passing the high fence above the swimming pool. He peered down at the tanned forms below, and then said:

"He writes very good verse. Of course, he's quite undeveloped, but there may be a possibility of growth in him. A very nice boy. He has a certain talent. A real gift for description."

When he did not go on, Mabel asked: "Is he going to be here this summer?"

"No. He's gone abroad. To France and Italy. He may never come West again."

Bits of foliage were catching at Mabel's skirt. She exclaimed:

"Oh, everybody always goes away."

"Yes, everybody." Burton turned toward her. "I suppose you're leaving Berkeley for the summer?"

"No, I don't believe so. I may for a while later on. But I'll be here next year."

"I'll probably be here all summer. A student, a young fellow named Aaron Berg, wants me to go on a walking trip with him for a couple of weeks, and I may do that. Somewhere in the Coast Range probably. But I'm not sure. If we find an apartment, I'll stay here and help mother get settled."

"Oh, I adore your mother," said Mabel.

Burton continued: "She has just heard that her nephew Wayne is coming out to California. He was in business in New York last year, but he's not very well and he's going to try this climate. I've asked Tom Gresham if he can help him get a job in San Francisco, but I'm afraid Tom can't do much. He's all excited about some saw-mill or other in Humboldt County."

At the end of the road, beneath a dense live oak, they sat for a while on a bank of dry grass, and talked of their plans for the coming year. And when it grew cooler, they rose and brushed the twigs from their clothes and started home.

Burton left her on Telegraph Avenue and walked north toward the campus. She watched him go away, and thought that next year, perhaps during the summer, she would see him. Why had she not talked to him more frequently these past few months? Oh, well, there would be time. Now she must have dinner, for she was going this evening to visit a friend of her sister's, who had come recently to San Francisco.

In the cafeteria, as she carried her tray behind the long line, she noticed that nearly all the people around her were strangers. Many of them were school teachers from small towns who had come to spend the summer in Berkeley. Burton had called them "gold fish swarming to be fed." She moved on, taking from a white pile before her a knife, fork, and spoon rolled tightly in a napkin, Even the students working behind the counter were new. A fresh tide had risen and filled the town and the buildings of the university.

When she reached the end of the counter and stood before the cash register waiting for the girl to add up her plates and give the check, she saw a young man not far away who reminded her of Carl. Bearing her laden tray to a table, she hoped Carl would be successful in the store. Then she began to lift the full dishes off and arrange them before her. But several times she looked over at the young man sitting nearby. He might be interesting to know.

THE END

A Note About the Author

Clarkson Crane (1894–1971) was a novelist and English professor. Born in Chicago, he was raised in a prominent family on the city's Near North Side. In 1910, he moved with his parents to California, where he would attend the University of California, Berkeley, graduating in 1916. During the First World War, he served as an ambulance driver in France and was awarded the Croix de Guerre for bravery. He returned to the United States in 1919 and was honorably discharged from the Army before embarking on a career as a writer, publishing stories in *The Smart Set* and *The Dial*. In 1925, while in Paris, he published *The Western Shore*, his most acclaimed novel. The following year, he became a lecturer in English at the University of California Extension School. Soon, Crane would meet Clyde Evans, with whom he would develop a lifelong relationship. Recognized as a pioneering LGBTQ author, Crane was a fixture of the San Francisco literary scene in the early twentieth century.

A Note from the Publisher

Spanning many genres, from non-fiction essays to literature classics to children's books and lyric poetry, Mint Edition books showcase the master works of our time in a modern new package. The text is freshly typeset, is clean and easy to read, and features a new note about the author in each volume. Many books also include exclusive new introductory material. Every book boasts a striking new cover, which makes it as appropriate for collecting as it is for gift giving. Mint Edition books are only printed when a reader orders them, so natural resources are not wasted. We're proud that our books are never manufactured in excess and exist only in the exact quantity they need to be read and enjoyed. To learn more and view our library, go to minteditionbooks.com

bookfinity & MINT EDITIONS

Enjoy more of your favorite classics with Bookfinity,
a new search and discovery experience for readers.
With Bookfinity, you can discover more vintage
literature for your collection, find your Reader Type,
track books you've read or want to read,
and add reviews to your favorite books.
Visit www.bookfinity.com, and click on
Take the Quiz to get started.

Don't forget to follow us
@bookfinityofficial and @mint_editions